1999

P9-DFP-811

———————— ★ ————————

The body lay on its side just inside the door. Male, light sandy-colored hair, slim, fortyish—all this Paget noted in the first swift glance, but his eyes kept coming back to the pitchfork half-buried in the man's chest.

Paget swallowed hard and forced himself to breathe slowly, deeply, until the last of the nausea subsided.

At least one of the curving tines must have pierced his heart, but there was surprisingly little blood, and no sign of a struggle. The man must have dropped dead within seconds of being struck.

Paget recalled the man only too well. He was the same man he'd seen talking to—or had it been arguing with?—Andrea McMillan on Boxing Day. The connection, tenuous though it might be, filled him with foreboding.

———————— ★ ————————

"...suspenseful from the start, uncovering its tangled web of relationships—conventional and otherwise—at a leisurely pace: a sturdy '90s version of the British procedural, with Inspector Paget a model of the gentleman copper."

—*Kirkus Reviews*

Previously published Worldwide Mystery title by
FRANK SMITH
STONE DEAD

Forthcoming from Worldwide Mystery by
FRANK SMITH

CANDLES FOR THE DEAD

FATAL FLAW

FRANK SMITH

W❂RLDWIDE.

TORONTO • NEW YORK • LONDON
AMSTERDAM • PARIS • SYDNEY • HAMBURG
STOCKHOLM • ATHENS • TOKYO • MILAN
MADRID • WARSAW • BUDAPEST • AUCKLAND

If you purchased this book without a cover you should be aware
that this book is stolen property. It was reported as "unsold and
destroyed" to the publisher, and neither the author nor the
publisher has received any payment for this "stripped book."

FATAL FLAW

A Worldwide Mystery/December 1999

First published by St. Martin's Press, Incorporated.

ISBN 0-373-26331-7

Copyright © 1996 by Frank Smith.
All rights reserved. No part of this book may be reproduced
or transmitted in any form or by any means, electronic or
mechanical, including photocopying, recording or by any
information storage and retrieval system, without permission
in writing from the publisher. For information, contact:
St. Martin's Press, Incorporated, 175 Fifth Avenue,
New York, NY 10010-7848 U.S.A.

All characters in this book are fictitious, and any resemblance to
actual persons, living or dead, is purely coincidental.

® and TM are trademarks of Harlequin Enterprises Limited.
Trademarks indicated with ® are registered in the United States
Patent and Trademark Office, the Canadian Trade Marks Office
and in other countries.

Visit us at www.worldwidemystery.com

Printed in U.S.A.

Denise Dietz

**AN ELLIE BERNSTEIN/
LIEUTENANT
PETER MILLER
MYSTERY**

Throw Darts at a Cheesecake

Fat Free Murder

At the weekly meeting of Weight Winners, losing is everything. Group leader Ellie Bernstein herself has shed fifty-five pounds, along with a cheating husband and an unfulfilling life. But she quickly discovers losing weight is not only murder, it's downright lethal.

One by one, the group's Big Losers are being murdered. Is some jealous member of the Friday meeting a secret killer? Motive aside, Ellie's got to watch her back as well as her calories before she finds herself on the most permanent diet of all...death.

Available December 1999 at your favorite retail outlet.

WORLDWIDE LIBRARY®

Visit us at www.worldwidemystery.com

WDD334

DEADLY VINTAGE

A JACK DONNE MYSTERY

WILLIAM RELLING JR.

In California's wine country, a heady bouquet of money, rivalry and murder gives ex-Treasury agent-turned-vintner Jack Donne a case that turns deadly.

Neighboring vintner and universally loathed Ozzie Cole makes an outstanding product. So when Ozzie comes to Donne, claiming somebody is counterfeiting his best pinot noir, Donne reluctantly agrees to look into it.

But Donne soon learns blood is thicker than wine and there's a lot of it being spilled—in his direction.

Available December 1999 at your favorite retail outlet.

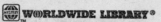

WORLDWIDE LIBRARY®

Visit us at www.worldwidemystery.com   WWR330

FATAL FLAW

FRANK SMITH

ONE

HE DIDN'T *LOOK* DANGEROUS as he stood there on the doorstep, the cold November rain dripping from the hood of a cheap plastic mac. But then, he never had, she thought. He'd always looked as he did now; shy and diffident, with that little-boy air of wanting to please.

Instinctively, she looked past him, down the path to the rain-swept street, and saw that it was empty. She gripped the door more firmly and wondered whether he would try to stop her if she closed it.

He saw the apprehension in her eyes and stepped back a pace, raising his hands, palms outward in a gesture of reassurance. Colour tinged his pallid face.

'I'm sorry if I startled you; I didn't mean to,' he said.

His voice—it was softer than she remembered. Strange. In her memory it was harsh, more menacing. She'd prayed she'd never have to hear it again.

'What do you want?' She had to force the words out.

He looked down at his feet. 'To—to say I'm sorry,' he said. Then, with a rush: 'I know it can never make up for what I did, but I had to come. To tell you myself, and to tell…' His eyes shifted, probing the empty hallway.

'She's not here,' the woman said sharply. 'Did you really expect she would be?'

'I didn't know. I thought perhaps…' He shrugged resignedly and trailed off into a troubled silence. 'I'd like to talk to her. To say I'm sorry. That's all. If you could…'

'I don't know where she is.' The lie came out bald and

flat. 'Even if I did, there's nothing to be said. She has a new life now.' Why had she said that? There'd been no need.

'I—I see.' He began to turn away then stopped. 'Would you tell her, that is if you should happen to hear from her, that I'm truly sorry? I know it can't change what happened, but I've changed. They helped me in there—they really did. There was this psychiatrist who used to come once a week…'

His eyes searched for some response from the woman, but she gave no sign of even having heard what he'd said.

'I'd better be on my way, then.'

She watched him go down the drive and into the street. He turned to the right and walked to the bus stop. She closed the front door and locked it, then went to the window, standing well back so that he wouldn't see her watching him.

But he'd know.

He stood there a good ten minutes in the rain before a bus came, never once glancing back at the house. She saw him get on, but the windows of the bus were misted over and she couldn't see where he sat. The bus swung out, spray flying from its wheels as it gathered speed, and, faintly, she heard the hiss of tyres as it went by. She watched until it disappeared from view, then sat down abruptly on the edge of the chair and tried to stop her hands from shaking.

Friday, 13 November

THE ALARM WENT OFF at seven as usual, but the woman was awake long before that. She'd spent a restless night listening to every single creak and groan of the old house. And yet she must have slept because she'd dreamt. Dreamt of him.

Fancy him coming back like that! Just walking up to the door and ringing the bell, bold as brass. She lay there trying to recall the dream, but it wouldn't come. Better not to remember it, she told herself as she threw back the covers.

The rain had stopped some time during the night. It was still dark outside. Only the light from the street lamp filtered past the curtains. She shivered as she thrust her feet into slippers beside the bed, then pulled on a woollen dressing-gown and wrapped it tightly around herself. She really must get the gas put in the bedroom this winter. She'd been thinking about it on and off for years, but she'd always put it off.

The puddle of water on the tiles at the bottom of the stairs didn't mean anything to her when she first saw it. It would be from her umbrella yesterday, she reasoned. And yet she couldn't remember it being there when she went to bed. It nagged at her in a fitful sort of way as she put the kettle on, but she wasn't worried about it—until she saw the second puddle beside the back door, and the shattered glass lying on the mat.

She just stood there staring at the jagged hole in the back door window, and in her mind's eye she saw a hand reaching through to turn the key in the lock. His hand. He'd been here. Right here in the house while she slept. And he wanted her to know he'd been. Her knees began to tremble and she clutched at the wall for support.

Her handbag! She hurried into the front hall and felt a wave of relief when she saw it was still where she'd left it on the side table yesterday when she'd returned from the shops. Quickly, she went through it. Money, keys, credit cards, nothing seemed to be missing. But he'd been through it; she was sure of that. Puzzled, she checked the cupboard where she kept an extra fifty pounds, but the money hadn't been touched. So it wasn't money he wanted, but the thought did nothing to cheer her.

Slowly, methodically, she went from room to room but nothing seemed to be missing; nothing was disturbed. What *did* he want?

Her gaze fell on the piano. The photographs!

The police. She must telephone the police. The woman picked up the phone and began to dial, then stopped and put it down again. No, there was something else she must do first. She picked up the phone again and began to dial a different number.

TWO

IT WAS DARK BY THE TIME she came out. She was late to-night. Almost half an hour late. He watched as she de-scended the broad steps and made her way purposefully to her car in the area reserved for staff parking. He kick-started the bike, pulled his visor down, and went through the gates ahead of her. A bus pulled into the kerb, and he tucked in behind, waiting for her to go by.

She drove a Peugeot hatchback, white with grey trim. That hadn't changed at least. She'd always been partial to the Peugeot. He let two more cars pass before swinging out into traffic, cutting off a Vauxhall Cavalier as he fell in behind. He ignored the furious bleating of the Cavalier's horn, and kept his attention focused on the Peugeot. He was sure it would follow the same route as it had the night before, and the night before that, but it didn't do to take anything for granted.

He closed the gap as one of the cars ahead of him turned off. The traffic seemed to be particularly heavy tonight, and he didn't want to be left behind at the lights. Automatically he moved into the right lane ready for the turn into Bridge Street, then realized that the Peugeot was still in the left lane. Odd, that. She didn't usually leave it till the last min-ute.

She went straight through at the lights. With a hasty glance over his shoulder, he cut back into the left lane and found himself right behind the Peugeot. Not that it mattered, really. He was quite sure she had no idea she was being followed.

When they came to the roundabout she took the Wood-bourne exit and he was able to drop back as they slid into the steady flow of traffic leaving the town for the weekend. The traffic thinned as the new housing estates dropped behind, but the Peugeot continued steadily onward. Obviously she wasn't going home. So where was she going? He smiled in the darkness. Perhaps this was what he'd been waiting for.

The road became narrower, winding, yet the Peugeot never slackened speed. She must know the road well, he thought, closing up to avoid losing her altogether. But not too close; no sense warning her that he was there. *He* would choose the time and place. *He* was in control. He slammed a gloved fist on the handlebars. 'That's right!' he shouted into the wind. 'I'm in control now.'

The Peugeot was drawing ahead, its front-wheel drive holding well on the sharp curves of the country lane. He opened the throttle wide, but had to slow almost immediately for a nasty little S-bend. He felt the back wheel begin to slide. Christ! Not now, he thought, as he fought to keep the bike upright. He couldn't lose her now. The back tyre thumped against the high grass verge, spewing gravel as it caught, and he was out of the skid and still astride the bike. He settled himself more securely in his seat and peered ahead.

The Peugeot was no longer there. The road ahead was straight for perhaps three hundred yards. She couldn't have gone that fast, it was impossible. Then, out of the corner of his eye, he caught a glimpse of the Peugeot's rear lights disappearing up a driveway as he shot past the entrance. He rolled slowly to a stop, running the bike up the verge and into the trees before cutting the engine. He walked back and stood looking up at the sign above the open gates.

Glenacres Stables. Of course! He should have guessed.

He hummed softly to himself and did a little dance in the road as he walked back to the bike. She was making it easy for him. Dead easy.

Saturday, 5 December

'ALL READY FOR CHRISTMAS over at Glenacres, then, are you, Ernie?'

Ernie Craddock grimaced. 'Don't remind me, Reg. Anyway, there's three weeks to go before Christmas, and to tell the truth it's a bit slow at the moment. We'll be busy, though, if the weather holds through the holidays.'

'They still going to have the hunt on Boxing Day over at the Hall this year, then? I heard it might be called off after all the trouble they had last year.'

Craddock shrugged. 'As far as I know it's on,' he said. 'Where'd you hear that?'

Reg Lyman shuffled his feet. 'Oh, somebody was on about it in here the other night,' he hedged. The landlord of the Black Swan had no intention of taking sides in the ongoing dispute between the pro-and anti-hunt forces, both of whom patronized his pub from time to time.

'Well, it's on as far as I know,' Craddock said. 'In fact, from what I've heard, there should be a good turn-out— depending on the weather, of course.' He picked up his glass, realized it was empty, and set it down again.

The man behind the bar looked at the glass and cocked a quizzical eye, but Craddock shook his head. 'No, I'd better not,' he said. 'I've got the car out back.' He looked at his watch. 'Time to be going in any case. See you, Reg. 'Night all,' he called as he made for the door.

He stood for a moment allowing his eyes to adjust to the darkness. It wasn't a bad night. A bit parky, but not bad for December. He buttoned up his coat and made his way around the side of the pub to where his car was parked at the back.

There wasn't much light back there; just a single bulb over the back door, but it was enough. His car was the one down at the end. He always tried to park it there, out of the way of the yobbos who had trouble finding their way out of the yard after half a dozen pints.

There was a motor bike parked beside his car, and the helmeted man astride it seemed to be having trouble starting it.

'Being a bit stubborn, is she?' Craddock said as he came up to his car.

'Doesn't like the cold weather,' the man said as he dismounted. He pulled a small torch from his pocket and switched it on. 'It just takes a bit of tweaking. Would you mind holding this a minute for me? Save me having to push it over to the light.'

'I can switch the car headlights on if you like,' Craddock said.

'No need for that. This will only take a second.' The man handed the torch to Craddock. 'Just shine it down there for me,' he said. 'A bit lower…'

Craddock squatted down, torch focused on the engine. 'How's this?' he asked.

'Couldn't be better,' the man said softly, and brought the heavy spanner crashing down on Craddock's head.

Thursday, 17 December

THE LIGHTS OF THE TOWN glowed softly beneath the mist that lay like strands of lucent gauze across the valley. Up here the air was clear, but the road was narrow where the hillside had given way and Paget drove with care. You never knew when some idiot would come careening round a corner on your side of the road. The local council had been debating what to do about the slippage for two years that he knew of, and probably long before that, but nothing had been done. Nor would it be, he thought, until the road-bed gave way and some poor sod went over the edge.

Not that he was in a hurry for the evening to end. He flicked a sideways glance at the woman beside him, and was rewarded with a smile.

'Warm enough?' he asked, turning his attention back to the road.

'Warm and sleepy,' she said lazily. 'I think it must be the wine. Just ignore me if I start to snore.'

He smiled in turn. He enjoyed being with Andrea Mc-Millan. She was so down to earth; so—uncomplicated. They got on well together. No strings; no obligations. Just friends who spent time together whenever they could. Which wasn't as often as he would have liked, but between his impossible hours as a detective chief inspector, and hers at the hospital, there was little chance of it changing.

The lights were against him at the top of the hill and he had to stop. There was almost no traffic about; it was after eleven and most people would be home by now, but the lights remained stuck stubbornly on red.

Yet why was it, he wondered, that he always felt so guilty when he was with Andrea? He looked forward to being with her; anticipated their infrequent evenings to-gether, and yet his feeling of guilt kept nagging away at the back of his mind.

Was it because he felt that by going out with Andrea he was in some way being disloyal to the memory of Jill? He considered the question but dismissed it. Why was he doing this to himself? he thought irritably. It wasn't as if he and Andrea were lovers, for God's sake.

The light was green. He'd been staring straight at it but he hadn't seen it change. Annoyed with himself for allow-ing his mind to wander, he swung the wheel hard over and the tyres squealed in protest as he made the sharp turn into Crescent Road.

He cast an apologetic look in Andrea's direction, but her eyes were closed and there was a half-smile on her face. She looked lovely, he thought as he turned his attention back to the road. She looked...

It wasn't as if they were lovers!

The phrase echoed and re-echoed in his head as he stared into the darkness. Was that what this was all about? Even as the question formed in his mind, he knew the answer, and his immediate reaction was to reject it.

It couldn't happen, he told himself. It couldn't. Not after Jill. He was suddenly warm; uncomfortably warm, and he felt sure that Andrea could see or at least sense his discomfort. He was almost afraid to look at her, but it was as if he had no choice. Her eyes were still closed; the half-smile still on her face—and he knew he wanted her. He wanted her more than anything in the world.

He looked away quickly for fear she would open her eyes and read what must be written all over his face. Don't be a fool, he told himself. Don't spoil what you have.

Without quite knowing how he'd got there, Paget found himself in Northumberland Place. He pulled over to the kerb and stopped the car outside number 57. It looked like any other in the row of imposing terraced houses built almost a century ago, but in fact it marked the entrance to a block of flats.

'Did you get it all sorted out?'

Paget turned off the engine. 'Sorry?' he said. He thought he must have missed something. His mind was in such a turmoil. 'Did I get what sorted out?'

'You were miles away,' she said. 'And you looked so fierce! Heaven help whoever you were thinking about.'

'Sorry,' he apologized, not daring to look directly at her. 'Must have been day-dreaming there for a minute.'

Andrea unfastened her seat-belt, then leaned back and closed her eyes, unwilling, at least for the moment, to leave the comfort of the car. 'Impossible,' she said. 'You can't day-dream at night. What were you really thinking about, Neil? You looked terribly serious.'

He groped for an explanation. 'Christmas,' he said. It wasn't really a lie; he had been thinking about Christmas earlier in the evening. 'I was wondering if you have any plans. Do you?'

Andrea opened her eyes, but she didn't look at him; neither did she answer right away. 'It's—difficult,' she said at last. 'We're still terribly short-staffed, and it's hard to plan ahead. I'm afraid I won't have much time off until after the New Year.' She hesitated as if about to add something else, but apparently thought better of it. Instead, she said: 'What about you?'

'It will be much the same for me,' he said. 'There's no point in sitting around the house all by myself on Christmas Day when someone with a wife and kids could be enjoying the holiday. Even Mrs Wentworth, my daily housekeeper, will be away, so I might as well work.'

Andrea put a hand on his arm. 'You're a sweet man, Neil Paget,' she said softly. 'Not at all the surly policeman I first thought you were.'

He forced a smile as he covered her hand with his own. 'You're not so bad yourself, Dr McMillan,' he said. The light from a distant street lamp was reflected in her eyes, and he longed to touch her face.

Andrea sensed the change in him; saw what was in his eyes, and she panicked. No! He mustn't. Not now. Especially not now. In the split second it took for the thoughts to enter her mind, she withdrew her hand and glanced down at her watch.

'I'm on early shift again, tomorrow,' she said as naturally as she could, but she could hear the quaver in her voice. 'I had such a lovely time this evening, Neil, but I'd better get some sleep or I'll be nodding off on rounds tomorrow.'

She opened the door. 'No, don't get out,' she said as he began to open his own door. 'It's only a few steps.' She leaned over and brushed his cheek with her lips, then slipped out of the car. 'Thanks again for a lovely time. I'll ring you as soon as I know how things will be after the holidays. And in case I don't see you before, merry Christmas.'

'We might manage a quick drink around Christmas Eve,' he called after her. 'I'll ring you.'

She seemed to hesitate in mid-stride, then went on. 'Yes,' she called back. 'That would be nice, Neil. Goodnight.'

He watched as Andrea ran up the steps and opened the door. She turned and waved, then disappeared inside. The faint smell of her perfume lingered, and for a brief moment he was tempted to follow her. But no. He'd have to buzz her on the intercom; make up some excuse or other... He sighed. It was no good. Besides, it was late and she had said she was on the early shift at the hospital.

He leaned his head against the head-rest and let out a long breath. What *had* he said? He went over every word in his mind. It didn't make sense. One minute they were just chatting as people do at the end of a pleasant evening, then...

She must have sensed the change in him. That was the only explanation. He groaned aloud. 'I told you not to spoil it,' he growled beneath his breath. 'You're a fool, Paget. No. You're a damned fool!'

He started the car and made a sweeping U-turn in the middle of the deserted street.

From the darkened window of the flat two floors above the street, Andrea McMillan watched him go. She wished she could relive those last few seconds in the car. As the car turned the corner and disappeared from view, she pulled down the blind and snapped on the light beside the bed. For a long moment she stood there, looking down at the gilt-framed picture that stood alone on the bedside table.

She sat down on the bed. No, she thought wearily, that would have only made things more complicated than they were. Besides she reminded herself, Neil Paget was a policeman, and a policeman was the last thing she needed in her life right now.

THREE

'GOOD-NIGHT, MONICA.'

Jane Wolsey closed the door and shook her head in a puzzled fashion as she made her way to her own room at the end of the upper hall. She hoped Monica wasn't going to be ill again. That *would* put the cap on it for Christmas. But the girl was too bright-eyed, too flushed, and far too excited. Something had happened at the party; Jane was sure of it, but Monica had insisted it was nothing.

'It was the wine, Miss Wolsey, that's all,' she'd said, adopting her most contrite expression. 'I know I shouldn't have had it, but I didn't think a little bit would hurt. And everyone else was having such fun. I'm sorry, but I shall be fine in the morning, honestly, Miss Wolsey, you'll see.'

I should have gone with her, Jane thought guiltily, then brushed the thought aside. She had not been invited, and she could hardly insist on chaperoning a seventeen-year-old. Monica had only herself to blame. She knew very well what alcohol could do to her. She'd been told often enough. It was a good job Sally had been there to bring her back to the school. What a state the girl had been in. Shivering, flushed, over-excited—thank God Crowther hadn't seen her before they got her up to her room and into bed.

Jane sighed heavily. It was understandable, she supposed. Monica Shaw had little enough to be happy about this Christmas, and she'd so looked forward to the party at the stables. It had been the one bright spot in what would otherwise have been a dreary holiday for her.

Christmas Eve, and she was spending it here at Thornton Hill; the only girl left in the school over Christmas. Jane found it hard enough herself, and she was used to it. What must it be like for a girl like Monica.

Damn that woman anyway.

Jane Wolsey opened the door of her room and went inside. In school parlance it was the housemistress's 'private quarters'. Anywhere else it would have been called a bedsit. As sixth form housemistress she was entitled to larger, separate quarters, but she had given up that privilege years ago in favour of the much needed extension to the library. The room was small but comfortable—a bit cramped when she had the girls in, but she didn't mind that. At least up here she was close to them. It was like having your family around you. Her family; the only real family she had ever known.

It was too early for bed. Perhaps a cup of tea and a bit of television if there was anything decent on. Her mind went back to Monica Shaw, as she filled the kettle at the sink. Or rather to Monica's mother, Julia.

Two days before end of term, she'd rung up. Couldn't possibly get home from Brussels in time for Christmas—the European Community conference, you know. And I'd be so worried if I thought Monica was at home in that big house all by herself, especially over Christmas. Jane had not been privy to the conversation but she could imagine how it had gone.

And she could imagine the head's reaction. Yes, Mrs Shaw. No, Mrs Shaw. Of course I understand perfectly, Mrs Shaw. No, of course not, Mrs Shaw. It won't be any trouble at all. We'd be delighted to have Monica stay with us over Christmas. A gift for her from you? Of course we'll arrange it. Did you have anything in particular in mind? No? Well, I'm sure her housemistress, Miss Wolsey, will know exactly what to get her. Yes, something personal of course.

Julia Shaw was a Thornton Hill 'Old Girl', and one whom Crowther loved to talk about. 'She'll be Prime Minister one day, you mark my words. You should be very proud of your mother, Monica. We here at Thornton Hill are very proud of her. Pity you aren't more like her.'

God, but Crowther could be thick sometimes. Couldn't she see what she was doing to the girl? Monica was *not* like her mother and never would be, and thank heaven for that at least. Julia Shaw was a self-centred, hard-driving career woman, plain and simple. She should never have had children at all. Monica was an embarrassment to her, and she didn't even bother to hide the fact. Conference indeed! Who ever heard of a European conference continuing over Christmas? The woman simply didn't want to be bothered with the girl.

Jane Wolsey sighed again as she made the tea and sat down before the television set. Monica's gift—from her mother—was there beside the TV, all wrapped and waiting to be opened in the morning. Jane eyed it apprehensively. She hoped Monica would like it.

Even more fervently, she hoped the girl would be all right. She was sure there was *something* Monica wasn't telling her. Perhaps she should ring Sally. She glanced at the clock. It was a bit late to ring now. Sally would have to be up early in the morning. Still, she'd like to know...

Friday, 25 December

THE CLOCK IN THE TOWER above the chapel struck the hour of one, its tone muted by the falling snow. Thick, wet flakes stuck to the trees, weighing down the branches until some of them touched the ground, and snow-capped bushes looked like giant mushrooms.

But the girl who stumbled blindly up the path leading to the back door of Braden Hall saw none of this, oblivious even to the tracks she'd left behind. The door stuck again as it always did in winter, and she had to put her shoulder to it before it opened. She stumbled inside and pushed the door shut, wheezing as she fought for breath, blood pounding in her ears like storm-tossed waves crashing against the shore. She wanted desperately to rest, but there was something she must do. The sound inside her head grew louder; engulfed her...

She was in her room, leaning against the door, panting hard. Her head ached abominably and she wanted to be sick. She doubled over, arms wrapped tightly around herself and the object she was carrying, holding back the shakes she knew must come, and biting back the urge to scream.

Jumbled thoughts hammered inside her head as she staggered to the bed and flung herself face down. Her small, sharp teeth bit deeply into the pillow as tremors racked her body. Her shoulders heaved convulsively, yet she made no sound as she waited for the storm to pass.

Slowly, painfully, she pulled herself up and propped her back against the wall. She remained like that for a long time, eyes closed, teeth clenched, and breathing hard. When, at last, she did open her eyes, it was to stare sadly around the room as if seeing it for the first time—or perhaps the last. Her eyes fell on the mirror, and her lips parted in a mirthless smile.

She wanted to cry but the tears refused to come.

FOUR

'HER NAME IS MONICA SHAW, SIR.' The uniformed constable spoke softly as if afraid of waking the girl on the bed. 'Her housemistress, a Miss Jane Wolsey, found her like this first thing this morning. Said she was bringing her a Christmas present from her mother.' He shook his head sadly. 'What a thing to have happen at Christmas. She was only seventeen.'

Why should its being Christmas make a difference?

The thought passed fleetingly as Paget looked down upon the huddled form so small and still amid the tangled bedclothes. Surely the death of anyone so young was a tragedy at any time of year.

Long, dark hair all but covered the girl's face, and a slim white arm stuck out incongruously above her head. The arm was cold and stiff to his touch, rigor well advanced. Carefully, so as not to disturb the body, he pulled the bedclothes away and was surprised to see that the girl was fully dressed except for shoes. Her hair fell away to reveal a small, pinched, chalk-white face, and Paget felt the all too familiar cold, hard knot forming in the pit of his stomach. He felt the muscles convulse and he swallowed hard. He had never become used to this part of the job, and he knew, no matter how often he had to face it, he never would. He lowered the bedclothes gently.

Seventeen, Maitland had said. She looked to be about twelve!

The bedside lamp was on, its rays pale and feeble, competing as they were with the probing light of a wintry sun. But it was what lay on the table that drew Paget's attention:

a plastic syringe. Paget bent closer to examine it. There was a small, dark stain on the tip of the needle. Blood, most likely, dried and crusted. He sniffed, but if there was any odour he could not detect it.

'She was diabetic,' Maitland offered. 'Miss Wolsey told me. She said that would be her insulin.'

'I see.' Paget's tone was non-committal. 'And you say Miss Wolsey rang for the ambulance? Surely she must have realized that the girl was dead?'

'She said she thought the girl had gone into some sort of coma, sir. She said her first thought was to get her to hospital.'

'And it was the ambulance men who called us?'

'That's right, sir. When they saw how things were, they rang us straightaway. Said they'd seen enough suicides in their time to know when to leave things alone. I have statements from them, but I had to let them go because they had another emergency call just after I arrived.'

Suicide. They were probably right. Christmas was always a bad time for those who were alone, the depressed, and the chronically ill. He remembered his own first Christmas alone after Jill died, and how he'd felt himself. Not suicidal, exactly, but he could understand the frame of mind that might lead to such a measure.

The sound of muted voices came from the corridor, and a tall, thin, gloomy-looking man appeared in the doorway. He looked half asleep, but his hooded eyes missed nothing as they swept the room.

'You certainly know how to pick 'em, I'll say that for you, Paget,' he greeted the chief inspector. 'I suppose you do *know* what day this is? Or didn't they use to have Christmas up in London?' He sniffed loudly, whether from the cold or in disgust was impossible to tell.

'Damned nearly went into the ditch a couple of times on the way over,' he went on. 'The road's a sheet of ice.' He rubbed his hands together as if they were cold, but Paget had come to recognize the gesture. Charlie was about to get down to business. 'What is it this time?' His eyes went to the night table. 'Drugs?'

'Hard to say, Charlie,' Paget said. 'I'm hoping you and Starkie can tell me.' Inspector Charlie Dobbs was in charge of the Scene-of-Crime forensic team, and Dr Reginald Starkie was the Home Office pathologist.

'Speak of the devil,' said Charlie as a short, plump, bald-headed man appeared beside him. 'Merry Christmas, Reg.' The pathologist glowered as he paused to catch his breath after climbing the stairs. 'Sounds like you could do with losing a bit off that spare tyre,' Charlie observed. He patted the man's ample belly none too gently. 'No Christmas pud for you today, my lad.'

'And a merry Christmas to you, too, Charlie!' Starkie wheezed as he pushed past. 'Got nothing better to do on Christmas Day, then, have we, Paget?'

Paget ignored the jibe. 'Thanks for coming out so promptly,' he said. After all, it *was* a hell of a way to spend Christmas.

Starkie grunted and set his bag aside. He broke the seal on a packet of latex gloves and began to pull them on. 'I was supposed to be reading the lesson this morning,' he grumbled to no one in particular. 'Something to do with peace and goodwill and not being called out to look at dead bodies on Christmas Day.' He sighed heavily. 'Ah, well, let's take a look, then.' He made a note of the time and bent to his task.

Paget moved aside to allow Starkie room to do his job, and looked around the room. It was a dreary little place. What had once been a larger dormitory had been made over into smaller, separate rooms that were little more than cubicles. Private to be sure, but small and cramped and barely adequate for one person.

It was sparsely furnished. There were two chairs; one straight-backed with a padded seat; the other an old-fashioned leather armchair that had seen much better days. A portable radio, together with earphones, lay on the floor beside the chair. Along one wall, parallel to the bed, was a cupboard whose upper shelves and hangers contained the bulk of the girl's clothing, including two complete school uniforms. The lower shelf was a jumble of undergarments, some soiled and waiting to be washed by the look of them, piled on top of several pairs of shoes. Beside the cupboard was a desk-cum-dressing-table made of pressed wood, and mounted on the wall above it was a mirror. A strip of Sellotape was stuck to the glass as if something had been taped there recently and taken down again, but whatever it was, it was not in evidence now.

The dresser top was strewn with jars and bottles containing creams and sprays, a brush, a comb, hair grips, a lipstick holder, a box of tissues, and a hand-held hair-drier with its flex writhing like a snake through everything.

And there was glass. Tiny shards glinting in the light. Paget looked around but could see nothing broken. Neither was there anything in the wastepaper basket except some cotton wool wadded into a ball.

The cupboard and dresser were painted white—or had been many years ago. Now the surfaces were scuffed and scarred and yellowing with age. School books almost filled a shelf beside the dresser, but mixed in with them were several well-thumbed paperbacks, all of them romances, judging by their titles.

There were no pictures. No photographs. No posters; nothing even stuck on the inside of the cupboard doors. And yet there was ample evidence that there had been in the past. The distant past. Dried bits of Sellotape, hard and brittle to the touch, still clung determinedly to the paint, and yet Monica Shaw had put up no pictures of her own, and he wondered why.

And lastly there was the bed. Small, narrow, utilitarian, little more than a cot, really, but adequate, he supposed, for a young girl. Sadly, he shook his head. Not much of a place to be spending Christmas, he thought. Why was she here? Why wasn't she at home?

As he was about to leave he room, he stopped to examine a coat that lay in a crumpled heap on the floor at the foot of the bed. It was a heavy winter coat, and an expensive one. Blue, teal blue, if he wasn't mistaken. And a pair of winter boots lay some distance away, apparently kicked off and left where they fell. They lay in a small puddle of water that had begun to dry at the edges on the wooden floor. He felt the coat. It, too, was quite damp, and he made a mental note to find out exactly when it had stopped snowing.

'OH, FOR HEAVEN'S SAKE, Jane, do try to pull yourself together.' Samantha Crowther paced back and forth before the gas fire in the housemistress's room, back and forth, back and forth until Jane Wolsey wanted to scream.

It was all very well for Crowther; she hadn't been close to Monica. Not the way she had. For that matter, thought Jane ungraciously, she doubted whether Crowther had ever been close to anyone in her life. All she ever thought about was the school and its reputation; never mind the people. She kept going on and on about how difficult this could make things for the school. What would the other parents think? How would they react? What about the board? And what was she going to say to Monica's mother—*if* she could ever get hold of her. All of the government offices were closed for Christmas, of course, and there seemed to be no way of finding out exactly where Julia Shaw was.

Did it matter? Jane wondered dully. Did Julia Shaw have any feelings at all for her daughter? How many times had she even *seen* Monica since she'd deposited her almost six years ago at Thornton Hill? Ten? A dozen at the outside. She couldn't even be bothered with her at Christmas.

Jane felt the tears begin to form again and closed her eyes, but the image of Monica's cold, white, lifeless face refused to go away. She wished Crowther would go away. Just go away and leave her alone with her thoughts.

'I CAN'T BE SURE,' Starkie said when Paget asked him how long the girl had been dead. They were in the corridor, and the pathologist was gathering his instruments together. 'There are conflicting signs, here. At a rough guess, I'd say she died somewhere between midnight and two this morning. I can tell you one thing, though. She was really trying to make a job of it. I found two more syringes mixed up in the bedclothes, both empty, and there are three separate puncture marks.'

'Which means?'

'Hypoglycaemic shock, if it was insulin,' he said. 'As a diabetic, this girl would know that. It's not something she would do by mistake.'

'And that would kill her?'

Starkie pursed his lips. 'It's not quite as cut and dried as that,' he said. 'Initially, she would experience rapid heartbeat, sweating, dizziness, and mental confusion. That could be followed by the loss of consciousness, and possibly death.'

'Is there any way you can tell whether it was self-administered?'

Starkie snapped his bag shut. 'The angle of entry is consistent with what I would expect, assuming she was right-handed, but that's hardly conclusive. I hope to be able to tell you *what* was administered, but *how* it got there I leave to you, Paget. That's your job, not mine, thank God. The only other thing I can tell you at the moment is that there are scratches and contusions on her upper arms, inner thighs and abdomen; fairly recent ones, I'd say. I'll have more for you tomorrow.'

'Tomorrow. I don't suppose…' Paget began, but Starkie anticipated him. 'Don't even suggest it,' he said firmly. 'This may be your idea of how to spend Christmas, Paget, but it certainly isn't mine. The only carving I intend to do today is on turkey and a joint of beef.'

He was half-way to the stairs when a thought struck him. 'What happened to Sergeant Tregalles?' he asked Paget. 'I thought you two always worked together. Not ill, is he?'

'No, he's not ill,' Paget assured him. 'He's got the long weekend off, that's all, and there didn't seem to be much point in dragging him away from his family when I can manage here on my own.'

Starkie snorted. 'You must be going soft in your old age,' he said. 'If it were me, it would be the other way round, I can tell you. Anyway, I'm off. Talk to you tomorrow. Merry Christmas.'

Merry Christmas. Not much chance of that, thought Paget gloomily.

Trouble was, he had allowed himself to hope that this Christmas might be different. To be truthful, he'd fantasized a bit about spending at least part of Christmas with Andrea, but he'd heard absolutely nothing from her since that night a week ago. He'd telephoned, but there was no answer at the flat. He'd left a message at the hospital, but she had never called him back. He knew they were rushed off their feet over there—so had he been this past week— but surely she could have found time to phone back.

That he'd misjudged the situation was becoming painfully obvious, he thought glumly. The way she had withdrawn—almost bolted from the car. Things had been going so well up till then. He should have…

'Sir…'

Paget jumped, startled by the sudden appearance of Maitland at his elbow. 'For God's sake, man! Stop creeping about the place like that,' he growled irritably. 'What is it?'

The constable stared at Paget, then looked down at his boots. The chief inspector must be going deaf. 'Sorry, sir,' he said, 'but Inspector Dobbs would like a word.'

There was no note. At least, his people hadn't found one, Charlie said. 'All sorts of notebooks, paper and pencils in the desk. She wasn't short of material. But as far as I can tell, it looks like suicide. I have to go, but if you need anything, ask Grace Lovett. She's in charge.' He nodded in the direction of a slim, fair-haired young woman on her hands and knees beside the bed. 'As for the rest,' he shrugged, 'it might be a few days before we have much for you, what with the holidays and all, but we'll do our best.'

No note. Paget stood in the doorway and looked at the now empty bed. It might mean something or it might mean nothing at all. It wasn't unusual for suicides not to leave a note. But the question still remained: was it really suicide?

THE WOMAN WHO OPENED the door in answer to his knock was tall, slim, and striking in appearance. Iron grey hair, beautifully coiffed, framed a strong, handsome face. Her brow was broad, her eyes steady, her chin firm, and her mouth was set in a thin, straight line as if something had displeased her. Apart from a tailored blouse of dazzling white, she was dressed in tones of grey; grey shirt, grey cardigan, and grey shoes whose heels must have been at least three inches high. Jade leaf-shaped ear-rings were half hidden by her hair, and her fingers were adorned with several rings.

Paget judged her to be somewhere between forty-five and fifty.

'Yes?' The voice matched the image perfectly.

'Detective Chief Inspector Paget,' he said, displaying his

warrant card. 'I'm looking for the housemistress, Miss Wolsey.'

The woman didn't respond immediately, but her eyes took in every detail, and he had the feeling that he'd been stripped down and reassembled in that brief moment. It was not a pleasant experience.

'You'd better come in, Chief Inspector,' she said as she stepped aside. It was less an invitation than a reluctant acceptance of the inevitable. 'I am Samantha Crowther, headmistress of Thornton Hill. *Miss* Samantha Crowther,' she emphasized. 'I am responsible for the school and its good name, you understand, and before we go any further, I'd like to know how long those cars and vans will be parked out there in the driveway in front of the school for everyone to see?'

As Paget stepped over the threshold, a second woman rose to her feet from the depths of an armchair, and came forward to meet him. 'I am Jane Wolsey…' she began, but Miss Crowther cut her off with a wave of her hand.

'In a moment, Jane, *if* you please. Chief Inspector?'

Not a word about the young girl who lay dead at the other end of the corridor, he noted. Her manner irritated him, but there was nothing to be gained by getting off on the wrong foot with the headmistress.

'The school is quite well screened from the road,' he pointed out, 'and once the forensic team have all their equipment out, I'll have them move the vans to the back of the school.'

Miss Crowther nodded as if she had expected no other answer. 'I really don't see why all this is necessary,' she said. 'We are, of course, shocked and saddened by Monica's death, but it's hardly a matter for the police. The girl was a diabetic, and much as it pains me to say it, I suspect it was her own refusal to adhere to the strict regimen required to maintain her health that caused her death. This isn't the first time, you know. She has done this sort of thing before—disregarding her doctor's instructions, to say nothing of mine—with the result that she had to be rushed into hospital to—to do whatever it is they do in such cases.'

'Stabilize her,' Jane Wolsey said quietly. 'And it was only once, Miss Crowther.'

'Yes. Well, but you do see what I mean, Chief Inspector? The ambulance men clearly exceeded their authority in calling you. Miss Wolsey should have consulted me before any such call was made.'

'I did try...' Jane Wolsey began, but the headmistress brushed the words aside. 'Really, Jane, you know I always go for an early morning walk,' she said as if that explained everything.

'They had very little choice in the matter, Miss Crowther,' Paget told her. 'They are obliged to call us when, in their opinion, a suspicious death has occurred.'

'Suspicious death?' Samantha Crowther stared at Paget in disbelief. 'You can't possibly be serious?'

'I'm very serious, Miss Crowther. There are a number of unanswered questions concerning exactly how Miss Shaw died. There will probably be an inquest.'

'Oh, dear!' The headmistress looked quite shaken. 'Whatever will I tell the board?'

'Her parents haven't been notified, I take it?'

Miss Crowther shook her head. 'No. I did try to reach her mother, but being Christmas Day, it's difficult. Monica's parents are divorced. Her father remarried years ago and went abroad, I believe. Her mother is Julia Shaw.' She paused as if waiting for the name to register, but it meant nothing to Paget. 'She's a member of the British delegation at the Common Currency conference,' she explained. 'She's in Brussels, but I've no idea where, and I can't get hold of anyone with all the offices closed today. I left a message with the embassy, but I'm not at all sure that it will get to her. I also tried the house in Hampshire on the off chance, but there was no reply. Perhaps…?' She eyed Paget speculatively.

'I see,' he said. 'In that case, we will contact Brussels and ask them to have Mrs Shaw get in touch with us immediately.'

'You will make sure she understands that we did everything possible, Chief Inspector? I'm sure Miss Wolsey…'

'I'm sure Miss Wolsey will tell me herself,' said Paget smoothly, 'so I won't detain you any longer, Miss Crowther.' Gently but firmly he herded her towards the door.

Samantha Crowther seemed reluctant to leave. 'I shall be in my study if I am needed,' she said. She paused at the door and adopted a more confidential tone. 'You will make sure that Mrs Shaw understands that there was nothing we could have done to prevent Monica's death, won't you, Chief Inspector?' She eyed him anxiously. 'I mean, the school cannot be held responsible; you do see that, don't you?'

'I'm sure Mrs Shaw will want to speak to you herself, Miss Crowther,' said Paget soothingly.

'Yes. Well…' The headmistress looked anything but cheered by that prospect.

He began to close the door behind her, but Miss Crowther wasn't quite finished yet. 'You won't forget about the vans will you?' she said. 'Their presence here invites curiosity, and that is the last thing we want at Thornton Hill. After all, we do have a reputation to uphold. Please have them removed as soon as possible.'

FIVE

'PLEASE SIT DOWN, Chief Inspector.' Jane Wolsey indicated an armchair beside the fire. The room was warm and Paget removed his coat before sitting down. Now, with the departure of Samantha Crowther, he was better able to focus his attention on the housemistress.

She was younger than he'd first thought; mid-forties perhaps, but with her tear-stained face so pinched and drawn, and her hair so liberally streaked with grey, she looked older. She sat on the edge of the chair, hands folded in her lap, hunched over like some old crone, submissive, waiting. Her large, spaniel-like eyes followed his every move as if fearful of what he was going to say.

As the silence between them lengthened, her hand fluttered self-consciously to her hair as if suddenly aware of its disarray. She used her right hand. Her left hand remained immobile in her lap, curled and shrivelled, its shape more closely resembling that of a claw than a human hand. Nor was it only the hand that was misshapen, he realized; her left arm was withered and shorter than the right.

'I know this must be painful for you, Miss Wolsey,' he began, 'but I'd like you to tell me in your own words exactly what happened this morning. Tell me what you saw and what you did when you went along to Monica's room. I'm told you were taking her a Christmas gift?'

Jane Wolsey's eyes went to a large, square package beside the television set. It was wrapped, he saw, in a heavy, gold metallic paper embossed with Merry Christmases in flowing copperplate. Broad red ribbon shot through with gold and silver threads encircled it, and a bow containing

a cluster of tiny bells topped it off. The wrapping alone
was a work of art; a bit overdone for his taste, but a beautiful creation nevertheless.

'Yes,' she said dully. 'It was to have been Monica's gift
from her mother.'

'Mrs Shaw had it sent here to you?'

Miss Wolsey shook her head. 'No, no. I bought it and
wrapped it myself,' she said. 'You see, when Mrs Shaw
found that the Common Currency conference was going to
continue on over the holidays, she asked the head—that is,
Miss Crowther—to buy Monica a gift on her behalf. Miss
Crowther turned the task over to me. Oh, not that I minded,
of course, but I wanted it to be just right for Monica.' Her
eyes became moist, and Paget thought she was about to
cry, but she lifted her head and carried on.

'Girls of that age can be very difficult to buy for, you
know, so I wanted to be there when Monica opened her
gift. To make sure that she liked it. That's why I took it
along first thing this morning.' She paused, frowned, and
looked down at her hands. When she looked up again,
Paget could see tears glistening in her eyes.

'To be honest, there was another reason as well,' she
confessed. 'You see, Monica was supposed to have gone
home for Christmas like all the other girls, but when her
mother telephoned at the last minute to say she couldn't
leave Brussels, there was no alternative but for Monica to
remain here. I—I didn't think she should be alone when
she first woke up on Christmas morning. I felt *someone*
ought to be there.'

The housemistress went on to say that when she received
no answer to her knock she had entered Monica's room.
At first, she thought the girl was playing some sort of game,
pretending to be asleep. 'She was all wrapped up in the
bedclothes as if she'd rolled herself in them,' Miss Wolsey
explained. 'It was only when I went to shake her that I

realized...' A tear escaped and rolled slowly down her cheek. 'I didn't know what to do. She was so stiff. I kept telling myself she must have had some sort of seizure.' Her voice dropped to a whisper. 'And yet I knew... In my heart I knew.'

'The ambulance men said you told them to hurry because the girl was very ill,' Paget said. 'Why did you say that if you knew she was dead?'

She avoided his eyes. 'I—I couldn't bring myself to say the words,' she said huskily. 'I really couldn't. I know it must sound silly, but I was hoping—praying that I was wrong. She... Oh, God!' Jane Wolsey jammed a tiny handkerchief against her mouth and stifled a sob. Tears filled her eyes and ran down her cheeks. 'Why?' she choked. 'She was so young.'

Paget remained silent. There was nothing he could do or say that would help the housemistress in her grief. He waited patiently, and only when she was calm again did he continue.

Jane Wolsey said the last time she had seen Monica was somewhere between nine and nine thirty the previous evening. 'I went in to make sure she was all right.' With a gesture that spoke of habit she pulled the long sleeve of her dress down until the buttoned cuff almost covered her deformed hand.

'You see, she'd been to a Christmas party at Glenacres in the afternoon. Glenacres is the riding stables where we send our girls for equestrian training. You may have seen the sign on your way here today. Actually, their lower paddock borders our own property behind the school, so it's very convenient. The girls can walk across the fields and go in the back way rather than go all the way round by road.

'Monica had some wine at the party—in fact she spilled some of it on her anorak. I took it from her as soon as she got back to try to get the stain out, but I'm afraid it may be there to stay.' She rose and went over to a chair where a snow-white anorak had been spread to dry, and showed it to Paget. 'You see?' she said, holding it out like an offering. 'She can't possibly wear it like that. She can't…' Abruptly, she crushed it to her in a fierce embrace as if it were the girl herself, and began to weep.

Paget rose and went to her. He took the jacket from her and spread it once more on the chair, then led the housemistress back to her own seat before the fire. 'Perhaps a cup of tea…?' he suggested, but she shook her head.

'I'll be all right,' she said. 'It was just…I'll be all right.' She wiped away the tears. 'I'm sorry, Chief Inspector; what was it I was saying?'

'You said Monica had some wine,' he reminded her.

Jane Wolsey nodded. 'Yes. I've no idea how much she had to drink, of course, but she should have had more sense. She knows—knew what it could do to her.' She swallowed hard and forced herself to go on. 'Unfortunately, at seventeen, rules don't mean very much, I'm afraid. Luckily, Sally Pritchard was there and realized what might happen, so she brought Monica back here in her car. Sally works at Glenacres,' she explained.

'Not that Monica was actually ill, you understand, but being diabetic, she had to be careful. Any change in her routine such as over-exertion or excitement, and any change in her diet, especially something like wine, could bring on an attack, so I was glad Sally brought her back in the car when she did.'

'This was late in the evening?'

'Oh, no. The party was in the afternoon. It must have been about six when Sally brought her home in her car. I could see that Monica had overdone it; her eyes were too bright and her face was flushed. Just excitement, that's all it was. That's all it was,' she repeated softly as if to reassure herself.

She remained quiet for a moment before going on. 'I made sure that she checked her blood glucose level, of course. And had something to eat, and she took her insulin before getting into a warm bath. When I looked in later, she was already in bed and seemed to be settling down for an early night, so I said good-night and turned the light out so that she could get some rest.'

'I see. Tell me, did you see her take her insulin?'

The housemistress looked puzzled by the question. 'Yes, I did. As a matter of fact, but I don't see...'

'Was Monica right-handed?'

'Yes.'

'Where did she inject herself? What part of her body?'

'In her tummy,' Miss Wolsey said promptly, and smiled slightly as Paget grimaced. 'It's the best place, really,' she explained. 'And it doesn't hurt much if you pinch the flesh between your fingers. And I made sure the bath water was not too hot. It makes a difference, you see. It can alter the rate at which the insulin is absorbed into the body.'

'I see. You seem to be very knowledgeable on the subject, Miss Wolsey. Have you had some previous experience?'

She shook her head. 'No, but when you have young girls in your care, you have to be prepared for every eventuality, so I made it my business to learn.' Tears welled up in her eyes again. 'But even that wasn't enough, was it? I wasn't prepared for what happened.'

He didn't give her time to dwell on that. 'Tell me, Miss Wolsey, was the light on when you entered Monica's room this morning?'

She nodded. 'Yes, it was. And the reading lamp beside the bed was on as well. That's why I thought Monica was playing some sort of game, all huddled up in the bedclothes like that.'

'Did you touch anything? Move anything, or take anything from the room?'

Jane Wolsey looked distressed. 'No. No, of course not. Why should I?'

'You mentioned taking the gift along to her room, but I see you brought it back.'

'Well, yes, but it wasn't ever *in* the room itself,' the housemistress explained. 'I had set it down just outside in the corridor while I went to make sure Monica was awake, and when the ambulance men came I brought it back in here. It would have been in the way where I was.'

'Did you see what Monica was wearing in bed?'

Miss Wolsey shot a quizzical look at Paget. 'Her pyjamas, I should think,' she said. 'Monica preferred pyjamas.'

'But you didn't actually *see* what she was wearing, Miss Wolsey?'

The woman looked mystified. 'Well, no. She was all wrapped up in the sheet, and when I touched her; when I realized…I—I'm sorry, Chief Inspector, but all I could think of was to get help.'

'So you don't know she was fully clothed?'

The housemistress stared at him.

'There was a coat on the floor at the foot of the bed,' he went on. 'A blue coat and a pair of boots. They do belong to Monica, I take it?'

Jane Wolsey nodded. 'Yes, that's right, they…' She stopped in mid-sentence. 'That's right! It was her new coat. I meant to pick it up—she'd never even worn it. It was on the floor, and I remember wondering… Her boots; they were wet and muddy when she came back from the stables, so I put them on a piece of newspaper to dry. I'm afraid I don't understand this at all, Chief Inspector.'

'Neither do I,' he confessed, 'but at a guess I'd say Monica got dressed and went out again some time during the night.'

Jane Wolsey looked shocked. 'Oh, no,' she insisted, 'she wouldn't do that. I left her in bed. Besides, it had started to snow, and Monica hated the cold.'

'Nevertheless, she was dressed, and there were wet patches on the floor where I suspect snow melted after she returned. Do you happen to recall whether it was snowing when she returned from the party?'

'No, it wasn't. It started shortly after, I believe. I looked out about nine and it was quite deep on the window-sill by then.'

'I see. Now, is there anywhere Monica might have gone? Did she have friends around here? What about these stables? Could she have gone to see someone there?'

'No!' The word came out sharply, too sharply—and too quickly in Paget's opinion, and the woman herself looked faintly startled by her own vehemence. 'No,' she said more softly. 'There would be no reason for her to go there.'

He decided to leave it for the moment. 'How would you describe Monica?' he asked her. 'What sort of girl was she?'

The housemistress raised her eyes to his. 'That's not an easy question to answer,' she said sadly. 'To be honest, not many people liked her. She had no friends, at least not among the girls. She was quiet; too quiet, perhaps.' She gave a small gesture of apology. 'I'm sorry if I sound negative, Chief Inspector,' she said, 'but Monica made it very difficult for anyone to be her friend. I don't know a lot about these things, but I think she was afraid that if she did reach out to someone, they might let her down in some way.

'You see, there was no love in Monica's life. It was an emotion that was foreign to her. Perhaps I shouldn't say this, but I suspect she'd never known love, even as a child.

Her parents were divorced when she was three years old, and she's never seen or heard of her father since that time. As for her mother...'

Jane Wolsey stopped abruptly, cutting off whatever it was she was about to say. Her mouth set in a thin, hard line. 'I tried in my own small way to be her friend,' she went on after a moment, 'but it wasn't enough.' She shook her head sadly. 'Not enough,' she repeated softly.

'You say she discouraged friends, yet she went to a Christmas party at the stables,' Paget said. 'And you mentioned this girl, Sally, who brought her home. Wasn't she a friend?'

'Well, yes, she was in a way,' the housemistress said. 'But Sally is at least ten years older than Monica, so it's not quite the same thing, is it? She's one of the instructors at Glenacres. As a matter of fact, she was a Thornton Hill girl herself some years ago. I had the juniors, then. She's a nice girl. Sensible; level-headed. I asked her to keep an eye on Monica when she was over there at the stables.' Miss Wolsey stopped, perhaps thinking she was wandering from the subject, but under Paget's compelling gaze felt obliged to go on.

'You see, lately, Monica has been spending more and more time over there, and I was, well, frankly, Chief Inspector, I was worried.' She paused as if selecting her words carefully before continuing. 'She was not a rider—Monica was actually very awkward on a horse—but lately she's been spending every spare hour over there, and I didn't want her to overdo it.'

'Was her condition *that* critical?' Paget asked. 'I was under the impression that people with diabetes can do just about anything they choose as long as they monitor themselves carefully.'

Unaccountably, a flush appeared in Miss Wolsey's cheeks. 'Well, no, it wasn't *critical,* but Monica was...I know Miss Crowther thought I was being over-protective, but seventeen can be such a difficult age for a girl, and she had no one else to look out for her.'

Paget phrased his next question with care. 'We don't know yet exactly how Monica died,' he said, 'so we have to explore every possibility. Did Monica ever speak, even obliquely, of taking her own life?'

For a moment, Paget thought she hadn't heard the question. The housemistress continued to stare into the fire, eyes moist, unseeing. A tremor ran through her small frame, and she wrapped her arms around herself as if she were cold. She plucked nervously at the sleeve covering her left hand.

'No,' she said at last. The word was little more than a whisper. 'If I'd thought she would…' She pressed her knuckles to her mouth and closed her eyes. Paget waited, but the woman remained silent.

'You saw no note when you found her this morning?'

The housemistress shook her head. 'There was no note,' she said with infinite sadness. 'Nothing.'

There was a knock on the door, but Jane Wolsey remained seated, seemingly oblivious to the sound. Paget rose to his feet and opened it to find Maitland standing there.

'Excuse me, sir, but there's a Miss Gray downstairs,' he said quietly so that only Paget heard. 'She says she's come to take Miss Wolsey and Miss Shaw to church. I asked her to wait in the common room, seeing it was empty. WPC Turner is with her. I hope that was all right?'

'Quite right, Maitland,' Paget said. He turned to Miss Wolsey. 'Were you expecting a Miss Gray?' he asked her.

Jane Wolsey rose from her chair. 'Sylvia?' she said, obviously puzzled. 'No.'

'She says she has come to take you and Miss Shaw to church.'

Jane Wolsey's hand flew to her mouth. 'Oh, dear! Oh,

how thoughtless of me. I should have telephoned. But it was Sally who was coming to pick us up.'

'Tell Miss Gray I'll be down in a couple of minutes,' Paget told the constable. 'You haven't told her what's happened here, have you?'

'No, sir.'

'Good. Don't. Oh, and there's one more thing. It seems that there's a problem getting hold of Monica Shaw's mother. She's in Brussels at the Common Currency conference. Get the details from Miss Crowther and phone them into Division. I want someone on it right away. The sooner Mrs Shaw is found and notified, the better. And there's to be no mention of suicide. For the moment, all we know is that the girl died in her sleep. All right?'

Maitland nodded. 'Right, sir.'

SIX

THORNTON HILL SCHOOL was built in the shape of a squared-off U. The main building, Crowther Hall—named after the founder, Miss Crowther's great-grandfather—formed the base of the U, while Cameron Hall and Braden Hall formed the two sides. Miss Wolsey's quarters, and those of the upper and lower sixth form girls, were in Braden Hall.

The common room was at the rear of the main building. It was a long, narrow room, with tall windows that looked out on a broad expanse of lawn, now blanketed in snow. Beyond the lawns were tennis courts, nets down and put away for winter, and beyond them was a grove of trees.

A young woman was looking out of one of the windows. She had her back to him but turned quickly when she heard the door. She was very young; eighteen or nineteen, perhaps, with the fresh complexion of one who spends a lot of time outdoors. She was a pretty girl, with chestnut hair and green eyes, but she looked troubled and apprehensive.

'Miss Gray? I am Detective Chief Inspector Paget.' He smiled as he saw alarm flare in her eyes. 'Please don't be alarmed,' he said. 'I'd just like to ask you a few questions.'

Alarm gave way to wariness. 'I don't understand,' she said. 'What has happened?' Her eyes went to the police-woman beside the door. 'No one will tell me what is going on.'

He nodded apologetically. 'I'm sorry, but that was my fault,' he said. 'Won't you sit down?' He indicated one of the chintz-covered chairs.

The girl sat down, but the question remained in her eyes as he took a seat facing her.

'Miss Wolsey seemed surprised to hear that you had come to take her and Monica to church,' he began conversationally. 'She thought Miss Pritchard would be here.'

'Yes, well she would have except she's a bit under the weather this morning,' the girl said, 'so she asked me to take them and bring them back.'

A feeling of disquiet came over Paget. 'Did Miss Pritchard say what was wrong?'

'She said it was nothing serious—probably something she ate or drank at the party yesterday—but her stomach was still a bit queasy and she thought it best if she didn't leave the house today. But she'd promised Miss Wolsey that she would take her and Monica to church this morning, so she rang and asked me if I would come over instead.'

'You live at Glenacres, do you?'

'That's right. I share a room with another girl, Penny Wakefield.' Sylvia Gray smiled ruefully. 'I lost the toss, so I had to stay behind while she went home for Christmas.'

'Are you a friend of Monica's?'

The girl hesitated. 'I know her,' she said cautiously, 'but we're not what you would call friends, exactly. Why? What's happened? Is she in some sort of trouble?'

'I'm afraid it's more serious than that,' he said quietly. 'Monica died last night.'

Her eyes grew even wider, and her mouth formed the word 'died?' but no sound came out. 'How…? What happened?'

'We're not quite sure. That's why we're here. That's why I wanted to talk to you. Were you at the Christmas party yesterday?'

The girl nodded.

'How did Monica seem to you then?'

Sylvia Gray shrugged. 'All right, I suppose—for Monica.' Colour began to rise in her face. 'I'm sorry, I didn't mean that to sound…' She stopped and looked away.

'Then what *did* you mean, Miss Gray?'

The girl shifted uncomfortably in her seat. 'It's just that Monica isn't—wasn't—all that easy to get along with,' she said. No doubt she would have stopped there, but under Paget's unrelenting gaze felt compelled to continue. 'It's not that she didn't try. She was a hard worker; Sally only had to suggest a job and she was off like a shot. It was just that she was, well, awkward. No one wanted to work with her because she always seemed to mess things up some-how. I think Sally was the only one who could get along with her. There was a bit of a joke around the yard that if you wanted a job to take twice as long, you should get Monica to help you.' She grimaced apologetically. 'I'm afraid that doesn't sound very nice, does it?'

'So you tended to avoid her. Is that it?'

The girl nodded. 'Yes, I'm afraid I did.'

'Tell me what you did see of her yesterday.'

Sylvia Gray thought about that for a moment. 'I remem-ber she knocked over a bottle of wine,' she said slowly. 'She was filling up the glasses—well, plastic cups, actu-ally—and she turned round to get another bottle and knocked it over. Somebody grabbed it, but most of it had run out by then.' She shrugged. 'But that was Monica. She just couldn't seem to get it right, somehow. I know Mr Lucas wasn't all that pleased. It was some of his best wine.'

'Do you recall anything else?'

The girl looked away as if trying to think, but there was a subtle change in her voice when she said: 'No, I don't think so.'

'Are you quite sure, Miss Gray?'

Colour tinged her face. 'Sorry, but I can't think of any-thing,' she said.

'What about later, when Miss Pritchard brought her back here? Did you see them leave?'

A guarded look came into Sylvia Gray's eyes. 'Yes.'

'And?'

'I—I'm not sure what you mean.'

Paget allowed his irritation to show. 'Come, now, Miss Gray. I'm told that the girls usually walk back and forth between the stables and the school. Why did Miss Pritchard bring her back in the car?'

Sylvia Gray avoided his eyes. 'You'd have to ask Sally about that,' she said evasively.

'Oh, I will,' Paget assured her, 'but in the meantime, I'm asking you, Miss Gray. Why was it necessary for Monica to be taken back to the school by car? Was she drunk?'

The girl looked startled by the suggestion. 'No. At least, I don't think so. She was diabetic, so she couldn't drink much at all.'

'Then why the car, Miss Gray? Was she ill, perhaps?'

'I don't know. I saw them getting into the car, but that's all. It was dark.'

'There are no lights?'

'Well, yes, the yard lights were on, but they're not all that good. And it was just for a few seconds.'

The girl seemed to be trying to distance herself from whatever had taken place the day before. It might mean something or it might mean nothing. Paget decided to let it go for now. 'How did Monica seem to you at the party?' he asked her. 'Did she seem to be enjoying herself, for example? Did she seem happy? Sad? Was she with anyone in particular?'

Some of the tension seemed to drain away as the girl considered the question. 'I don't think she was any different,' she said at last. 'As I said, she didn't have any real friends, so she was sort of outside the circle, if you know what I mean. To tell you the truth, I don't know why she came to the stables at all.'

'Why *did* she come, do you think? Was she paid for her work?'

'Oh, no. She just came over whenever she had time to spare. She doesn't even have a horse. She just seemed to like being there. To be fair, she did work hard when she was on her own. It was just that she could never work *with* people.'

'Did she ever say anything that might suggest she was unhappy enough to consider taking her own life?'

Sylvia Gray sat very still. 'So *that's* it!' she breathed softly. 'I've been wondering why you were here; what all these questions were about.' She frowned in concentration. 'No, I can't say she ever said anything like that to me. I'd have remembered if she had.'

'Did you ever see Monica take her insulin shots?'

'No. I know she did take them sometimes when she was over there, but I never actually saw her. She carried a kit with her all the time, though.'

'I see.' Paget stood up. 'Thank you, Miss Gray. You've been very helpful. But I must emphasize that we really don't know exactly how Monica died. There could be any one of several perfectly natural explanations.'

Sylvia scrambled to her feet. 'You mean she may not have committed suicide?'

'Do you know of any reason why she should?' he countered.

'Well, no, but I thought you said…'

'I said we don't know, Miss Gray.' He led the way to the door.

'Poor Miss Wolsey,' the girl said as they left the room. 'She'll be ever so upset. May I go and see her? I think I should. Is it all right?'

'Quite all right as far as I'm concerned,' he told her. 'I believe she is still in her room. Do you know the way?'

'Oh, yes. I've been here before.'

As the girl ran up the stairs, Paget followed her with his eyes and wondered what it was she was holding back. Perhaps it had nothing to do with the way Monica Shaw had met her death, but all the same he'd like to know. He didn't like loose ends.

'APART FROM MISS WOLSEY and I, there were only two other people on the premises last night,' Miss Crowther said. 'The rest are either away for the holidays or they live outside.' The headmistress went on to explain that in order to survive financially, it had been necessary to take in more girls, which meant there was less room for staff on the premises.

'I'm afraid it is becoming very difficult for the smaller independent schools such as Thornton Hill to survive these days,' she explained. 'The staff didn't like it, of course, but we only have a certain amount of space, and when it was put to them it was either that or staff cuts, they agreed—reluctantly. Most of them managed to find accommodation close by, but several of them travel here each day from Broadminster.'

In answer to his questions regarding Monica herself, Miss Crowther seemed somewhat vague, and it soon became apparent that her knowledge of the girl came as much from hearsay as personal contact. 'We try to instil a sense of community, a team spirit in our girls here at Thornton Hill,' she said. 'In fact we pride ourselves on it, but Monica simply resisted any and all attempts to include her in the circle. I regret to say she was a wilful girl; quite difficult to deal with—and quite unlike her mother.'

'I must say I'd gathered a rather different view of Miss

Shaw from her housemistress,' Paget ventured, but Samantha Crowther was shaking her head gently but firmly.

'Poor Jane. You mustn't take what she says too literally,
Chief Inspector. She does so want to believe the best of
people, but some of the girls simply walk all over her, and
she doesn't seem to realize it. She means well, of course,
but you can't afford to let the girls get ahead of you. They'll
try it on every time, especially with someone like Jane.'
Miss Crowther sighed. 'Unfortunately, with her, shall we
say, "limitations", we do have to make allowances. I'm
sure you understand.'

Paget understood only too well. There was nothing to be
gained by spending any more time with Samantha
Crowther. 'You mentioned two others who were here last
night,' he said as he rose to go. 'If I could have their names,
and you can tell me where I might find them...?'

'Of course. One is Mr Lambert—he takes maths and
computing sciences, so essential these days—and the other
is Mrs Frobisher. She's modern languages. I can ring
through on the house phone to see if they are in, if you
wish.'

HAROLD LAMBERT TOLD PAGET that he had gone to bed
about eleven the previous evening, and knew nothing of
what had happened until Miss Crowther rang him about
eight o'clock that morning. Lambert seemed to be genuinely shaken, but when asked for his opinion of Monica
Shaw, he shifted uncomfortably in his seat.

'I'm afraid she wasn't one of my better students,' he said.
'The unfortunate thing was that she could have been if
she'd been prepared to apply herself. She could have been
in the top two or three. But she seemed...' He stopped,
searching for the right phrase. 'This may sound absurd to
you, Chief Inspector, but it sometimes seemed to me that

she was bent on *not* learning. It was as if she took some sort of perverse pride in failing.'

'What about the girl rather than the student? What was your impression of her?'

Lambert shook his head sadly. 'She had no social skills, I'm afraid. Consequently she had no friends. She was a very moody girl; uncommunicative, even sullen. Trying to talk to her was like talking to a wall. She'd simply stand there staring off into the distance as if you weren't there at all. Most frustrating.' Lambert spread his hands apologetically. 'I'm sorry, but you did ask.'

Mrs Frobisher confirmed everything Lambert had said, including the fact that Monica could have been, in her opinion, a much better student if she hadn't spent so much time 'day-dreaming', as she put it. 'She did just enough to get by…' Mrs Frobisher stopped. 'No, that's not true,' she amended. 'I might as well be honest even though she's dead, poor soul. She did *not* do enough to get by. I'm sorry to have to say it, Chief Inspector, but if I'd had my way, Monica would have left this school long ago. I'm not telling you anything I haven't told Miss Crowther many times before, but I was always overruled. Monica Shaw was here because her mother is who she is, and it was her wish that Monica remain here. That's the truth of it.'

Unwanted and unloved. Was this to be Monica's epitaph?

The chief inspector's footsteps echoed hollowly as he made his way through empty halls. What a wretched life the girl must have had. How long had she been here? Six years?

To Monica Shaw it must have seemed an eternity.

SEVEN

BEFORE LEAVING THORNTON HILL SCHOOL, Paget went back upstairs and surveyed the corridor outside Monica Shaw's room. Almost directly opposite her room was a door leading to the back stairs. They were long and steep and narrow. He descended slowly to the ground floor, examining each step as he went. There were several damp patches, but how long they had been there it was impossible to tell. The school heating system, which seemed adequate in the rooms, did not extend to the stairwell.

The ground floor corridor led off to his right towards the front of the school. It would, he surmised, eventually lead him to Crowther Hall and the main entrance. Doors off the corridor led to store-rooms and kitchens, now dark and deserted. To the left of the stairs was the back door, thick, metal-clad, and made even thicker by innumerable layers of paint. It was fitted with a mortise lock, complete with a large, old-fashioned key, and there were bolts at the top and bottom of the door. The bolts were drawn back and the door was unlocked.

The flagstone floor just inside the door was stained and wet, and the reason was soon made clear when Paget opened it. Snow swirled around the covered entry and blew over the sill to settle on the floor even as he watched.

Outside, he could see the outline of the path as it went past a couple of greenhouses and continued on towards the tennis courts, but if there had ever been any tracks they had long ago filled in. He closed the door and made his way along dark corridors to Crowther Hall.

Miss Crowther was standing in the middle of the entrance hall, staring intently at something on the wall. As Paget approached, she turned towards him, a puzzled expression on her face.

'Is there something wrong?' he asked.

'I don't know whether there is anything wrong,' she said slowly, 'but it is very strange. There's a picture missing. A photograph of one of our governors.'

The framed photographs were mounted in a line along the wall opposite the main entrance. There were five of them, but there should have been six. The space between numbers two and four was empty.

'It's of Lady Tyndall,' Miss Crowther explained. 'I don't understand it at all. Lady Tyndall was here herself, yesterday, and I'm quite sure it was here then.'

Paget examined the hook on which the picture had hung. It was bent out of shape as if the weight had been too much for it or someone had pulled down on it. 'Is it possible that Lady Tyndall herself could have taken it?' he asked. 'Perhaps to replace it with a more recent photograph?'

'It's possible,' the headmistress said. She sounded doubtful. 'But I'm sure she would have said something to me. Besides, these photographs are less than six months old, so why would she wish to change it?'

'I have no idea,' said Paget. 'Perhaps she can tell you herself.'

The headmistress looked distressed. 'I suppose I shall have to ring her,' she said. 'About Monica as well. But Lady Tyndall's not going to like it, you know. She won't like it at all.'

She turned without another word and went back towards her study, but it was unclear to Paget which item of information Miss Crowther thought would upset Lady Tyndall more: the death of Monica Shaw or the disappearance of her picture. For that matter, neither was he sure which was the more upsetting to Miss Crowther.

MID-AFTERNOON, AND IT WAS beginning to get dark. Large, splodgy flakes of snow settled wetly on the windscreen as Paget passed through the school gates and turned right on the Malford road. Slush rumbled beneath the car as he picked up speed, and he eased back on the accelerator as he felt the rear end begin to fishtail. He turned right again at the crossroads, and followed the country road for about a quarter of a mile before he saw the stone pillars marking the entrance to Glenacres on his right.

'Sally Pritchard's cottage is on the left about a hundred yards beyond the gates,' Miss Crowther had said. 'You won't see it from the road because it's hidden behind a hedge, but you'll see the opening. It's all by itself, so you can't miss it.'

And there it was. Paget began to turn in, then saw the drift of snow across the drive. It wasn't large, but it had all but filled in earlier tracks, and he decided not to risk getting stuck. He got out and checked to make sure the car was off of the road, then made his way to the house on foot.

The cottage was small, but it looked even smaller beneath a blanket of snow that sagged below the eaves to form a scalloped edge above the windows. The lights were on inside, and he saw movement behind the curtains as he came up to the door and knocked. A green Fiesta with rust spots on the doors was parked a short distance from the house, and it, too, was covered with snow, although the parking space between it and the house was comparatively bare.

A young woman opened the door. 'You must be from the police,' she said before he could introduce himself. 'Sylvia rang to tell me what happened.' She passed a shaking hand across her brow. 'I still can't believe it. It seems so... I'm sorry.' She stood aside. 'You'd better come in.'

Paget kicked the snow off his shoes and ducked to avoid

hitting his head on the low lintel as he went inside and introduced himself.

Sally Pritchard was a surprise, and a very pleasant one at that. She was small and slender and her eyes were large and blue, set wide beneath a mop of short, unruly hair. But her face was pale, and there were dark circles beneath her eyes. In fact, she looked as if she hadn't slept all night.

She wore a chequered shirt, open at the neck, blue jeans, and floppy knitted slippers. An oval pendant set with a stone he did not recognize hung from a slender chain of gold around her neck, but apart from that she wore no jewellery. She motioned him to a seat and settled in a chair herself and tucked her feet beneath her.

The entire front of the cottage had been made into a single room. It still wasn't large, but it had an old-world charm that was made even more inviting by the addition of a tinselled Christmas tree adorned with gleaming ornaments, and festive decorations were strung from beam to beam. Through a curtained archway he could see a tiny kitchen, and another door led to what he presumed to be the only bedroom.

'I must apologize for disturbing you,' he said. 'Miss Gray did say that you weren't feeling well, but it is rather important that I ask you a few questions if you feel up to it.'

'It's nothing serious,' she assured him. 'Probably too much rich food and wine at the party yesterday, that's all, but I didn't know how long it was going to last when I asked Sylvia to stand in for me this morning. I'm all right now, thank you.' She paused, hesitating as if afraid to put the next question. 'Sylvia said that Monica committed suicide…' Her voice dried up in her throat and she coughed several times to clear it. 'Is that true, Chief Inspector?'

So much for trying to keep the record straight, thought Paget. 'It is only one of several possibilities,' he told her.

'Miss Shaw died suddenly during the night. My job is to try to find out why. Which brings me to why I've come to you. I understand that you took Monica back to the school after the party yesterday?'

'Yes, she was upset...' Sally Pritchard seemed to be having trouble with her voice.

'Tell me about it,' he said quietly. 'Tell me from the beginning. How did she come to be at the party in the first place? I understand she didn't ride.'

Sally cleared her throat once again as she clasped her hands together and looked down at them. 'I invited her,' she said. She spoke softly, reflectively, as if to herself. 'Perhaps...' She shrugged the thought away and began again.

'Monica was—well, I don't like to say this, Chief Inspector, but she wasn't exactly popular around the stables. She had a way of alienating people, but it was just her way. She tried too hard; came on too strong, and people didn't like that. But she's worked hard there, and when I found out that she was going to be all alone over there at the school at Christmas, I felt the least I could do was to invite her to our party.

'Anyway, she came and seemed to be enjoying herself— at least for the first part of the afternoon. I don't know exactly when it was that she started into the wine; it must have been well on into the afternoon, but there were so many people coming and going that I lost track of her for a while. All I know is that suddenly she was becoming a problem. She was talking too loud, breaking into conversations, laughing for no apparent reason. It was embarrassing, especially with so many of our clients there.

'You see,' she explained, 'we invite our clients, and the local people with whom we do business, to drop in during the afternoon, and there were quite a few of them there. Well, with Monica acting up the way she was, I was afraid that if Mr Lucas saw her—he's the owner of Glenacres—

he'd have her out of there in a second. If he thought she was upsetting clients, he might even have banned her from coming to Glenacres ever again, and I didn't want that to happen. God knows, the girl had little enough pleasure as it was; if she couldn't come to Glenacres, she'd have nothing.'

Sally Pritchard drew in a long breath and let it out again. 'Which was why I took her aside and gave her a good talking to. I told her to go for a walk and pull herself together. I warned her about what could happen if she didn't. But when she's like that, you can't tell Monica anything.' Her face clouded. '*Couldn't* tell her anything,' she amended softly. 'She went off up the yard in a huff, so I let her go on with it. I wish now…' The blue eyes clouded and she trailed off into a brooding silence.

Paget had to prompt her to get her started again.

'It must have been about an hour later when I noticed that her anorak was still hanging on the peg,' she went on, 'and I began to wonder where she'd got to. I didn't think she'd have gone home without it, but with Monica you could never be sure about anything. Chances were she was out there in the yard somewhere, sulking more than likely, and probably freezing to death. So, I went looking for her.'

'Just so that I can keep things straight in my mind,' Paget said, 'where exactly was the party held?'

'In the red barn,' she told him. 'Have you been over to Glenacres?' He shook his head. 'Well, you can't miss the old place. It's the oldest building there, and the first one you come to on the right as you go up the drive. It should have been pulled down years ago, but then we put the yard office in it, and all the odd bits of equipment we don't know what to do with seem to end up there. It's a bit of a tip, really, but a rather essential one. We have the party there every year. There are too many of us to go up to Mr Lucas's house, and besides, there's still work to be done, so you'd have people tracking muck in from the yard. This way we can come and go as we please and we don't have to worry about the mess. Mr Lucas supplies the food and the wine, of course.'

'I see. Thank you. Please go on. Did you find Monica?'

'Yes. She was at the top end of the yard—the barn is at what we call the bottom end. And she was just standing there, shivering and crying.'

'Did she say why?'

Sally remained silent for a long moment before replying. 'She said someone had—molested her.'

Paget sat up straighter. 'Did she say who it was?'

'No. She said she didn't know who it was.' Inexplicably, colour began to rise in Sally Pritchard's face, and she hurried on. 'It was in the shed,' she explained. 'It was dark. It's a storage shed where we keep supplies and special feed supplements and things like that. Monica said someone grabbed her and pulled her inside.' She looked down at her hands. 'It could have been one of the lads playing a bit of a joke.'

Paget looked sceptical. 'Do you think it was a joke, Miss Pritchard?'

The young woman regarded him levelly. 'You have to understand, Chief Inspector, that Monica was a very emotional girl. Hers was not a happy life. She fantasized about a lot of things. She was a very lonely girl, so she made up stories. Besides…' Abruptly, Sally Pritchard fell silent.

'You were about to say…?' Paget prompted.

She shook her head as if puzzled, but answered the question. 'I thought she might be making it up to spite me for telling her to behave herself,' she said. 'Now, I'm not so sure.'

'I see. Did you see anyone else about?'

'No, but then it was dark.'

'But I'm told the yard lights were on.'

Her expression did not change, but he sensed a withdrawal. 'The light over the door of the shed was out,' she said.

'Did you look in the shed?'

'Yes. There was no one there. I turned on the inside light and checked. There's nowhere for anyone to hide.'

'Is there another door or window to the shed?'

'Yes. There's a back door. It's on a spring lock. Someone *could* have gone out that way when they heard me coming.' A wry smile touched her lips. 'I'm told I'm not exactly light on my feet when I have my boots on,' she said.

'Anyway, I went back to Monica and did my best to calm her down, but to tell the truth I still thought she was making the whole thing up. Anyway, I decided that the best thing to do was to take her back to the school. The party was all but over in any case, so that's what I did.'

'How was she physically?' Paget asked. 'Did you see any signs of a struggle?'

'Her clothes were a bit messed about, but a stable isn't the cleanest place, so that could have happened in any number of ways.'

'Am I right in assuming you did not tell Miss Wolsey what you've just told me?'

Sally Pritchard grimaced guilty. 'I couldn't,' she said simply. 'Jane is a good friend, but Monica pleaded with me to say nothing about what had happened. She said she'd never be allowed to come over to the stables again, and she was probably right. I agreed, partly, I must admit, because I wasn't convinced that anything *had* actually happened to her. I thought it best to say nothing and let the whole thing blow over.'

Paget rose to his feet. 'Thank you, Miss Pritchard. You've been a great help,' he said, 'but I'm afraid I must ask you the same question I asked Miss Gray. Did Monica ever say anything to you that suggested she was considering taking her own life?'

Sally Pritchard stood up. Her head barely came to Paget's shoulder. The question seemed to trouble her, and she took a long time to answer. 'No,' she said in a voice so low that Paget barely heard her. 'If I'd even thought she might… No.' She walked to the door and opened it.

'There is one more thing you can do for me,' Paget said. 'I'd like you to give me a list of the people who were at the party yesterday, if you will. I can pick it up tomorrow morning on my way to Glenacres.'

'You mean you are going to talk to *everyone* who was there?' She looked dubious. 'I'm not sure I can remember them all.'

'It may not be necessary to talk to them all,' he said, 'but I would like the list to be as complete as possible just in case.'

'I'll see what I can do,' she said, 'but there's no need to call in here. I shall be at work myself, tomorrow. It's a big day for us. It's the Warrendale Hunt, and everyone will be picking up their horses at Glenacres. Warrendale Hall is only about half a mile down the road, so most of them will get sorted out at Glenacres and ride over to the hall from there. That is unless the weather turns bad overnight, of course.'

Another thought occurred to her. 'I hope you weren't planning on talking to everyone at Glenacres tomorrow,' she said. 'We'll be short-staffed as it is, what with people off for the holiday and the hunt and all. It would be much better if you could wait until Monday.'

'I'd rather not leave it any longer than I have to,' he said. 'Could you spare me half an hour tomorrow morning?'

Sally Pritchard looked doubtful. 'I might after everyone has gone,' she said, but her tone was not encouraging.

Paget said goodbye, and was surprised when she followed him out on the step. She stood there for a moment as if about to speak, then apparently changed her mind and stepped back inside and closed the door.

There was a cold, clammy dampness in the air, and Paget pulled his coat around him as he followed his own footprints in the snow to where he'd left the car. Sally Pritchard seemed to be sincere and quite straightforward—for the most part. She'd been uncomfortable about something, though. She probably felt guilty about not taking Monica seriously. That was understandable, but it didn't explain why she had followed him outside. What had she been going to say before she changed her mind? And why, as she turned away, had she been shaking like a leaf?

EIGHT

ASHTON PRIOR WAS A SMALL village that lay off the beaten track some twenty minutes' drive from Broadminster. It had neither the charm of its more famous Cotswold cousins, nor any historical significance to attract the tourist or the scholar. Neither had it been 'discovered' by urban dwellers seeking rural solitude, only to destroy it by dragging bag and baggage with them. In fact, it was one of those wonderful rarities, a village without character—and its residents liked it that way.

Four o'clock in the afternoon, and the light was almost gone as Paget entered the main street. It lay silent and empty beneath a fresh mantel of snow. Apart from a few dimly lighted windows suggesting life within, the village might have been deserted.

He turned right at the church and dropped into a lower gear as he passed the pub on the corner and went down the hill to the bridge at the bottom. The hill wasn't all that steep, but it was treacherous in winter, and Paget had learned to treat it with respect. He picked up speed as he crossed the narrow bridge, and shot up the other side, turning into his driveway just as his tyres began to lose their grip.

It had begun to snow again as he put the car away, and he wondered whether they would have to call off the Warrendale Hunt tomorrow.

He went through the house turning on lights. After all, he reminded himself, today was Christmas Day. There should be light! He stopped before the Christmas tree Mrs Wentworth had bought and decorated. She'd done a lovely job and she wasn't even there to enjoy it. Oh, what the hell, he thought, she'd gone to all that trouble. The least he could do was plug in the lights.

The lights came on. They glowed brightly for an instant, then dimmed. There was a frying sound, a smell of burning, and they all went out.

He sighed and pulled the plug. 'Merry Christmas, Neil,' he said aloud. The sound echoed hollowly in the room. 'And let's not forget "Joy to the World",' he muttered beneath his breath. He stood there, irresolute, in the middle of the room.

Carols. That was it. Let's have some good old-fashioned carols…

He didn't have any carols on tape or disc. Packed away somewhere were some old 33s, but he didn't know where and he wasn't in the mood to start looking. In desperation, he turned on the radio and spun the dial through a series of stations pumping out everything from rock to chat shows. When he came to one where someone was droning on about what to do with holly after Christmas, he turned it off in disgust.

'I could tell you what to do with your bloody holly,' he muttered, 'but I can guarantee you wouldn't like it.'

He dropped into a chair, put his head back and closed his eyes.

He thought of ringing Andrea. Wondered how she was spending Christmas. *Where* she was spending Christmas, for that matter. It occurred to him that he knew practically nothing about her friends and relatives. She never talked about herself, her background, parents, anything. He knew she was divorced. That much she had told him, but she had never mentioned the matter again.

And she had never invited him in. Come to think of it, she had always been down at the door, waiting, when he went to pick her up. But that was probably just her way.

Andrea deplored tardiness; didn't like to keep anyone waiting.

She must be working. He should have stopped off at the hospital, but… No, not a good idea. What was the point? If she had wanted to talk to him she would have called before this. Perhaps she'd gone away for Christmas. But then, she'd said she'd be working over the holidays. Besides, she would have mentioned it. Wouldn't she?

His stomach growled, reminding him that he'd had nothing to eat since breakfast. He heaved himself out of the chair and went to the fridge. Mrs Wentworth had left all sorts of things for him to choose from, but there was nothing there he really fancied.

In the end, he scrambled some eggs, tossed in a few bits of cheese and made some toast. Then he sat down in front of the TV to eat while he watched the show he'd taped the night before—*A Christmas Carol* with Alastair Sim. He and Jill had watched it faithfully every year.

But his mind was restless, and the image of Monica Shaw intruded. Had she *really* committed suicide? Certainly, by all accounts, she had no friends—with the possible exception of Sally Pritchard, but even she seemed to have befriended the girl more out of a sense of duty than anything else. Or pity. But was that enough to drive a girl of seventeen to take her own life?

Paget punched the Off button on the remote control, and closed his eyes.

It wasn't the same, watching it on his own.

NINE

Saturday, 26 December

PAGET KNEW IT WAS A MISTAKE as soon as he turned into the driveway leading up to the stables. There were cars and bikes and horse-boxes parked all the way up the drive. He continued on, looking for a place to turn round, but every inch of space was taken and he was forced to back all the way down again and park farther down the road.

The Warrendale Hunt was quite obviously on.

He was annoyed with himself for not having realized what it would be like this morning, but then, he'd never attended a hunt before—or at least the preparations for one. He should have heeded Sally Pritchard's warning, but it was a bit late to think of that now.

But it wasn't just that. He'd been irritable ever since four o'clock this morning when he'd finally given up trying to sleep. Silly thing to do, dropping off like that in the chair last night. He'd slept for almost three hours, and as a consequence had tossed and turned for half the night before finally getting up at four. He breathed in deeply as he got out of the car, but his head still felt as if it were stuffed with cotton wool.

At least he'd had the good sense to toss a pair of wellingtons in the car, and now he put them on. A warm front had moved in overnight, and the gravelled drive had turned to rutted slop with the passage of so many vehicles.

The stable yard was even more congested than the driveway. He really should have thought to ask Sally Pritchard what time the hunt started. He hadn't counted on there being this many people. The yard was full of them; people and horses, all milling about in what seemed like aimless confusion. And yet, beneath it all, he sensed some sort of order, and with it an undercurrent of excitement and anticipation. Riders conversed earnestly with grooms and with each other, while others stood about chatting in small clusters of three or four, seemingly oblivious to grooms and horses trying to get through.

Black appeared to be the favoured colour in jackets, although dark green and navy were presented, together with light-coloured jodhpurs and well-polished boots. But there were a few red jackets, Paget noted. What did they call them? Pinks, that was it. Though why such blazing red should deserve the name 'pink' was beyond him.

The small group stood apart, aloof from the plebeian mob, stern-faced and serious, eyes roving critically even as they talked among themselves. Shepherds ever conscious of their flock.

He stood to one side, watching. He couldn't escape the feeling that the scene transcended time; that had he been here fifty, sixty, seventy, or even a hundred years ago, everything would have been much the same.

He began to move again, and as he eased his way through the shifting throng, he picked up snippets of conversation.

'...sturdy legs. Plenty of bone. Should go for a good price, if I'm any judge. Still, we'll see next week...'

'...simply impossible to get to, now. But then, what can you expect? It would never occur to British Rail to ask the people who actually use the confounded thing. All they can think about is...'

'...and all I can say is that she knew bloody well when the hunt was, so if she was so anxious to ride she should have taken it into account when she got herself put up the spout. I mean, really!'

'…not worth a damn. Mind you, I still think there's good potential, long term, in the mining stocks. You see, it all depends upon…'

'Mind your back, sir. Coming through.' Paget stepped smartly aside to avoid being trodden on by a big grey as it clattered over the cobblestones, sending slush in all directions. 'Sorry about that, sir,' said the young groom apologetically. 'You have to look sharp with this one. Loves to tread on people's feet, does Busker.'

He made his way to one side, trying to stay clear of what had now become a steady parade of horses moving down the cobbled yard, and he caught a glimpse of Sally Pritchard. She was standing in the doorway of what had to be the red barn she'd spoken of the day before. Her head was down as she listened closely to a tall, dark-haired woman who punctuated her words with quick, emphatic gestures.

The woman was beautiful. She was tall and slender, her gestures graceful, almost languid. From a distance, at least, her olive-coloured skin was flawless, and her hair was as black as midnight. There was an air of authority about her, and she looked vaguely familiar, but Paget couldn't place her. Whoever she was, she certainly seemed to have a lot to say to Sally, and from the expression on Sally's face, she wasn't buying it. At one point she shook her head vigorously from side to side, and said something the woman didn't like. The woman turned as if to leave, but Sally put a hand on her arm. She seemed to be pleading with the woman. Paget thought she looked quite desperate.

Two horses stopped in front of him, blocking his view, and by the time they moved on, the woman to whom Sally had been talking was no longer there. He began to move towards the girl, but she was immediately surrounded by a group of young riders all talking at once.

'Excuse me…' Paget stopped one of the grooms. She was a big-boned, fair-haired girl with an open, friendly, freckled face. 'What time does the hunt start? When does all this—' he swept an arm around the yard '—activity die down?'

'The hunt starts at eleven o'clock,' said the girl. He could see the question in her eyes as she took in his suit and tie. 'But the yard should be clear by ten at the latest. They'll go to the Mocking Bird first. They always stop at the pub on the way to the Hall.' She lowered her voice conspiratorially and grinned. 'Some of 'em need it to give 'em the courage to take the jumps,' she confided.

Paget smiled in turn. 'I see. Thank you,' he said.

The girl looked as if she were about to say something else when someone called: 'Penny! I need help over here,' and she was gone.

Paget glanced at the time. Just turned nine thirty. Not long to wait. In fact, even as he continued to watch, some riders began to move off down the drive, presumably to assure themselves of a place at the bar.

'I don't believe we've met?' The words were spoken softly, but there was no doubt about the challenge they implied. 'My name's Lucas. Jack Lucas. I'm the owner of these stables.'

He was a big man, about fifty, heavy-set, florid, balding on top. And he wore a red jacket. He stood before Paget, feet apart, shoulders slightly hunched like a boxer sizing up his opponent. His eyes were neither friendly nor unfriendly, merely questioning.

Paget introduced himself and produced his warrant card. 'I was hoping to have a word with you later on this morning,' he said.

'Detective Chief Inspector?' Lucas said, glancing at the card. The look he shot at Paget was no longer neutral. 'Surely to God you're not here about the hunt?'

Paget shook his head. 'I'm investigating the death of one

of the girls over at the Thornton Hill School. Monica
Shaw.'

Lucas didn't seem to know whether to look relieved or
sad, but finally chose sad. 'Yes, young Sylvia told me,' he
said, shaking his head. 'Terrible business. Very sad indeed,
especially at Christmas. Suicide, wasn't it?' He left the
question hanging, but Paget wasn't to be drawn. 'But I
don't see what it has to do with me.'

'She was here at the party on Christmas Eve shortly before she died,' Paget explained, 'and I'd like to talk to
anyone who may have spoken to her that day.'

Lucas eyed Paget sharply. 'I hope you weren't planning
on doing that today,' he said. 'My people simply haven't
got time for it. They've got more than enough to keep them
busy without this sort of thing.'

'Miss Pritchard explained that to me yesterday,' Paget
told him. 'But we will have to talk to them, so I'll have
someone out here first thing Monday morning. It shouldn't
take long.'

'Well…'

'Did *you* talk to Monica, yourself, on Thursday, Mr Lucas?'

'Me? No.' Lucas shook his head vigorously. 'I knew her
to see her, of course, but that's about all. Saw her at the
party, but didn't talk to her. Mind you, I wasn't there more
than an hour. I had business in town. I left about three and
didn't get back till seven.'

He glanced around. 'Look, can this wait?' he said. 'The
others are ready, and it's almost time to be off.' He inclined
his head towards a group of people who, Paget had noticed,
kept glancing in their direction.

'Of course,' said Paget agreeably. 'Until Monday, then.'
Lucas grunted an unintelligible reply and nodded curtly before striding off to join his friends.

The yard was emptying rapidly. Paget began to walk

towards the big red barn at the bottom end of the yard. Sally Pritchard had mentioned an office in the barn, and he hoped to find her there.

He was half-way down the now almost empty row of box stalls when a woman came round the corner leading a big grey—the same horse, if he wasn't mistaken, that had almost trodden on his foot. The man who walked beside her was speaking quietly, low, insistent words, yet almost deferential. The woman stopped, turned, and said something to the man, and it was only then that Paget recognized her.

Andrea!

Surprised, but pleased to see her, he was about to step forward. But something about the way the two of them had their heads together made him draw back.

Andrea was speaking now, her voice low and seemingly urgent. He gained the impression that she was explaining something very carefully to the man. She stopped speaking, turned and mounted. The horse began to move off but she reined him in sharply as the man spoke again.

Softly. Insistently.

Paget saw her stiffen. Suddenly, she rose in the stirrups and raised her riding crop. He was sure she was going to strike the man, but he made no move to defend himself. He just stood there, a half-smile on his face as he looked up at her.

The crop hung there as if frozen in mid-air, and Paget saw the hand that held it begin to shake. Slowly, Andrea sank back in the saddle, hand still shaking as she took up the reins. She dug her heels deep into the horse's flanks. Startled, the animal moved forward and would have knocked the man down if he had not stepped aside. But even then his movements were unhurried. It was as if he had anticipated the move, and was contemptuous of it. He watched as horse and rider left the yard, then slowly turned and walked away.

WITH THE SCENE HE'D JUST witnessed still uppermost in his mind, Paget opened the door of the red barn and peered inside. It was a cavernous building, and certainly the oldest of all the buildings he'd seen so far. And Sally Pritchard was right; it was a bit of a tip. There were odd pieces of rusting farm machinery stacked against the far wall; broken shafts and wheels, the remnants of a dog-cart, and a variety of poles and jumps that had seen better days. There were folding tables stacked one on top of another, and chairs piled high beside them. Directly opposite the door was a big, old-fashioned work bench, its surface strewn with tools. Beside it were a large oil drum, a couple of petrol tins, and a shiny tin marked 'Grease'. Odd bits of tack hung everywhere from hooks and pegs and nails. Apart from the chairs and tables, it all looked like junk to Paget—but then, what did he know about stables?

These things he observed almost peripherally, because his attention was drawn to the small boy who was watching him from his seat on a swing. The swing was suspended from a heavy lateral beam that ran from high above the doorway where Paget stood, to a point above the bench on the opposite wall. The boy would be about seven or eight, Paget judged, fair-haired, pale and solemn-eyed.

'Would you give me a push, please?'

And polite. Paget waked over to the swing and gave it a push. The boy gripped the ropes and wriggled his bottom more firmly into place. 'Harder, please. I like to go high.' He began to pump with vigour after each push.

'I'm not sure you should go much higher than that,' Paget said. The beam to which the swing was attached was some twelve or thirteen feet above the floor, and the arc the swing described as formidable. Paget wasn't a small man by any measure, but even he was having to stretch to keep the swing going.

'I've been higher,' the boy said, continuing to pump.

'Perhaps,' said Paget, 'but I'd rather you didn't while I'm here. What's your name?'

'James. Everybody calls me Jimmy, but it's really James. Except Sally. She calls me James. Sally put the swing up for me.'

'Do you know where Sally is? I came to see her.'

James skewed round on the seat to look at him and the swing wobbled dangerously. 'Are you her boy-friend?' he asked.

Paget steadied him on the next back swing. 'No. I'm here on business.'

'Oh.' James lost interest. 'She's in the office.' He uncurled one finger from the rope and pointed as best he could.

At the far end of the barn was a loft, and beneath it a corner had been partitioned off to form an office. The door was slightly ajar, and Paget could hear the murmur of voices beyond.

'I want you to let the swing die down, now,' he told the boy. 'I have to go and talk to Sally. All right?'

'I shan't fall off,' said James. 'Sally lets me go higher.'

'I'm sure she does, but I'm not Sally, and I'd feel much better if you'll promise me you'll let the swing die down.'

'Will you give me another push before you go?'

'Only if you do as I say.'

'All right.'

Paget knocked on the door and heard Sally Pritchard call 'Come in'. He stuck his head inside and saw that she was on the phone. One hand covered the transmitter. 'Sit down,' she mouthed, 'I'll only be a minute.'

He'd barely taken a seat when Sally hung up the phone and sat back in her own chair. 'You've come for the list, I suppose?' Her voice was flat, civil enough, but little more. She looked cold and pinched about the face, especially around the eyes. Yet it wasn't cold. An electric heater was blasting heat across the tiny office.

'The boy, James—he'll be all right, will he? He likes to go high, he tells me.'

Sally Pritchard smiled, but it was obviously an effort. 'He'll be all right,' she told him. 'Why? Did he con you into pushing him? He's perfectly capable of doing it himself, you know.'

Paget smiled. 'I seem to remember doing much the same at his age,' he said. 'He seems like a nice lad. James…?'

'Lucas, the owner's boy.' Her face softened as she glanced through the open door. 'He'd spend hours on that swing if you'd let him, but his father… Well, that's not what you've come to talk about, is it, Chief Inspector?'

'No. Do you have the list?'

Sally unbuttoned the pocket of her shirt and pulled out a folded piece of paper. 'I sat down and wrote this out last night,' she told him. 'I knew it would be a madhouse here this morning.' She handed the paper to Paget. 'Apart from Monica, everyone on the first page either lives or works here. The ones on the second page are the people who dropped in for a drink. Clients, people we do business with, and some of the girls who work part-time here to help pay for boarding their horses.'

Paget glanced at the second page. 'Did any of these people know Monica well?' he asked.

'No. None of them did as far as I know.'

Paget continued to look at the list. 'I see,' he said as he folded it and put it away. He stood up. 'Perhaps we could have a look at that shed, now?'

Sally Pritchard half rose to her feet, then sank back into her chair again. 'I'm sorry,' she said, 'but I'm waiting for a telephone call, so I'll give you the key and you can look for yourself, if you don't mind. The shed's at the top end of the yard. It's the small, metal one. You can't miss it.' She opened a drawer and took out a ring containing several keys. 'It's the smallest one,' she told him as she handed him the ring. 'You will let me have them back when you're finished, won't you?'

'Of course. Tell me, is the door to the shed usually kept locked?'

She nodded. 'It's supposed to be,' she said, 'but I'm always having to get after someone for leaving doors unlocked. When you're in and out all the time, you don't want to be bothered with locking and unlocking doors if you can help it, but we've had more than our fair share of pilfering, and sometimes the horses get into things they shouldn't. Mr Lucas gets very upset if he finds a door unlocked. It was open when I found Monica, of course. It shouldn't have been, but it was.'

'Who has access to the keys to the shed?'

'Everyone—that is, all the regular staff. They all have their own keys.'

'I see.' Paget was about to leave when another thought occurred to him. 'I saw you talking to a tall, dark-haired woman earlier this morning,' he said. 'I have the feeling that I should know her, but I can't for the life of me think where I might have seen her. Do you know who I mean?'

He had asked the question out of simple curiosity, but Sally Pritchard's reaction was strange. She became very still, and her eyes went completely blank. 'I spoke to a good many people this morning,' she said. 'I'm afraid I don't know who you mean. Sorry.'

'No matter,' he told her. 'I was just curious. No doubt it will come to me when I least expect it.'

He moved to the door. 'I see Dr McMillan is riding today,' he said. 'Is that her horse? The big grey?'

Sally nodded. 'That's Busker,' she said. 'He's a bit of a handful, but she's a good rider.'

'Come here often, does she?'

A frown creased Sally's brow. 'Does this have something to do with Monica?' she asked him.

Paget smiled disarmingly. 'No. Just curious,' he said. 'Thank you, Miss Pritchard.'

James was waiting for him as he left, and true to his promise, Paget stopped and gave the boy a push. 'I can go higher,' the boy told him as Paget moved away. 'Watch me.'

'Just for a minute, then.'

James kicked out, sending the swing higher and higher while Paget stood in the doorway and watched. It was like being at Wimbledon, he thought, as his head swivelled from side to side, following the sweep of each arc. But James was showing off, now, trying to impress him, so Paget waved goodbye and went off to find the shed.

of Pushing reheated thoughts had expectation of suicide had made it fair in race people's minds. However, since the murder of... faded out...

TEN

THE STORAGE SHED WAS AS Sally Pritchard had described it. She was right; there was nowhere for anyone to hide, but someone could have slipped out of the back door quite easily. Paget opened it and looked out. There was a wire fence about ten feet away, and beyond it was the schooling ring. It afforded little in the way of concealment, but Monica's assailant—if indeed there had been any such person— had only to run a few paces either way along the inside of the fence to gain cover among the other buildings backing on to the ring. And it had been dark.

He examined every inch of the floor, but it was impossible to tell whether or not a struggle had taken place. It would be a waste of time to have Charlie and his people go over it, he concluded. Too many people had access to the shed for any findings to be of value.

On his way back to the red barn to return the key, Paget met the girl he'd spoken to earlier about the hunt. She had a bucket in each hand, and was eyeing him with open curiosity as he approached. On impulse, he stopped and introduced himself.

The girl set the buckets down. 'Penny Wakefield,' she said. 'Syl said she thought you'd be coming round. I did wonder when I saw you earlier today.'

'Syl being Sylvia Gray, I take it?' he said.

'That's right. She said you thought Monica had committed suicide. Is that right? Did she?'

'It's because we don't know how she died that we're asking questions,' Paget explained carefully, although privately he thought he was probably wasting his breath. Sim-

ply asking whether Monica had ever spoken of suicide had
made it fact in most people's minds. However, since the
subject had come up, he might as well put the question.
'Did she ever mention any such idea to you?'

'No. She never was what you might call happy, but suicide? No.'

'Were you at the Christmas party here on Thursday?'

'Till about half-past five. I had to leave then to catch the
bus. See, I had Christmas Day off, so I went home.'

'I see. Tell me, did you know Monica very well?'

The girl shrugged. 'I don't think anyone knew Monica
very well,' she said. 'But she used to talk to me sometimes.
She had some funny ideas, but she wasn't a bad kid.'

'Funny ideas? About what? Can you give me an example?'

Penny sighed. 'I don't suppose it can do any harm if I
tell you now,' she said. 'Poor kid. They were about her
mother, mostly. She was always making up stories about
her. How important she was, and how much she wanted
Monica to be with her, but something always seemed to
come along to prevent it. She would even tell me that she'd
been up to London—even Europe—to visit her mother on
the weekends when I knew very well she'd never been any
farther than Broadminster that weekend. And no matter
where it was, her mother always had this fabulous flat, and
they would go out together to all the best shops and the
finest restaurants.

'It was all a load of old rubbish, of course, but I never
let on that I didn't believe a word of it. If it made her feel
better to tell all those stories about her mother, where was
the harm?'

'But did *she* believe them?' Paget asked.

The girl thought about that carefully before she replied.
'I think she did while she was telling them,' she said slow-

ly, 'but deep down I'm sure she knew them for what they were. Sad, really, when you think about it.'

Sad wasn't the word for it, thought Paget. Monica Shaw was emerging as a pathetic figure virtually abandoned by her mother, yet desperately denying it even to herself.

'Do you know if she told these stories to anyone else?'

Penny shook her head. 'I don't know,' she said. 'No one else ever mentioned that she had, and I'm sure someone would have if she'd told them anything like that.'

'Why you, then, Miss Wakefield? Don't misunderstand me, but it's just that I had gained the impression that Monica rarely shared her thoughts with anyone.'

Again, the girl shrugged. 'I don't know,' she said, 'unless it was because I was one of the few who would put up with her. She was always pestering Sally for something to do, but most of the gang around here wanted nothing to do with her, so Sally used to send her along to help me. See, Monica wasn't what you might call well co-ordinated. You had to be patient with her. Perhaps I was a bit more patient than the others.'

'Tell me about Thursday. Did you talk to Monica then?'

'Not much. Not what you'd call real talk. You know what it's like at a party; everyone talks but nobody listens. Not that it matters as long as they're having a good time. I saw her there, of course, but that was about all. Anyway, I was up the yard half the time, trying to get finished before I left.'

'Did you by any chance see Monica anywhere near the shed up there?' Paget nodded in the direction of the storage shed. 'Say somewhere between five and six that afternoon? Perhaps with someone else?'

Penny looked at him sharply, then glanced towards the shed, a strange expression on her face. 'That was Monica?' she said, her voice rising. 'I never thought...' She broke

off and turned back to Paget. 'Are you *sure* it was Monica?'
she asked him.

'Perhaps you had better tell me exactly what it was you
saw that afternoon,' he said.

'It wasn't so much saw as heard,' she said slowly. Penny
Wakefield sounded slightly bewildered. 'The little devil! I
never dreamt…' She looked at Paget. 'Sorry,' she apologized, 'but it comes as a bit of a shock. If I'd known it was
her he had in there…'

'From the beginning, if you don't mind, Miss Wakefield,' Paget prompted her.

'Yes. Well, I'd just finished up, and was on my way up
to the room to change, you see. Syl and I have the end
room above the stalls, next to the shed.' She pointed to a
row of small windows beneath the eaves. 'I saw Maurice
go into the shed, but I didn't think anything of it at the
time. I was in a bit of a hurry because my bus was due in
twenty minutes, and I had to get down to the gate to catch
it.

'Anyway, I changed and was on my way out when I
noticed that the light over the shed door was out, and that
made me wonder whether Maurice had locked the door
when he left. He's always leaving it open,' she explained,
'and he always says it wasn't him, so I went over to check.'

'Did you put the light on?'

'No. The bulb was gone.'

'Gone? You mean burnt out?'

The girl shrugged. 'I suppose so,' she said.

'I see. Please go on.'

Penny Wakefield shifted her weight from one foot to the
other and glanced over at the shed. 'Well, when I got to
the door, I could hear voices, and I realized that Maurice
had…well, there was someone in there with him.' She
stopped, but under Paget's quizzical gaze reluctantly went
on. 'They were…well, you know…'

Paget played dumb. 'I'm afraid I don't know,' he said blandly. 'They were what?'

Colour began to creep into the girl's face. 'They were having it off,' she said baldly.

'Try to remember exactly what you heard,' he said. 'It may be important.'

Penny Wakefield looked doubtful, but furrowed her brow in concentration. 'I didn't exactly hang out,' she said, 'so it wasn't much. He was…well, coaxing her, you might say. I don't remember the exact words.' The colour in her face was rising fast.

Paget waited. His eyes never left Penny's face.

'He said something like "It's all right. I won't hurt you…" something like that. Like I said, I didn't hang about.'

'And what did she say?'

Penny shook her head. 'I didn't hear her say anything. Just noises, you know.'

'Noises?'

Penny laughed nervously. 'More like squeaks,' she said, looking more embarrassed than ever. 'There was a lot of thrashing about.'

'As if she were struggling?'

'Yes. She…' She stopped as the implication of the question sank in. 'I don't mean…' she began, and stopped again.

'*Could* she have been struggling? Trying to get away? Could someone have had a hand over her mouth, for example? Is that why you only heard squeaks, as you call them?'

'I—I suppose,' Penny admitted reluctantly, then more defiantly: 'I didn't know it was Monica. I thought… Well, it could have been anybody, couldn't it?' Her voice took on a belligerent tone. 'I mean, with Maurice about, even the cat isn't safe.'

'Who is Maurice?' Paget asked the question although he thought he knew the answer from the list given to him by Sally.

'Maurice Blake. He's head trainer and instructor.'

'I was under the impression that Sally Pritchard occupied that position,' he said.

'She should,' the girl said with surprising vehemence. 'She can run circles around Maurice. But no, she's mainly responsible for Thornton Hill; she must have close to forty girls from over there now, so a lot of her time is spent on training. But Maurice brings the women in and that pleases Mr Lucas. Not that he'd be very pleased if he knew everything Maurice does around here,' she added darkly. 'And since Ernie Craddock was killed the other week, Maurice thinks he's cock-of-the-walk.'

The name stirred a memory. 'Craddock,' he said. 'Was that the chap who died after being mugged outside a pub?' he asked. He hadn't handled the case personally, but he remembered some of the details.

The girl nodded soberly. 'Bastards! He was a good old stick, was Ernie,' she said. 'Never did anyone any harm. And he knew more about horses than Maurice will ever know.' She drew in a long breath and let it out again. 'Maurice was cocky enough before, but now, with Ernie out of the way, he reckons he's got a clear field.'

He remembered, now. It was thought at first that Craddock had been run over, but according to the pathologist's report, someone had cracked his head open with a heavy instrument, probably metal, and had then left him lying under the back wheels of a van parked in the yard. It was dark when the owner got in to drive away, and he drove over Craddock's head. The driver went into a state of shock when he realized what he'd done. He thought he'd killed Craddock, of course, but the post-mortem revealed that Craddock was dead before the van went over him.

That Penny Wakefield didn't like Blake was obvious, but she was being remarkably candid, and Paget asked her why.

The girl glanced around although no one was in sight, and lowered her voice. 'Because I'm giving in my notice at the end of the month,' she told him. 'I've got a better job lined up at Church Stretton, but I haven't told anyone yet.'

'Are you leaving because of Maurice Blake?'

Penny shook her head. 'No, not really. He doesn't bother me all that much, although with Ernie gone there'll be no holding him. No, it's just that the new job is closer to home and there's more money in it. And I know the people, so that helps.'

Paget questioned her closely, especially with regard to Blake. How could she be so sure that it was Blake she had heard inside the shed? But Penny Wakefield wouldn't be shaken. She said she'd recognize his voice anywhere, and he saw no reason to disbelieve her.

When he asked where he could find Blake, the girl told him he had been there earlier but had left for Birmingham as soon as the yard was clear, and wouldn't be back until Monday.

He was copying down the address of the place where Penny Wakefield would be working after she left Glenacres, when Sally Pritchard called to him from the door of the red barn.

'Telephone for you,' she told him as he approached.

It was the duty sergeant. Julia Shaw's London office had notified him that Mrs Shaw was flying in from Switzerland. She would be driving down to Broadminster, and expected to be there by late afternoon. Would Paget be there when she arrived?

'I'll be there,' he told the sergeant.

Before he left the yard, Paget went back to the shed and tried the outside light. It was working now.

JULIA SHAW LIT ANOTHER cigarette and blew a stream of
smoke towards the ceiling. She was tall, willowy, and quite
beautiful in a brittle sort of way. She reminded him of a
picture he'd seen in a book of fairy tales as a child. The
Snow Queen, cold, distant, and unapproachable. Yet, beneath that cool exterior, Julia Shaw was a bundle of nervous
energy. Except for a very short time there in the mortuary,
she had chain-smoked ever since her arrival.

'Suicide?' she said. Her eyes met his across the desk in
a blaze of blue. 'I must say I find that a rather remarkable
conclusion with so little evidence to support it, Chief Inspector. Monica was never what you might call an outgoing
child, but suicide…? Oh, no. I don't mean to sound callous,
but she wouldn't have had the courage for one thing.'

'I said it was a possibility we had to consider, Mrs Shaw.
We will know more after the post-mortem.'

Julia Shaw shuddered delicately. 'That dreadful place!'
She drew deeply on her cigarette.

Paget had taken her directly to the mortuary to identify
the body. Not that he'd ever had any doubt that the body
was in fact that of Monica Shaw, but coroners could be
sticky about things like that.

It was impossible to read her expression as she stood
looking down on the pale features of her daughter. If anything, Julia Shaw appeared to be more annoyed than sad or
distraught, but it was hard to judge people's feelings under
such circumstances.

'Yes, that is my daughter, Monica,' she said in answer
to his question.

They drove back to the station in silence. There were no
tears to mar the flawless make-up, Paget noted.

Another stream of smoke. 'I sincerely hope you haven't
released any of this speculation to the press,' she said
sharply.

'Nothing has appeared as yet,' he said. 'No doubt there

will be something in the papers tomorrow, but no details will be released until we know more ourselves.'

Julia Shaw eyed him for several seconds. 'Good,' she said at last. 'If, as you seem to be suggesting, Monica took more insulin than she should have, I'm quite sure it was by accident.' She tapped her cigarette in a brief tattoo against the ashtray. 'Why, in God's name, would a young, healthy girl like Monica want to take her own life?' she asked irritably. 'It's ludicrous to even suggest it! She had everything. God knows I've sent enough money to that school over the years. She's been well looked after.'

'She *was* the only girl left in the school over Christmas,' Paget pointed out. It wouldn't take much for him to dislike Julia Shaw. 'Her housemistress, Miss Wolsey…'

'Jane Wolsey?' The housemistress was dismissed with a disdainful snap of the cigarette against the ashtray. 'What would the likes of Jane Wolsey know? Monica understood the situation. She was well aware of the demands of my job, and she accepted it. If I could have returned home for Christmas, I would have, but it was impossible. These meetings are important; crucial to the country's future. I'm sure you understand that yourself, Chief Inspector. You can't just leave in the middle of them, Christmas or no Christmas. It isn't as if she were a child. She was almost eighteen.' Julia Shaw lapsed into brooding silence.

Paget was finding it difficult to even talk to this woman. From the very start it had seemed to him that she was more put out by having to fly back to England than she was about the death of her daughter. And why from Switzerland and not Belgium?

He assumed a puzzled expression. 'I was given to understand that the talks were being held in Brussels,' he said, 'and yet I believe you said you flew in from Switzerland?'

She ground out her cigarette. 'I hardly think that is relevant to your investigation, Chief Inspector,' she told him.

'But if you *must* know, I went there for a few days' rest. These meetings have been dragging on for months. I was utterly exhausted. I needed to get it away. Completely away.' She took out another cigarette and lit it.

'Did Monica know that, Mrs Shaw?'

She shook her head impatiently. 'I thought it best not to tell her,' she said. 'She would have wanted to join me there, and I simply couldn't stand…' She took a deep breath. 'I needed rest. I told the Crowther woman that the meetings were continuing over Christmas because I knew Monica would understand that. I knew…'

She stopped abruptly. 'But why I'm explaining all this to you, I don't know,' she said as she rose to her feet.

Paget stood up as well. 'There is the matter of the inquest, and of course, the funeral arrangements,' he said.

'My private secretary will see to all the details.' Julia Shaw took out a card case and handed him a card. 'His name is Brown. Jeremy Brown. He can be reached at that number.'

'And you, Mrs Shaw? Where can you be reached?'

She pulled on her gloves. 'I hardly think that will be necessary,' she said, 'but in the event, that number will serve. Now, if that is all, Chief Inspector, I must get back to London tonight. That is,' she added ominously, 'after I've had a few words with Miss Crowther at Thornton Hill.'

ELEVEN

Sunday, 27 December

PAGET SPENT SUNDAY AT HOME. He rose late and had a
leisurely breakfast, then spent the rest of the morning reading the newspaper and catching up on the news.

But his thoughts kept drifting back to the tableau he'd
witnessed in the stable yard the day before. Andrea rising
in the stirrups, arm upraised, and this man, this stable hand
or whatever he was, just standing there grinning at her. If
looks could kill...

And why had she told him she would be so busy at the
hospital over Christmas that she wouldn't have time to see
him? Because, he told himself, she didn't *want* to see him.

He thought back to that night just over a week ago; went
over every word, every look, every detail. They'd enjoyed
the evening. Andrea had said several times that she had had
a lovely time, and he was sure she meant it. She'd been so
relaxed on the way home. All the way to the flat, in fact.
Even after he stopped the car, she had shown no inclination
to get out. And yet, within seconds, she was anxious to be
gone. What *had* he said?

There was only one way to find out. He picked up the
phone and dialled her number. No answer. He rang the
hospital, and was told that Dr McMillan was not available.

Angrily, he put the phone down. No matter what he'd
done or not done, the least she could do was talk to him.
He was disappointed in her. She must know he'd been calling. And if she had time to go riding, then she'd certainly

had time to ring him back. Well, enough was enough. If Andrea wanted to talk to him, she knew where to find him.

For lunch he made a pot of coffee and a sandwich, then cast round for something to read; something light to take his mind off brooding over what had gone wrong. His eye fell on the gift from Mrs Wentworth, still wrapped in Christmas paper, but unmistakably a book. He stripped the paper off and groaned aloud.

It was the latest book by Dick Francis, and there on the cover was a damned great grey that looked for all the world like Busker.

Monday, 28 December .

DETECTIVE SERGEANT JOHN TREGALLES stuck his head inside the open doorway to DCI Paget's office and cocked a quizzical eye at the chief inspector. Paget was on the phone. He motioned the sergeant to a seat while he continued the conversation.

Tregalles slumped into a chair and smothered a yawn. Too many late nights and too much food over the holidays: that was his problem. And not enough exercise. The crease in his belt, normally covered by the buckle, was clearly visible one notch over. No doubt about it, he thought gloomily, he was putting on weight.

Not that he was exactly fat. Tregalles had the broad shoulders and compact body of the athlete; the build of a dedicated swimmer who had been collecting trophies since the age of ten. He was younger than Paget by some four years, but deep furrows in his forehead and around his eyes and mouth gave his face an oddly crumpled look that made him appear much older.

'Smudged while it was hot,' Audrey used to tease him, but she said it with affection, and wouldn't have had it any other way.

Paget was looking better these days, Tregalles thought. In fact the chief inspector had been downright perky these past few weeks. He'd put on a bit of weight as well, and looked the better for it. He would be quite good-looking in a craggy sort of way if he'd just let himself relax and ease up a bit.

The chief inspector was thirty-six, according to Leona in Personnel, but he'd looked more like fifty when he'd first arrived. He rarely smiled. But then, from the little Tregalles had been able to glean about the chief inspector's past, he hadn't had much to smile about. Lost his wife, they said. Some sort of explosion. And he'd been ill. Not that he'd ever mentioned it. He wouldn't, though, would he? Kept himself to himself, the chief inspector did. Aloof. That was the word for Paget.

Paget hung up the phone, sat back in his chair, and eyed Tregalles over steepled fingers.

'A seventeen-year-old girl by the name of Monica Shaw died Christmas morning,' he said. He made it sound like an accusation, thought Tregalles. What happened to 'Good morning, Sergeant. Have a nice Christmas, did you?' So much for perky.

'The evidence suggests it was a suicide attempt. The girl was diabetic, and the amount of insulin she pumped into herself would have been sufficient to bring on hypoglycaemic shock. According to Dr Starkie, that might have been enough to kill her, especially if no one found her for several hours. I say ''might'' because the actual cause of death was an aneurysm in what he calls—' Paget consulted a notepad on the desk '—the Circle of Willis. It's a ring of arteries located at the base of the brain, and one of them simply burst. The technical term for it is subarachnoid haemorrhage, if you're interested. Starkie says almost anything could have triggered it—even something as simple as turning the head.'

Paget pushed the notepad aside. 'It will be up to the coroner to decide, of course, but under the circumstances there's bound to be an inquest, so we'd better have some answers ready. The girl attended a Christmas party at Glenacres Riding Stables just hours before she died, so I want to get out there later on this morning, and I'd like you with me to take care of some of the interviews. I was at the scene on Christmas Day, and I've done some follow-up since, but we'll need more. It's all in here.' He pushed a folder across the desk. 'Read it, then get back to me by—' he looked at the clock '—ten thirty.'

Tregalles took the folder and stood up. 'Time of death?' he said.

'Roughly between 1 and 2 a.m. Give or take half an hour each way at the outside.'

'Any suggestion of foul play?'

Paget didn't answer immediately. 'Only the girl's fingerprints were found on the syringes,' he said. 'And apart from the fact there was no note, everything seems to point to the suicide theory. But we'll see. Read it for yourself; I think you'll see what I mean.'

'Right.' Tregalles tucked the file beneath his arm, and made his way back to his own small cubicle. It was typical of Paget that he'd not even asked what else the sergeant had on his plate. The man became so immersed in whatever he was doing that he expected others to be ready to jump in at a moment's notice. He just assumed that you'd clear the decks and get on with it.

Still, he'd rather work with Paget than some he could think of. He worked you hard and he was a bugger for detail, but you always knew where you stood with him. Tregalles felt comfortable with the man, perhaps because they shared a similar background and spoke the same language. Tregalles was from Cornish stock, but he had been born and raised in Bethnal Green, and despite his more than twenty years in the border country, he was still a Londoner at heart.

Tregalles surveyed the pile of paper on his desk. He'd better get cracking if he was to clear this lot by ten thirty. Paget wasn't a man to be kept waiting.

SUPERINTENDENT ALCOTT lit a cigarette and flicked non-existent ash in the general direction of an already overflowing ashtray.

'Sit down,' he told Paget. 'I've just had a call from Mr Brock.' Morgan Brock was the chief superintendent, and Alcott's immediate superior. 'He wants a full report on this business at Thornton Hill School for the Chief Constable. It seems Sir Robert received a telephone call from Lord Tyndall about it this morning. His wife, Lady Tyndall, is on the board of governors at Thornton Hill, and she is concerned about adverse publicity affecting the school.'

'I'm sure she is, sir,' said Paget. 'But I rather think that decision will rest with the coroner.'

Alcott drew deeply on his cigarette. 'What about our side of it? I thought I detected a certain—cautiousness in your report.'

'We still have a few people to talk to,' Paget said, avoiding a direct answer. 'Particularly about the girl's state of mind, and what happened before she died. According to Sally Pritchard—she's the one who took Monica back to the school on Christmas Eve—Monica claimed to have been attacked by a man and dragged inside a shed in the stable yard. You'll see by the report there were bruises and scratches on her arms, thighs and lower abdomen, but they were relatively superficial, and there was no penetration. I'm not saying she *wasn't* attacked, but there are things about her story that bother me. Forensic did find traces of skin beneath the girl's nails, but it was her own. They say that's not unusual if, for example, she was trying to pry the attacker's fingers loose from some part of her body, but they would have expected to find foreign elements as well.

'And then there's the matter of what happened after she returned to the school. I believe she got up, got dressed, and went out again after Miss Wolsey left her in bed. But where she went or why, I have no idea as yet.

'When she returned, she dropped her coat on the floor, kicked off her boots, and flopped down on the bed, still fully clothed. Not long after that, if we're reading the signs right, she attempted to take her own life by giving herself several injections of insulin. Whether she would have succeeded in killing herself is open to question. Perhaps she merely wanted to draw attention to herself, but whatever her motive, the aneurysm completed the job.'

Alcott looked sceptical. 'She was a bit young to be having an aneurysm, wasn't she?'

'According to Dr Starkie, it can happen at any age,' said Paget. 'If there is a weakness in the wall of the artery, it can rupture without warning, and when it occurs in that particular area beneath the brain, death follows almost immediately. If, for example, she was having convulsions, that might well have been enough to cause the rupture.'

Alcott rocked back and forth in his chair. 'Is there any doubt in your mind that the injections were self-administered?' he asked.

Paget hesitated. He and Starkie had discussed at length the possibility of someone else having given her the injections forcibly, but it had been the pathologist's opinion that Monica Shaw had administered them herself. 'The entries were clean,' he told Alcott. 'There were no signs of tearing or bruising of the skin such as you might expect to find if there had been a struggle. However, Starkie did mention one other possibility. The injections could have been administered by someone else while the girl was unconscious.

'I think the most likely explanation is that Monica Shaw

did attempt to kill herself, but I'm not at all satisfied about what went on prior to her death. For one thing, it's been suggested that it was the wine that made Monica act the way she did at the party, but Starkie says there was virtually no alcohol in her blood. He did point out that, as a diabetic, even a change of food coupled with over-excitement could have brought about a change in her behaviour, but he says there is no way he can prove that now.'

Paget hesitated. 'I may be wrong, sir, but I get the feeling that there's something not right here, and I'd like to get to the bottom of it.'

Alcott stubbed out his cigarette, scattering ash across the desk. 'Very well,' he said, 'but let's not waste too much time on it. And keep the Press Officer informed, will you? He's had his instructions from the Chief Constable's office, so let him take care of the media. The last thing I need is Sir Robert on my back, and the last thing *he* needs is Lord Tyndall on his.'

'SORRY. MY FAULT. I wasn't paying attention, I'm afraid. Here, let me get them for you.'

Andrea McMillan knelt quickly and picked up the books she'd knocked from the hand of a stooped, grey-haired man. His name was Stanton. Dr Isaac Stanton, a senior member of the staff and her immediate superior. He stood back against the wall as others leaving the meeting flowed around the kneeling figure.

Andrea rose to her feet and handed him the books. 'I'm sorry,' she said again. 'Clumsy of me.' She turned swiftly and was about to leave when Stanton put out his hand and stopped her.

'I'll walk with you, if I may?' He didn't wait for an answer, but fell into step beside her. He walked slowly, deliberately, it seemed to her, so that she was forced to slow her own pace.

'Something is troubling you, Andrea,' he said. It was a statement rather than a question. 'You were miles away in the staff meeting, and you looked worried sick. In fact, you've not been yourself for several days, now. It's not like you. Is there anything I can do to help?'

The knot in Andrea's stomach tightened. Isaac was a good friend, but there was nothing he could do. Nothing anyone could do. She tried to brush it aside.

'I'm just tired, that's all,' she told him, summoning a smile. 'Too many long hours, and with Christmas...'

Stanton stopped, and she was forced to stop and face him. 'If it is none of my business, then tell me so, Andrea,' he said. 'But don't tell me you're just tired when I can see for myself that it is much more than that. I do not wish to pry into your life, but sometimes we need a friend to talk to.'

Oh, how she would have liked to tell him. To tell anyone. Just sit down somewhere quiet and let it all pour out. What a relief it would be. She saw the concern in Stanton's eyes and was tempted; sorely tempted, but she couldn't bring herself to do it. This was one thing she had to resolve on her own.

He saw it in her face, and nodded understandingly as he resumed walking. 'If you should change your mind, you know where to find me,' he said. 'But a word of advice, Andrea. You cannot go on like this. I tell you this not only as a friend, but as a doctor. Whatever it is that's troubling you, do something about it. You know as well as I do how destructive indecision can be.'

TWELVE

When Paget and Tregalles arrived at Glenacres, they found that Jack Lucas was away on business, and his wife had gone into town. Not that Paget had expected either of them to be of much help. Lucas had said he'd only been at the party for an hour, and his wife had not been there at all, according to Sally. 'She hardly ever comes into the yard,' she said. 'Georgie is afraid of horses.'

'In that case,' Paget told Tregalles, 'you take this chap, Tillman, and start on the grooms, and I'll take Blake and the rest.' He handed Tregalles a copy of the list Sally Pritchard had provided, then set off to find Blake.

Paget could see what Penny Wakefield meant when she'd said that Maurice Blake brought in the women. He was young, probably not much over thirty, and there was such a roguish charm about the soft-spoken man with just a hint of the Irish in his voice that it would be difficult to dislike him.

Blake lived in a caravan behind the stables, and that's where Paget found him brewing a mid-morning pot of coffee.

'Mr Lucas said you'd be coming round,' he said when Paget introduced himself. 'Come along in, then. You're just in time for a brew.' He turned and led the way inside. 'How do you like your coffee?' Blake indicated a chair as he busied himself at the tiny counter.

'Black with sugar, please.' Paget settled himself at the table.

The caravan was neat and clean, but it was probably there in violation of all sorts of local ordinances. The fact that it was tucked away behind a clump of trees suggested that it might not stand close scrutiny, but that wasn't why he was here. That was a matter for the local authorities as far as Paget was concerned.

Blake set a mug before him and sat down himself. He regarded Paget levelly across the rim of his own mug as he took a tentative sip. 'Now, then, what can I do for you, Chief Inspector?'

There wasn't even the hint of nervousness in the man's manner, and Paget couldn't help but wonder about Penny Wakefield's story. It wouldn't be the first time that a disgruntled employee or colleague had put the boot in, and the girl had made it plain that she had no time for Maurice Blake.

But he made no mention of that to Blake. 'What can you tell me about Monica Shaw?' he said.

The man leaned back in his chair and shook his head. 'A sad business, that,' he observed solemnly. 'She was a funny kid; hard to understand. But then, I didn't have a lot to do with her. I talked to her a few times—she always seemed to be over here—but I can't say I knew much about her. You'd be better off asking Sally or some of the girls about her.'

'What about last Thursday, Mr Blake? She was at the party. Did you talk to her then?'

Blake took a swig of coffee, then sat looking down at his mug, lips pursed, thoughtful. 'I don't think I did,' he said slowly. 'Not talked to her specifically, that is. I remember seeing her there, and there was a lot of chat going on; I suppose she took part, but that was about it. People were coming and going all afternoon, so it was a very loose sort of thing.'

'What about outside? I understand that Monica was wandering about in the yard somewhere around five or six o'clock.' Paget was deliberately vague. 'Did you see anything of her then?'

Again, Blake appeared to give the question careful consideration. 'No, I don't think so,' he said. 'I was out there myself somewhere about then, too. I went up to have a look at Crackerjack. He'd been off his feed for a couple of days. The vet took a look at him when he dropped in for a drink that day, but he couldn't find anything wrong. Still, there was something putting him off his feed so I was keeping an eye on him.

'What time would that be?'

'Oh, about half five, I should think. Somewhere around there. I can't be sure exactly.'

'Did you see anyone else out in the yard?'

'Someone was just leaving in a car,' said Blake, 'and I saw young Penny haring off somewhere. Why?'

'Where were you when you saw Penny?'

'Up the top end of the yard. That's where Crackerjack's stall is.'

'That would be somewhere up near the storage shed, I believe?'

'That's right.'

'Did you go into the storage shed for any reason, Mr Blake?'

Blake frowned as if thinking back, but his eyes no longer met those of Paget as directly as before. 'Yes, as a matter of fact, I did,' he said as if he'd only just remembered. 'I went in there for some ointment. Crackerjack had rubbed some skin off a hock. Nothing serious, but there's no point in taking chances. But what's that got to do with anything?'

'In a moment, Mr Blake. How long were you in the shed?'

Blake shrugged. 'A few minutes. Three or four, perhaps. I can't say I remember exactly.'

'Do you recall whether the outside light was on?'

Blake rose to his feet. 'More coffee?' he enquired.

'No, thank you.'

'I think I will.' Blake topped up his mug and resumed his seat. 'Sorry,' he said as if just realizing he hadn't answered Paget's question. 'What was that about the light?'

Paget repeated the question.

'No, it wasn't,' Blake said. 'I meant to put a new bulb in, but I forgot about it. Thanks for reminding me.'

'It's working now,' Paget said.

Blake cocked an eyebrow as if surprised. 'Someone must have changed it, then,' he said.

'Did you lock the door when you left?' Paget asked him.

Blake sat staring down into his mug and swirled the coffee round and round. 'I believe so, yes,' he said.

'Are you quite certain, Mr Blake?'

The man's eyes came up to meet Paget's own. 'I thought we were supposed to be talking about Monica Shaw,' he said.

'And so we are,' said Paget. 'So we are, Mr Blake. You see, Monica claimed she was attacked and dragged inside the shed about the time that you say you were there.'

Blake looked startled. '*Monica* said that?' he said as if he couldn't believe what he'd heard. His face darkened. 'Are you accusing me?'

'I'm accusing you of nothing,' Paget said. 'I'm merely pointing out that Sally Pritchard discovered Monica in the doorway of the shed shortly before six o'clock. According to Miss Pritchard, the girl was crying. She claimed that someone had dragged her inside the shed and tried to molest her. And there is physical evidence that tends to support her story. Naturally, I am interested in anyone who was in the vicinity at the time.'

'Well, it bloody well wasn't me!' said Blake indignantly. 'I went in, picked up the ointment, and left. That's it! And you can make what you like out of that! I wasn't the only man here that day you know.'

It was a fine, righteous show of indignation. Blake *might* be telling the truth, but Paget doubted it. From what he had learned so far, there had been no reason for Monica to go to the shed. It seemed more likely that someone had seen her wandering about in the yard and had lured her inside, probably on the spur of the moment. Perhaps someone who'd had a bit too much to drink. Or someone like Blake.

Always assuming, of course, that Monica had told Sally the truth in the first place.

'As you say,' said Paget quietly. 'Who were those others, Mr Blake?'

Blake eyed him warily for a moment. 'Well, there was Jack Lucas, of course—not that I'm suggesting that he was involved—but he was there. Then there was Bob Tillman, the stableman. He'd had a bit to drink come to think of it, and I don't remember seeing him when I left the barn. And Vic Prescott, the new man. He seems all right; knows his business, but we don't know anything about him. Sometimes it's the quiet ones you have to watch. Then there were the two lads, of course, Tony and Phil.'

'That's all?'

'That's all from here,' Blake said, 'but there were others dropping in during the afternoon. Clients and such. Anyone could have stayed behind.'

'For what reason?'

Blake banged his mug down on the table, slopping what was left of his coffee over the brim. 'How the hell should I know?' he asked belligerently. 'You wanted to know who was there; I told you.'

'What did you do after you left the shed?'

Blake glared at him for a moment. 'I went back to Crack-erjack's box, applied the ointment, then went back to the barn to join the others. The party was beginning to break up about then.'

'You didn't return to the shed?'

Blake took a deep breath and let it out again slowly. 'No, I didn't return to the shed,' he said evenly. 'Why should I?'

'Perhaps to return the ointment.'

Blake stood up, went over to the sink and picked up a cloth, then came back to the table where he proceeded to mop up the spilled coffee. 'I didn't take the ointment back,' he said. 'Not then. I thought I might need it later, so I put it in my pocket. As it happens, I didn't put it back until the next morning.' He dropped the cloth in the sink, then turned, folded his arms, and propped himself up against the counter.

'Was there anything else, Chief Inspector?' the sarcasm was thinly concealed.

Paget rose to his feet. 'I don't think so, for the moment,' he said. 'Thank you, Mr Blake. You've been very helpful.' He crossed the floor to the door. 'And thank you for the coffee. It was very good.'

BOTH PAGET AND TREGALLES spent the rest of the day at Glenacres, and it was after five o'clock when they arrived back in the office and sat down to compare notes.

Tregalles had talked to the stableman, Bob Tillman. He'd also spoken to the new man, Victor Prescott, and two of the grooms, Tony Gresham and Phil Boxwell.

'Tillman is forty-two years old, and the general dogsbody around there,' he said. 'He's a bit slow, if you know what I mean, but a hard worker, by all accounts.

'He says he was at the party all afternoon. I checked with Sally Pritchard. She said she *thought* she remembered him being there when she left to look for Monica, but she couldn't be absolutely sure. Neither could anyone else; not for certain. But he is the sort who tends to fade into the background, so it's hard to say exactly where he was.

'There was one thing, though. He said he liked Monica. He seemed to be very upset by her death. Said she was always nice to him; gave him a hand when she didn't need to; that sort of thing. He's the only one I spoke to who had anything good to say about her.'

Paget leaned back in his chair and put his hands behind his head. 'You heard Maurice Blake talking out in the yard this afternoon, didn't you?' he asked, and the sergeant nodded. 'Any chance that Penny Wakefield could have mistaken Tillman's voice for Blake's in the shed that night?'

'No way,' the sergeant said emphatically. 'Blake's got a soft voice. What is he? Irish? Tillman's a Welshman, and he sounds it. There's no comparison.'

'Okay. What about this other man, Prescott?'

'He's new. Came in at short notice a week after that chap, Craddock, died. He said he was in the process of moving up here from the south, and was looking round for a job when that happened, so Lucas took him on. Just temporary.'

Tregalles referred to his notes. 'Prescott says he left the party about three. Said he made the excuse that he had some last-minute things to do before Christmas, but he said the real reason was because he didn't feel he'd been there long enough to fit in. He said they were all reminiscing about things he knew nothing about, and he felt a bit out of it. He's a non-drinker and a bit on the shy side, I'd say. Says he went to his room and stayed there. He's living above the stalls along with some of the grooms.'

'Anyone able to verify that?'

'Not a soul,' said Tregalles. 'And as for Monica, he said he's seen her about the place, but he's never actually spoken to her. Which could be true. He's only been there a couple of weeks.'

'And Lucas claims he was in town from just after three until seven,' said Paget. 'He could be lying, but he didn't strike me as a stupid man, and he knows we'll check, so I'll accept what he said for the moment. What about the other grooms?'

'Tony Gresham and Phil Boxwell,' Tregalles said, grinning. 'They're just lads, both of them, and they were both in the barn when Sally went off to look for Monica. She remembers that quite clearly, because both of them were squiffed. She says they could barely stand up, let alone attack anyone.'

'And the two young grooms I spoke to, Lucy Dixon and Sheila Fulbright, are both accounted for as well,' said Paget. 'I'd say the money is still on Blake.'

THIRTEEN

Tuesday, 29 December

TO THE WEST, A MANTLE of fresh snow adorned the rounded peaks of Powys, but the country lanes that wound their way through the valley were wet with rain and slush. A watery sun made several half-hearted attempts to pierce the sullen grey, but it had given up the fight by the time Paget reached the school.

As he came up the driveway, Miss Crowther appeared at the top of the steps leading to the main entrance of the school. She was accompanied by a tall, dark-haired woman. The woman glanced towards the approaching car, said something to Miss Crowther, then descended the steps and got into a mud-bespattered Range Rover. By the time Paget had parked the car, the Range Rover was half-way down the drive.

Miss Crowther remained where she was. There was a guarded look in her eyes as he came up the steps. 'Chief Inspector,' she said. There was neither warmth nor welcome in the greeting.

'Good morning, Miss Crowther.' Paget turned and nodded in the direction of the departing Range Rover. 'I thought I recognized the lady who just left,' he said, 'but can't seem to place her.'

'Really?' Miss Crowther managed to convey surprise, reproof, and a sense of disbelief in the single word. She turned and led the way inside. 'Lady Tyndall is very well known to us *here*,' she said. 'She is a Thornton Hill Old

Girl, you know. Now, of course, Lady Tyndall heads our board of governors. It is her photograph that is missing.'

'I see.' Lady Tyndall. Of course! Wife of Lord Tyndall, who was a friend of Chief Constable Sir Robert Wyckham. So that's who she was! He recalled, now, having seen her photograph in the papers from time to time, opening a bazaar or fête or some such thing. But he had seen her in person more recently, for she was the woman who had been talking so very earnestly to Sally Pritchard outside the barn on Boxing Day.

But then, why shouldn't she have been talking to Sally? Warrendale Hall was the home of Lord and Lady Tyndall, and Lord Tyndall was Master of the Hunt. No doubt they found it convenient to stable their horses at Glenacres.

'You wished to see me?' Miss Crowther stood poised as if to show he was keeping her from something terribly important.

'As a matter of fact, I came to see Miss Wolsey,' he said. 'Do you know where I might find her?'

'In her room, most likely.' The headmistress made no attempt to hide her displeasure. 'I've tried my best to get her out of there, but I might as well have saved my breath for all the good it did. I told her that all this moping about won't bring the girl back again. What's done is done, regrettable as that may be. But will she listen to me? Oh, no. I told her she'll make herself ill if she keeps it up.'

Miss Crowther sighed the sigh of the long-suffering. 'I do hope she bucks up before the girls return after the holidays. I mean, it's not as if anyone is *blaming* her for what happened. But then, Jane could always find something to feel guilty about, so I let her get on with it.' She turned to leave.

Paget said: 'Did you by any chance ask Lady Tyndall about the photograph, Miss Crowther? Had she taken it?'

The headmistress shook her head. 'Lady Tyndall is as

mystified as I am,' she said. 'We can't think why anyone would wish to take it. I've looked everywhere, and I've asked everyone here about it. I can't think where it's gone. It's the oddest thing.'

'Is anything else missing?'

'No, and I have checked, believe me. Was there anything else, Chief Inspector?'

'No, thank you, Miss Crowther.'

'Good,' she said, and walked away.

Jane Wolsey looked terrible. Her face was grey and she looked as if she hadn't slept in days. Miss Crowther hadn't overstated the case when she said she feared the house-mistress would make herself ill.

'Oh, thank heavens, it's you,' she said, glancing up and down the corridor. 'I thought it was Miss Crowther again. Is there any news?'

'Regarding...?'

'The inquest, of course.' She put a hand to her head and frowned. 'No, not the inquest—I don't mean that. I mean the post-mortem.'

'According to the pathologist, the cause of death was an aneurysm,' Paget said.

'An aneurysm?' She stared at him.

'Yes. It's a...'

'Yes, yes, I know what an aneurysm is,' she said impatiently. 'But that's not the point, is it? Was Monica trying to commit suicide when it happened? I must know!'

'Perhaps we could go inside?' suggested Paget.

Miss Wolsey put her hands to her face and held them there for a long time. 'Yes. Yes, of course. Forgive me, Chief Inspector,' she said distractedly. 'Please come in.'

The room was hot and stuffy, and Paget removed his topcoat before taking a seat farthest from the fire. Miss Wolsey perched herself on the edge of her own chair, tugged the sleeve of her blouse down over her deformed hand in what was becoming a familiar gesture, and looked at him expectantly.

'It appears that Monica did inject herself with far more insulin than was good for her,' he said, 'and from what we've been able to learn, she was a very unhappy girl. What we don't know is what she hoped to achieve. It may have been no more than a desperate bid to draw attention to herself; an attempt that went terribly wrong.'

Paget paused and leaned forward to emphasize his next words. 'Miss Wolsey, now that you've had time to think about it, was there anything Monica said when she returned from the party that, in retrospect, might suggest that she was thinking of taking her own life?'

The housemistress looked away. 'No,' she said in a dead voice. 'I have tried to think; in fact I've done very little else since she died.'

'You said, I believe, that Monica was flushed and excited when Sally Pritchard brought her home. Do you recall anything she said? Anything at all?'

The housemistress shook her head slowly. 'Just that she was sorry. She kept saying she was sorry over and over again. I remember because it was so unusual.' Jane Wolsey coloured suddenly and looked embarrassed. 'I'm sorry,' she apologized. 'I shouldn't have said that, but it wasn't like her, you see.'

'I'm not sure I follow you. What wasn't like her, Miss Wolsey?'

'Well—' the colour deepened— 'Monica didn't like to admit mistakes. She would usually try to brazen it out, but in this case I think she must have realized she'd gone too far.'

'What, exactly, did Monica say she was sorry for?' Paget asked.

'For drinking too much wine, of course.'

'I see. What about Miss Pritchard? What did she say?'

Again, Miss Wolsey shook her head almost sadly. 'Poor Sally,' she said. 'I felt sorry for her because she seemed to think it was all her fault. She kept apologizing, too, but it wasn't her fault.'

'Did Monica mention the party at all? Did she say whether she enjoyed it, or mention anyone by name?'

'If she did, I'm afraid I don't remember,' the housemistress said. 'I'm sorry, Chief Inspector, but that's all I can tell you.'

The quiet of the room was broken by the ringing of the telephone.

The housemistress answered it. 'It's for you, Chief Inspector,' she said listlessly. 'A Superintendent Alcott.'

His conversation with Alcott was short, but even so the gist was clear to Jane Wolsey. 'There's not going to be an inquest, is there?' she said as he hung up.

He shook his head. 'No. The pathologist's report made it quite clear that Monica died of an aneurysm. In the absence of any evidence to the contrary, the coroner is prepared to accept that Monica died of natural causes, so there is no need for an inquest.'

'But what about the injections?'

'Not relevant,' he said, 'and I'm quoting, now. The two things cannot be connected medically. In the opinion of the pathologist, it would be impossible to say whether the amount of insulin Monica injected into herself would have led to her death had the aneurysm not occurred.'

'I see.' Miss Wolsey tugged at her sleeve with nervous fingers. 'Is that all?' she said. 'Doesn't anyone care about what happened?'

'It's not a matter of not caring, Miss Wolsey,' he said gently. 'You see, once the coroner is satisfied that death was due to natural causes, and no crime was involved, then that's the end of it as far as the law is concerned.'

'You're saying that no one is to blame?' Her words were bitter.

'I'm saying there was no criminal intent,' he said quietly. 'As for blame—I'm sure there are times when we all wish we had acted differently when someone close to us dies in such a tragic way, but there is nothing to be gained by looking back, Miss Wolsey.'

Jane Wolsey remained silent. Was it her own sense of guilt that was gnawing at her. Was she still blaming herself for Monica's death? Or was she simply looking for someone—anyone—to blame?

Not that he didn't have reservations of his own about the way Monica Shaw had died. There remained the question of where she had gone just prior to her death. What had prompted her to get dressed again and go out into the night in the middle of a snowstorm? And what part had the alleged attack played in the scheme of things, if any? These questions would remain unanswered now.

The housemistress continued to look at him, but there was no life in her eyes. The death of Monica Shaw had affected her deeply. He put out his hand and touched her shoulder. 'You're not to blame,' he said. 'There was nothing you could have done, Miss Wolsey. Nothing.'

She blinked. Her eyes came into focus and colour touched her cheeks. 'I—I'm sorry,' she apologized as she turned away. 'I'm afraid my mind was... Thank you, Chief Inspector; you are very kind, but I'm quite all right now.' She drew in a deep breath and let it out again. 'I think I'll put the kettle on,' she said. 'Would you like a cup of tea?'

FOURTEEN

Friday, 1 January

THE ENTRANCE TO THE BRIDLE-PATH was hard to see at night, and even harder to back into with the car. Guided only by the light of a waning moon, he eased it back a foot at a time. The snow had almost gone, washed away by the steady drizzle of the past two days, but the ground was still soaking wet and he didn't want to risk becoming stuck in the mud. He reached the shelter of the trees; switched the engine off and set the brake.

He yawned and stretched, then lit a cigarette and settled down to watch and wait.

It was almost an hour later when the car appeared. It drifted slowly down the lane, without lights and almost without sound. He watched as it rolled to a stop beside a giant sycamore just beyond the stable gates. The car was light in colour. Foreign, by the look of it, but he wasn't very good on cars, especially now that so many of the new ones looked alike.

The moon was almost down and it was hard to see. He picked up the binoculars from the seat beside him and focused them. He swore softly beneath his breath as the moon slid behind a cloud. Was that the outline of the driver's head he could see? Or was it just the moulded head-rest? 'Come on, you bastard,' he muttered to himself. 'What the hell do you think you're playing at? Get out of the car. Let's see your face!'

He swung the binoculars to the main gate, then to the second entrance farther down the road. Nothing stirred. He checked the time: 9.53, then scanned the road again. Nothing.

He would have to get closer.

Cautiously, he began to open the door, quickly closing it again as the overhead light came on. He reached up and moved the switch to Off, then slid out of the car and gently latched the door. He paused to listen as something rustled in the undergrowth. Silence. He bent down and felt around until his fingers touched a fallen twig. He tossed it in the direction of the sound, and was gratified to hear some small animal scurrying away.

Cautiously, he began to move towards the road.

THE CLOCK ABOVE THE CHAPEL struck the hour of ten, its mellow chimes wafting across the silent countryside like ripples on a pond. Miss Crowther, out walking in the grounds before going off to bed, paused to listen. She had been born to the sound of those chimes or so her father had told her, and they were one of her earliest memories. But listening to them now she felt sad. Four generations of Crowthers had spent their lives within the shadow of the chapel tower, and she would be the last. Perhaps, if she had married... She dismissed the thought as she had so many times before. She'd never had any inclination to marry; to follow in her father's footsteps as head of Thornton Hill School was all she'd ever wanted, and she was more than satisfied.

Thank God this business about Monica hadn't happened during term while all the girls were there. The publicity could have destroyed the school. Now it would be old news by the time the girls returned on Monday week. No doubt it would be the talk of the place for a day or two, but it would soon die down. It wasn't as if Monica had been a popular girl.

But she was going to have to do something about Jane.

In her small room beneath the eaves, Jane Wolsey heard the chimes as from a distance, and raised her head to listen. They seemed especially slow and sonorous tonight—as indeed they had these past few nights.

She wished she could have attended the funeral. It had all been such a jumble since that night. She didn't even know there had been a funeral until Crowther had mentioned it in that offhanded way of hers. At the country home in Hampshire, she'd said. Very private, of course.

The unfeeling bitch!

The small figure at an upstairs window also heard the measured strokes, but they barely registered. Wrapped up tightly in his eiderdown, he sat in the chair beside the window, eyes glued to the faint outline of the path below, waiting, trying not to cry. The last stroke faded, and his eyes began to close. He tried to stay awake, but his eyelids were too heavy and his head fell forward on his chest.

A shadow appeared beside the gate, paused, then moved quickly up the path towards the silent house. The back door latch made a rattling sound; the shadow froze. But the small boy in his chair beside the window did not hear the sound, for by then he'd drifted off to sleep.

Beneath the trees, the watcher heard the distant chimes and counted every stroke. Ten o'clock. Still no movement from the car. The watcher took another cautious step.

The final muted strokes drifted across the stable yard and died away, but the figure sprawled across the floor inside the barn did not hear them—nor ever would again.

FIFTEEN

Saturday, 2 January

THE BODY LAY ON ITS SIDE just inside the door. Male, light sandy-coloured hair, slim, fortyish—all this Paget noted in the first swift glance, but his eyes kept coming back to the pitchfork half buried in the man's chest.

Paget swallowed hard and forced himself to breathe slowly, deeply, until at last the nausea subsided.

At least one of the curving tines must have pierced the heart, but there was surprisingly little blood, and no sign of a struggle. The man must have dropped dead within seconds of being struck.

'Victor Prescott,' said Tregalles. 'The new man. He was on my list. I spoke to him the other day.'

Paget recalled the name and the man only too well. He was the same man he'd seen talking to—or had it been arguing with?—Andrea McMillan on Boxing Day. The connection, tenuous though it might be, filled him with foreboding.

Charlie Dobbs came over to stand beside Paget as they watched one of his men take photographs. 'Nasty,' he observed conversationally. 'Another inch and those prongs would be sticking out of the poor bastard's back.' Paget's stomach quivered in response. 'Better get another shot from over here,' said Charlie to the photographer. 'And get in closer to the chest, man. We'll need a close-up of those wounds. He's not going to bite you.'

Starkie, who had moved aside to allow the photographer

to work, returned to his task. 'Let's get this thing out of the way,' he said, indicating the pitchfork. 'But be careful.'

A plastic bag was slipped over the handle and pulled down as far as it would go, then tied. Two metal clamps equipped with handles were attached with great care to the pitchfork; one to the metal ferrule just above the tines; the other half-way up the plastic-covered handle. Starkie gripped one clamp while one of Charlie's men gripped the other.

'All right, pull,' said Starkie. The body began to move. 'Wait a minute.' Starkie threw a sheet of plastic across the dead man's chest, and stuck his foot on it. 'All right,' he said. 'Now pull, and don't let the pitchfork touch the floor.' With a sickening, sucking noise, the tines slid free, and Starkie quickly bagged the end.

While they waited for the pathologist to complete his examination, Paget surveyed the scene.

The position of the body suggested that the man had just come through the door when he was attacked. The tines of the pitchfork were sharp, but even so it must have taken a fair amount of thrust for them to penetrate as deeply as they had.

As for the barn, apart from all the forensic paraphernalia, nothing appeared to have been disturbed. The swing, he saw, had been hooked up to one of the beams to keep it out of everyone's way, but as far as he could tell, everything else looked the same. He went over to the office and looked inside. It, too, looked much as it had a few days before.

'Bit of a coincidence, don't you think, sir?' Tregalles said. 'I mean it's only been a few days since we were here about that suspicious death over at Thornton Hill.'

'Yes, I agree,' said Paget absently. He sounded as if his thoughts were miles away, and Tregalles glanced at him sharply. The chief inspector, usually so sharp and precise in everything he did, seemed a bit vague. Come to think of it, he'd seemed sort of preoccupied ever since Christmas. And short-tempered.

They watched in silence as the pathologist stripped off his gloves.

'I'd say he's been dead about eleven or twelve hours, but that could be revised after I've had him on the table,' Starkie said as he joined them. 'Died instantly. I think it's fairly safe to assume that it was the pitchfork that killed him,' he added drily. 'But I've never seen anything quite like it before. Whoever used that on him really drove it on. One of the tines smashed right through a rib and kept on going; didn't even slow it down. Penetrated the heart, of course. Still, the poor devil wouldn't have had time to feel much after being hit like that.' He began to gather his equipment together and put it away. 'For what it's worth, I'd say you're looking for a powerful man who hated this fellow's guts.'

'You're saying no woman could have done this?'

Starkie grimaced. 'A woman *could* have done it,' he conceded, 'but it seems more likely to me that it would have been a man. There was a lot of power in that thrust.'

He put on his coat. 'I'm not sure how long it will be before I can do the autopsy,' he said. He glanced at the time and clucked his tongue. 'Damned holidays. Mortuary always fills up on holidays. If it isn't road accidents, it's something like this.' He began to gather up his things.

Paget grunted sympathetically. 'Still, the sooner we have the results…'

'I know, I know,' said Starkie testily, 'but do me a favour, Paget. You managed to bugger up my Christmas, and now you've buggered up my long weekend. Next Saturday is our fortieth anniversary, and the family's planning a bit of a do. I'd hate to have to hold it in the mortuary, so try to keep it free of bodies, will you? I know my wife would appreciate it.'

Superintendent Alcott came out to take a look for himself, smoking three cigarettes in rapid succession while he listened attentively to what everyone had to say.

'Right,' he said briskly. 'I'll get back to Charter Lane and have an incident room set up. Cooper can be moved in to handle that end of the operation, so I can go to him for the day-to-day situation reports. But I shall expect a daily briefing from you each morning so that I have something for Mr Brock to take to the Chief Constable.' He looked around. 'You'll need a mobile unit out here as well, so I'll get Sergeant Ormside moving on that.'

He ground a cigarette beneath his heel, and lit another. 'Now, Paget, I assume you want to get started on interviews out here, so I'll leave you with it.'

It was Sally Pritchard who had discovered the body when she came to work that morning. Now, standing well clear of the cordoned-off area, she told Paget and Tregalles that she'd arrived as usual about twenty minutes to seven. When she tried to open the door, it had stuck half-way, and she'd had to shove hard to get through. It was only when she switched on the light that she saw what lay behind the door.

Somewhat shamefacedly, she said the sight had turned her stomach, and she'd lost her breakfast.

'I forced myself to go back inside,' she went on. 'It seemed impossible that Victor could be alive, but I had to make sure.' She shuddered at the memory. 'He was so *cold.*'

'Was it then you telephoned the police?'

'Yes. I went into the office and phoned from there. Then I rang Mr Lucas up at the house and he came down straight away.'

'Was anything missing or disturbed, as far as you could tell?'

'I don't think so, but I haven't really looked. But I will as soon as…' Sally looked as if she might be sick again.

Tregalles said: 'Do you have any idea who might have done this, Miss Pritchard? What can you tell us about him?'

She shook her head quickly. 'He was new, so I can't tell you much about him at all. He seemed all right. Pleasant. Very quiet. Kept very much to himself. A bit shy, I thought. But he knew his way around horses. He was very good with them. I think Mr Lucas was thinking of keeping him on.'

'How long had he been here?' Tregalles asked her.

Sally Pritchard thought back. 'He came just after Ernie died,' she said. 'That would be almost four weeks ago. He…' Whatever she was about to say remained unsaid as she lapsed into silence and looked puzzled. 'I just realized,' she said in a hushed voice, 'that three people I know have died in less than a month.' She looked at Paget as if she expected an answer to her unspoken question.

The same thought had crossed Paget's mind, but he sidestepped the implied question.

'You say the body was lying behind the door, and you had to push hard to get it open?'

'Yes.'

'Then how, I wonder, did the person who killed Prescott get out of the barn?'

'Through the other door,' said Sally promptly. 'It's behind the office. You probably didn't notice it when you were here the other day.'

'Are either of these doors normally kept locked?'

'No. There's no need. There's nothing of value in the place. We don't keep any money or anything like that in the office; just the records, that's all.'

'Records?'

'Yes. We keep the training schedules there, mine and Maurice's, and we keep the daily log in there as well.'

Seeing their enquiring looks, she went on to explain. 'You see, we keep a log on all the horses here; changes in routine—exercise, training, special diets, treatments by the vet, shots, things like that. As I said, nothing of value.'

'What about invoices, bills, cheques, petty cash—anything of that sort?' asked Tregalles.

'No. Anything like that is picked up by Mr Lucas at the end of the day and taken up to the house. Nothing is left here overnight.'

'I see. We think that Prescott died somewhere between nine and ten last night. What would he be doing in here at that time?'

'Probably doing evening rounds,' she said. 'Maurice said he was going to put him on soon. We usually do a final round between nine and ten each night, and we make a note of anything out of the ordinary. That could include such things as medication, or a horse that's, say, off its feed or seems a bit off colour; how a new one is settling down; things like that. It all goes in the log.'

'Can we take a look?'

'Of course.'

Inside the office, Sally took a book from a drawer and flipped it open. 'Here's the last entry,' she said, running her finger down the page. 'It's mine. I made a note that Firefly went out yesterday. His owner picked him up at four o'clock. He's moving up north—somewhere outside Glasgow, I believe he said. That's the last entry, so Victor couldn't have…' She sat down abruptly. 'Sorry,' she said. 'I'm afraid I'm not used to this.'

'It's not the sort of thing one wants to get used to,' Paget said with feeling. 'Just take your time, Miss Pritchard.'

Tregalles said: 'We found a clipboard underneath the body, but there was nothing on it. It's been taken away by forensic.'

'We carry that with us and make notes as we go,' said

Sally. 'He must have surprised someone when he came in. Someone who was in here already. But why would they be in here? And why did they have to kill him?' She closed her eyes and shuddered. 'It could have been any of us.'

Could it? thought Paget. Had Prescott just been in the wrong place at the wrong time? Or had someone been waiting for him, specifically, to walk through that door. 'Tell me, Miss Pritchard,' he said, 'what time did you leave here last night?'

'Six, ten past, something like that,' she said. 'Why?'

'You didn't come back for any reason?'

'No,' she said guardedly. 'Why? What are you suggesting?'

'I'm not suggesting anything,' he said, 'but I do want to know where everyone was last night. It's simply a process of elimination, that's all.'

'Oh. Well, I went straight home and stayed there until I came in this morning,' she said. 'I can't prove that, but then I would hope I'm not called upon to do so, Chief Inspector.'

Paget smiled. 'Let's hope not, Miss Pritchard,' he said pleasantly.

SIXTEEN

'THE HOUSE', AS IT WAS commonly referred to, was on a knoll behind the stables, half hidden behind a scrubby hedge of dogwood. Access to it could be gained along a separate driveway connecting with the road, but from the stable yard it was simpler and much quicker to use the gate behind the schooling ring.

As he approached the house, Paget could see it once had been two buildings. A small stone cottage and a large stone barn had been converted into an L-shaped house and two-door garage. Tregalles's 'That must have cost a bob or two' echoed Paget's own thoughts, and the same could be said for the pale green Mercedes parked outside the garage.

Jack Lucas came to the door himself, and invited them into what appeared to be the sitting-room but it seemed to serve the function of an office as well. A large desk littered with papers took up a quarter of the room. The ceiling was low, and beneath it Lucas looked even larger than he had outside. He indicated chairs and settled himself in an old-fashioned wooden swivel chair beside the desk, and lit a cigarette.

'Right,' he said briskly once they were seated. 'You said you had some questions; what is it you want to know?'

'I'd like you to tell me what you know about Victor Prescott,' Paget said. 'I gather he hasn't been here long?'

'Came here on the seventh of December,' Lucas said. 'I looked it up before you came. I'd just lost Ernie Craddock, and Prescott happened to be looking for a job, so I took him on. Good background, and he knew his business.'

'So you knew him, or knew of him before he came 1ere?'

'No. He came from Haslemere or Horsham—somewhere down in that part of the country; I forget, exactly. Worked for a man named Dennison down there.' He squinted at Paget through curling smoke. 'Do you know anything about this business, Chief Inspector?'

'Virtually nothing, I'm afraid,' Paget confessed.

Lucas nodded as if it confirmed his own suspicions. 'If you did you'd know that Dennison is something of a name in the trade. I've never actually met the man, myself, but apparently he'd heard of Glenacres. He rang me up. Told me that Prescott was coming up this way. Something to do with Prescott's girl-friend landing a good job up here, so he wanted to come up here to be with her. Said Prescott had worked for him for several years, and was a good man. He said he'd tried to talk him out of coming, but he wouldn't be persuaded, so Dennison said he'd phone round and see if there was anyone up here who could take him on until he could get himself sorted out. Decent of Dennison, considering.

'I told him I couldn't do it. What with things the way they are these days, you've got to watch the pennies. Prescott himself turned up the next day, but I had to tell him that I had a full staff. But I liked the look of him, so when Ernie Craddock got himself killed that same weekend, I got in touch. He'd left his number just in case I heard of anything, so I rang him and told him I'd take him on. On trial; daily wage, of course. I mean, I'd never seen the man before. Mind you, with Dennison recommending him, I didn't have too many doubts, but you can't be too careful.' Lucas tilted back in the chair and shook his head. 'Shame he's dead,' he said. 'I would have kept him on.'

'Seems a bit of a coincidence,' said Tregalles ruminatively. 'First, this man, Craddock, is killed, then the man who takes his place winds up dead. Odd, that.' He shot a quizzical look at Lucas. 'You don't keep racehorses here, by any chance?'

Lucas shook his head. He looked genuinely puzzled. 'Run of the mill mostly. There are a few good hunters here, but there's nothing special about them.'

'What about this girl-friend of Prescott's?' Tregalles asked. 'Do you know her name or where she lives or works?'

Lucas scratched his ear. 'I don't think he ever mentioned her,' he said. 'You might ask them down at the yard; he might have told some of them.'

'What about next of kin? When he signed on he…'

Lucas shook his head impatiently. 'I told you, he was paid by the day. I paid him out of my pocket. There was no "signing on". Apart from what I've told you, I know nothing about the man. Sorry, but that's all I can tell you.'

'Do you have this man Dennison's telephone number?' Paget asked. 'If Prescott worked for him presumably he'll have some sort of record.'

Lucas shook his head. 'No, but it will be in the breeder's directory.' He crushed out his cigarette and pulled a book from a shelf above the desk. 'Ah, here it is. Chaslow, near Dorking. I knew it was somewhere down in that country.'

Paget copied down the address and telephone number. 'We'll be having a look at Prescott's room,' he said. 'Perhaps we'll find something there that will help us. It's odd, but there was nothing in the way of identification in his pockets, not even a wallet.' He pulled a set of keys from his pocket. 'I assume one of these will fit the door of his room?'

Lucas looked them over. 'That one,' he said, pointing to the largest one of the bunch. 'The rest, except for that silver one, look like ours. The small one is probably for his bike. He parks it round the back behind the stalls.'

Paget stood up. 'Thank you, Mr Lucas,' he said. 'If you

should think of anything else, perhaps you'd let us know. We will be setting up an incident room this afternoon. It's a portable unit. There's a bit of ground behind the red barn, so we'll set it up there if you have no objection. It will be out of the way, and it should be a fairly simple matter for British Telecom to run phones in for us.'

'I suppose it will be all right,' Lucas said grudgingly. 'How long do you expect to be there?'

'Probably not too long,' said Paget, 'but there will be some police activity around here for a few days, at least. We'll try not to be too disruptive.'

Lucas lumbered to his feet. 'I hope you're not,' he said bluntly. 'I've still got a business to run, you know.'

'There is just one more thing,' said Paget as he and Tregalles made their way to the door. 'Can you think of any reason why someone might have been in the barn last night? I'm told that nothing of value is kept there.'

Lucas shook his head. 'Someone who knew about the office being there might have thought they'd find money,' he offered.

'I suppose that is a possibility,' said Paget. 'Were you by any chance around the stables yourself last night?'

The big man shook his head. 'Last time I was down there would be about four in the afternoon. I went down to see Firefly loaded, and to have a word with his owner.'

'You were home all evening, were you?'

Lucas poked at his ear again. 'No, I went into Broadminster,' he said. 'Darts match. I'm on a team at the Coach and Horses. Got back about eleven or thereabouts. Why?'

'Did you see anybody about when you returned?'

'You mean around the stables? No. But then, I came straight up the drive to the house, so I wouldn't, would I?'

'What about your wife? Perhaps she…'

'She's out,' said Lucas shortly. 'Took the boy with her to keep him from wanting to go down to the yard to see what was going on. She won't be back until this afternoon, but she wouldn't have heard anything.'

'How can you be so sure, Mr Lucas?'

'Because,' Lucas said with exaggerated patience, 'even if there was something going on down at the yard, she wouldn't hear it up here. Too far away.'

'I would still like to talk to her,' Paget said. 'Perhaps you'd be good enough to tell her that either I or Sergeant Tregalles will be back to talk to her when she returns. Good morning.'

PRESCOTT'S ROOM ABOVE the stalls was very small. It reminded Paget of a prison cell, albeit slightly larger and with a dormer window that overlooked the yard below. Everything was clean and tidy; everything in its place. A narrow cot was neatly made, an extra blanket folded precisely at its foot. A washstand in the corner contained fresh towels, toothbrush, shaving kit, and the usual assortment of odds and ends, all set out with such precision that Paget wondered if Prescott had spent time in the army.

Beside the washstand was a curtained-off set of shelves containing three shirts, three pairs of socks, and three sets of shorts and vests. The bottom shelf had been reserved for a motor-cycle helmet, a pair of heavy brogues, and a pair of lace-up boots. The rest of his clothes, a two-piece suit of medium grey, a plastic mac, a blazer and a pair of trousers, and a tie that looked vaguely regimental, hung from a metal rod above the shelves. That seemed to be the extent of Victor Prescott's wardrobe. Everything looked new—Paget fingered the material of the suit—and cheap.

The suitcase Tregalles dragged out from beneath the cot was locked, but a closer look at Prescott's key-ring revealed a small flat key that opened it. The case looked empty at first glance, but further inspection revealed a wallet and large envelope in the pocket of the lid. Paget riffled through the wallet.

'Ah-ha!' he muttered softly as he unfolded a piece of paper and quickly scanned it. He passed it over to Tregalles. 'Prison discharge,' he said. 'Dated November fifth. And his name wasn't Prescott. It was Palmer. Victor Palmer.'

While Tregalles scanned the discharge, Paget opened the envelope. It contained a photograph of a child; a fair-haired girl of about four or five with laughing eyes and a cheeky grin. She sat astride the top rail of a wooden gate, her long hair blowing in the breeze across her face, her expression clearly saying: 'Hey, look at me!'

But Paget's eyes were drawn to the person beside the girl, arms half extended as if fearful that the child might fall.

Tregalles looked over his shoulder. 'That's Dr McMillan from the hospital!' he exclaimed. 'Is that her little girl? Pretty kid, whoever she is. But why would Palmer have her picture?'

Why, indeed? Paget felt a chill go through him as he recalled the scene he'd witnessed in the stable yard a week ago. Andrea with arm upraised, face white with anger, looking down on the slyly smiling Palmer.

He drew a deep breath. 'Find out everything you can about Palmer,' he said. 'I want to know exactly who he was and what he was up to.'

Although he doubted if Palmer's room held any further secrets, Paget had Tregalles seal it until a more thorough search could be made, then sent the sergeant to check out the motor bike behind the stables.

Finding the photograph of Andrea MacMillan and the child hidden away in Palmer's suitcase had knocked the wind out of him. Andrea had never spoken of a daughter, but there was no doubt in his mind that the child belonged to her. The likeness was too striking to be coincidental. But why, then, had Andrea never mentioned her? Surely she would have...

Unless the child had died.

The chilling thought came unbidden to his mind, and he thrust it away. It was ridiculous to start speculating on so little information, and only Andrea could tell him the truth of the matter. But still the nagging thought remained: where did Palmer fit into all this?

Paget blew out his cheeks. The answer to that would have to wait.

The two girls, Penny Wakefield and Sylvia Gray, said they had stayed in the previous evening, and gone to bed early. 'You see, we were at a New Year's Eve party the night before. We didn't get to bed till about four, so we were dead tired last night,' Penny explained.

'When did you last see Victor?' Paget asked.

'About five, I should think it was,' said Penny, glancing at her room-mate for confirmation. Sylvia nodded. 'He was coming in from the paddock as we were going for our tea.'

'What about later in the evening?' said Paget. 'Say about nine or ten o'clock. Did you hear anything out in the yard? Any strange noises; someone calling out, perhaps?'

Both girls shook their heads.

'How well did you know Victor?'

The two girls looked at each other and shrugged. 'Can't say I really knew him at all,' Penny said at last. 'Syl's the one who goes in for older men, aren't you, Syl?'

Sylvia Gray turned scarlet. 'Penny! That's a rotten thing to say.' She looked to be on the verge of tears.

Penny Wakefield was immediately contrite. 'I'm sorry, Syl,' she said. 'I was only joking. You know me. I'm sorry.' She looked at Paget and shrugged apologetically. 'Sorry,' she said again. 'Whatever must you think of me?'

'Did he ever talk to you? Tell you anything about himself? Did he ever mention a girl-friend?'

The two girls shook their heads. 'He was ever so shy,' said Penny. 'I used to wonder about him. He seemed sort of sad, somehow. I used to wonder if he had children somewhere. I said that to you more than once, didn't I, Syl?'

'Yes, you did,' her friend acknowledged, but the words came grudgingly, and it wasn't hard to see that she was still annoyed.

'Why?' asked Paget. 'What made you think he had children?'

'It was the way he used to watch young Jimmy,' Penny said. 'He'd just stand there watching him. I told Syl I thought he was pretending that Jimmy was his own little boy.' She lowered her voice. '*And* he used to give him sweets when his dad wasn't around. See, Jimmy's got bad teeth, and Mr Lucas doesn't want him to have sweets, but Victor used to keep some in his pockets and he'd slip a few to Jimmy every now and then. 'Course, clumsy old me has to catch him at it, and Victor gets all embarrassed and walks away. I wouldn't have split on him, but I never had a chance to tell him.' She looked sad. 'That was rotten luck, him walking in on someone in the barn like that. Poor sod. Could've been any of us, though, couldn't it?'

Could it? Paget wondered.

Short, stocky, black-haired, and as Welsh as they come, Bob Tillman, the stableman, said he'd spent the evening at home in Malford where he lived with his elder sister. They, too, had spent the evening watching television, and after Bob's long-winded and detailed account of what they'd watched, Paget didn't doubt it for a minute. He asked him the same question he'd asked the two girls: 'How well did you know Victor?'

Bob scratched his head. 'Can't say I knew him well at all,' he said. 'Hardly ever spoke, see. He was all right, though. Good with horses, he was; you could see that. Gentle with 'em, too. He was all right, was Victor.'

And that was all Paget could elicit from the man.

Maurice Blake also claimed to have spent the evening watching television, and Paget wondered what everyone used to do before the arrival of the ubiquitous box. But when he asked Blake about specific programmes, the man began to hedge, and said he'd only fiddled with the thing, and had turned it off when he couldn't find anything he liked. He said he hadn't left the caravan all evening, neither had he heard anything unusual outside.

Blake went on to say that the last time he'd seen and spoken to Victor was about half-past five when they talked about four new horses that were due to arrive within the next few days.

'Did you talk about anything else?'

'I don't think so, no.' Blake frowned. 'Victor didn't talk much; kept himself very much to himself.'

'Mr Lucas said something about Prescott having moved here because of a girl-friend. Did he ever mention a girl-friend to you?'

Blake shook his head. 'I got the impression he didn't know anyone outside Glenacres,' he said.

Paget, who had been watching the man closely, said: 'Did you like Victor Prescott?' Neither he nor Tregalles had mentioned that Prescott was not the man's real name.

Blake took his time answering. 'I don't know,' he said soberly. 'He was all right, I suppose, but there was something about him I couldn't take to. Knew his job, I'll give him that, but I always had the feeling that he was—' he laughed self-consciously '—it sounds a bit stupid, now, but I had the feeling that he was *waiting* for something.'

'Waiting for something? Such as what?'

Blake shrugged his shoulders helplessly. 'I'll be damned if I know,' he said. 'As I said, it was just a feeling. I'm probably doing the poor devil a terrible injustice.'

SEVENTEEN

TREGALLES RECOMMENDED the Black Swan at Longley Marsh for lunch. 'They do a Gloucester sausage you wouldn't believe,' he told Paget. 'And the mustard...'

The Gloucester sausage was off, and they had to make do with what tasted like recycled shepherd's pie. Not that Paget seemed to notice. He remained preoccupied throughout lunch, and the sergeant's attempts at conversation drew little response. Wisely, the sergeant made no attempt to probe. No doubt Paget would reveal all in his own good time.

Abruptly, Paget pushed his plate aside, and picked up the conversation begun earlier in the car as if there had been no break. It was a habit of his, and one that could be disconcerting to those who failed to store previous conversations in their memory banks ready for instant retrieval.

'So,' he said softly, 'Victor Palmer did five years inside for sexual offences against children.'

Tregalles nodded. He had spent almost an hour on the phone tracking down Palmer's record. 'They reckon he was responsible for thirteen cases altogether, girls and boys around the age of four to six, but they could only prove two of them in court. I should be able to get a full printout when we get back this afternoon.'

Paget thought of what Penny Wakefield had told him earlier about Palmer trying to make friends with young James. James with his blond hair, fair skin and large brown eyes. He shuddered inwardly at the boy's narrow escape. What Penny, in her innocence, had thought to be a show of paternal affection, had been, in all probability, nothing more than an attempt to gain the confidence of the boy.

The motor bike had been stolen from outside a garage in Cheltenham on the fifteenth of November, ten days after Palmer was released from prison. And he turned up at Glenacres at the beginning of December.

Where had he been during these two weeks? What had he been doing? And why did he have a photograph of Andrea and the child in his case?

Paget rose and made his way towards the door. Tregalles quickly drained his glass and hurried after him.

As they reached the car, Paget said: 'What about this man, Dennison? Any luck there?'

'No. He's out and won't be back until this afternoon. I've left a message asking him to ring us when he gets in.'

'Right. In that case I think I'll get back to the office, but I'll drop you at the stables on the way in. Find out whether Charlie's people have come up with anything of interest. Also, I'd like you to have a look at the yard office again. Talk to Sally Pritchard; find out exactly what they keep in those files. Perhaps there is something of value there; something other than money. And keep an eye open for Mrs Lucas and the boy. I don't expect that she'll have seen or heard anything, but you never know.'

'And you, sir?'

'I have to stop at the hospital,' Paget told him. 'After that, I should be in the office.'

Tregalles got in the car. 'Ah, yes, Dr McMillan,' he said. 'Funny, that, Palmer having her picture in his case.' Paget made no comment, lapsing once again into a brooding silence. Tregalles took the hint and said no more throughout the drive to Glenacres.

As he drove into town, Paget continued to wonder how Andrea McMillan fitted into the scheme of things. The photograph in Palmer's case had come as a shock to him. What was the connection between Palmer and Andrea? And what of the child? The likeness was too great to be coincidental; the girl in the photograph had to be Andrea's daughter. But why, then, had Andrea never mentioned her?

Which led to the question Paget had been subconsciously trying to avoid. What did he *really* know about Andrea? Not much when it came right down to it, he thought wryly. She had always avoided talking about herself, except in a very general sort of way, and he hadn't pressed her. But she couldn't be mixed up with this convicted sex offender; the idea was preposterous. God knows, he'd been wrong about people before, but he couldn't be *that* wrong about Andrea. Not when he felt as he did about her.

But something didn't add up. For example: where was the child? He felt sure she wasn't living with her mother, so where was she? Was she with her father? And if so, why? When families split up, the courts invariably gave custody to the mother, unless, of course, there were reasons, such as abuse...

Paget brought himself up short. Oh, no. Let's not start jumping to conclusions, he told himself. Let's wait and see what Andrea has to say.

But Dr McMillan was not on duty, he was told when he enquired at the desk, and she was not expected back until Monday.

Neither was there a response when he pressed the button opposite Andrea's name at the flat. He looked down the list and pressed the button marked 'Manager'.

The manager was a short, plump, grey-haired woman who peered short-sightedly through gold-rimmed glasses at Paget's card. Her name was Mrs Ansell, and once she had assured herself that Paget was indeed a policeman, she told him that Dr McMillan had gone away for the weekend.

'At least, I assume she has. She usually does when she has the weekend off.'

'Do you know where she's gone?' he asked.

'To her mother's, I should imagine, to see young Sarah.'

'Sarah?'

'Her little girl. She's staying with the doctor's mother, though for the life of me I don't know why, the way she misses her.'

'Do you know where Dr McMillan's mother lives?'

'Devon. Somewhere in Devon,' the woman said. 'I don't know where, exactly. I'm sorry, but that's all I can tell you.' Mrs Ansell peered at him anxiously. 'Nothing's wrong, is it? I mean, there hasn't been an accident or anything like that?'

'No, nothing like that, Mrs Ansell,' Paget assured her.

'Sorry, but I'm afraid I can't help you,' she said.

'Do you happen to know when Dr McMillan left for Devon?'

Mrs Ansell frowned. 'She was late,' she said. 'It must have been going on nine when I saw her going out last night. That's why I was a bit surprised this morning when I saw her car was still gone. Being as it was so late, I didn't think she would be going at all, but she must have done. See, she likes to get on the road no later than seven when she's going down to Devon, so I thought something must have come up and she wasn't going after all. And because she didn't have her bag.'

'Her bag?'

'The one she calls her "weekender". It's a big floppy thing that holds everything she needs when she's going away for the weekend. She always takes it with her. But she didn't have it with her last night.' The puzzled expression on Mrs Ansell's face cleared. 'It was probably in the car already,' she said, 'and she'd just gone back upstairs for something she'd left behind when I saw her coming down again.'

'Did she say she'd left something behind?'

'Well, no. It was just that she was in such a hurry, and she had this envelope in her hand when she came down. I just assumed…'

'Did she say anything at all?'

Mrs Ansell frowned. 'No, she didn't, and that wasn't like her. Not like her at all. Still, like I say, she was in a hurry.'

'You've met her daughter, Sarah?'

'Met her?' Mrs Ansell looked at Paget wide-eyed. 'Oh, my word, I should say so,' she said. 'Why, I've looked after young Sarah since she was just a tot.' Mrs Ansell's face became sad. 'I really miss her. We always got on so well.'

'When did she go away?'

'Oh, let's see, now. It must be going on for two months.' The woman looked distressed. 'I thought she'd be sure to come home for Christmas, but the doctor said Sarah liked it at her gran's, and she wanted to stay over.' Mrs Ansell sighed heavily. 'It doesn't seem right, somehow,' she said. 'It doesn't seem right at all.'

As Paget made his way back to the car, he silently agreed. Something was not right, and the sooner he got to the bottom of it, the better.

IT WAS FIVE PAST THREE when Tregalles saw the Cavalier Estate go up the drive adjacent to the stables. He waited a few minutes, then made his own way over to the house and knocked on the door.

He waited. The Cavalier Estate was parked askew, its nose mere inches from the garage door. Faint ticking sounds came from its engine as it cooled, and Tregalles noticed that the interior light was on. The door on the driver's side had not been properly closed. He went over and pushed it shut; the light went out. He turned and knocked again.

The door was opened by a fair-haired boy with solemn eyes. 'Are you a policeman?' he asked.

'Yes, I am,' said Tregalles. 'My name is Tregalles. Detective Sergeant Tregalles. You must be James.'

The boy's eyes grew round. 'Detective!' he said and opened the door wider. 'Mummy?' he called over his shoulder. 'It's Detective Tre—Tre—'

'—galles,' the sergeant supplied. 'Tregalles.'

'It's Detective Tregalles,' called the boy.

Tregalles heard the click of heels on the tiled floor and a woman appeared behind the boy. She had a cigarette in her hand. 'Yes?' she said in a voice that lacked interest in his answer.

Tregalles stared. Having met Lucas, he was unprepared for such a young wife. And beautiful, for Georgie Lucas was a very beautiful woman indeed.

'I—aahh—Mrs Lucas?' he managed at last. 'Detective Sergeant Tregalles.' He displayed his warrant card. 'I'd like a word with you about what happened down at the stables last night. May I come in?'

'Can I see?' James reached up and tugged at Tregalles's sleeve. He examined the warrant card carefully, then looked up at his mother. 'Can I go and tell Sally?' he asked. 'Please?'

'I suppose it will be all right,' the woman said absently, touching her son's hair. 'But don't get in the way down there.'

'I won't.' The boy was off like a shot. The woman looked blankly at Tregalles for a few seconds as if she'd forgotten why he was there, then moved aside and motioned for him to come in.

'I don't know how I can help you,' she said as they made their way to the same room where he and Paget had spoken to her husband earlier in the day. 'I don't know anything about—about what happened down there.' She made a vague gesture with her hand that Tregalles interpreted as an invitation to sit down, but he remained standing, waiting for her to sit down first.

Georgie Lucas was younger than her husband by twenty years or more. Like her son, her hair was blonde, but unlike his close-cropped cut, it flowed like honey around the perfect oval of her face to form a golden pool across her shoulders. Its flowing lines melded with a body of voluptuous curves and long, exciting, slender legs.

She was dressed as if for spring; light-coloured suit with straight skirt ending well above the knees—and very nice knees they were, Tregalles thought appreciatively—with just a touch of deeper colour accenting the collar and false pockets. A silk scarf, almost hidden by the collar, was held in place by a rhinestone brooch—a large rhinestone brooch.

She saw him looking at it, and her fingers touched it lovingly. 'Do you like it?' she asked coquettishly.

'It's very nice,' he said. 'Very nice indeed.'

She tucked in her chin, trying to look down at it. 'It should be very nice,' she said, considering what Jack paid for it. They are real diamonds, you know.'

Good God! Tregalles thought. 'Oh, yes, I could see that,' he lied.

She looked pleased. 'Would you care for something to drink, Sergeant?' she asked. He was about to say that a cup of tea would be welcome, when she moved to a cupboard in the corner and opened it to reveal an array of bottles. 'Scotch? Gin? Rum? I think Jack has some beer somewhere…'

'Ah—no. Nothing for me, thank you, Mrs Lucas,' he said.

She drew heavily on her cigarette. 'I think I'll just have a small one,' she said, and poured a good three fingers of gin into a glass. 'Shopping with Jimmy can be rather wearing,' she said by way of explanation as she removed a fur coat from one of the chairs beside the fireplace and sat down. 'Do you have children, Sergeant?'

'Two,' he said, taking a seat across from her. 'Olivia is eight and Brian is six.'

'Jimmy's eight,' she said. Her eyes wandered round the room as if she'd lost interest in what she was saying.

'A nice lad,' Tregalles observed. 'Now, then, Mrs Lucas, perhaps you could tell me about last night. You were here in the house, were you?'

'Mm-hmm,' she said, regarding him over the top of her glass.

'All evening?'

She reached for an ashtray and butted her cigarette. 'Yes,' she said. 'All evening.'

'Mr Lucas was out, I believe?'

'That's right. Just Jimmy and I were here.'

'Did you have any reason to go outside during the evening?'

Again she shook her head.

'Do you recall hearing anything unusual? Shouts, cars starting up or anything like that?'

Georgie Lucas sipped her drink and appeared to think about it. 'I can't recall anything like that,' she said. She crossed her legs and her skirt slid over nylon with a sound like rustling grass.

Tregalles fixed his eyes firmly on her face. 'How well did you know Victor Prescott?' he asked her. 'Did you ever talk to him? Did he ever tell you anything about himself?'

Georgie Lucas reached for another cigarette and lit it before she answered. 'I didn't know the man at all,' she said. 'I saw him here when my husband took him on, but I don't think I ever saw him after that.' She leaned forward and lowered her voice as if about to impart a secret. 'You see, Sergeant, I'm afraid I don't share my husband's en-

thusiasm for horses. I seldom go near the stables. In fact I
hate them, so I'm afraid I can't help you at all. Sorry.'

TREGALLES, HAVING RETURNED to headquarters in Charter
Lane, was in the incident room when a WPC by the name
of Wooller cupped a hand over the phone and called out:
'Got a call for DCI Paget. Anybody know when he'll be
back?'

Tregalles looked up. 'Who is it?' he asked.

'Says his name is Dennison,' Wooller told him. 'He's
ringing from a place called Chaslow in Surrey.'

'I'll take that,' Tregalles told her, and picked up the
phone.

IT WAS LATE IN THE AFTERNOON by the time Paget returned
to the office. Tregalles followed him in, pausing only long
enough to pick up two cups of coffee from the machine.

'Dennison rang back,' he told Paget. 'He says he's never
heard of Prescott or Palmer.' He set the coffee on the desk
and sat down. 'He says he doesn't know Lucas, and he
denies ever talking to him on the phone. He could be lying,
of course, but he sounded straight enough. When I said
we'd probably be checking further, he told me to check and
be damned.'

'I suspect that Palmer himself made the call to Lucas,
purporting to be Dennison,' said Paget. 'Either that or he
had someone do it for him. But why? Why was he so anxious to get on at Glenacres? Why that particular stable?
And doesn't it strike you as a bit of a coincidence that Ernie
Craddock, a key man at Glenacres by all accounts, just
happened to be killed when Palmer was looking for an
opening there? The timing couldn't have been better if he'd
planned it.'

The day staff had gone home, and it was quiet in the
office except for the sound of a rising wind and the occa-

sional slap of rain against the window. Tregalles, who had been about to take a drink of coffee, paused and set the cup down again as he digested this new idea.

'You think it was Palmer who killed Craddock?'

Paget leaned back in his chair and massaged his face with both hands. He felt tired. 'I don't know,' he said wearily, 'but you must admit Craddock's death came at a very convenient time for Palmer. I had a word with DI Martin—he was on the Craddock case—and he tells me that one of the tyre impressions lifted at the scene was that of a motor bike. I told him about the stolen bike that Palmer was using, and he's going to check it for a possible match. If they do match, it could mean that Craddock's death was not a mugging gone wrong at all, but a very deliberate murder. It might also mean that Palmer's death was no accident either.'

'I'm not sure I follow you,' Tregalles said.

Paget sniffed his coffee, grimaced and set it aside. He wasn't *that* thirsty.

'Look at it this way,' he said. 'The first thing that came to mind this morning was that Palmer had surprised someone when he walked into the barn last night. Someone who panicked and hit him with the first thing that came to hand. The pitchfork. But, if that was so, what was the person doing there in the first place? We're told that there was nothing of value in the office; no money, no confidential files, in fact nothing of interest to anyone except the staff, and virtually everyone knows that. So why was the person there? No one in his right mind sets out to rob a barn. Which leads me to believe that whoever killed Palmer was there for some other reason.'

'To kill Palmer.'

'Or to meet him, and something went wrong. If our theory is correct, Palmer went to a lot of trouble to get into Glenacres. Everyone seems to agree that the man knew his job, so he's obviously worked around stables before. His file should tell us that. Which reminds me; what about his file? Do we have it yet?'

Tregalles shrugged apologetically. 'We have some stuff on computer, but we won't be able to get his complete file until Monday at the earliest.'

Paget grunted. Damned holidays, he thought irritably. How the hell were they supposed to work with everything closed down for days?

'It seems to me,' he went on, pursuing his original thought, 'that people who work with horses move around quite a lot. It may be that there is someone at Glenacres who used to work with Palmer, or at least knew him before he went to prison. Someone who may know more about this than they're telling us, so I want a background check made on everyone who works there.'

Tregalles frowned into his cup. 'What about that photograph?' he said. 'Did you talk to Dr McMillan?'

'No. She's away. She won't be back until Monday.' Paget's words were clipped and sharper than he'd intended.

'It wouldn't surprise me if Palmer intended to have a go at that kid of hers,' Tregalles said. 'With his record, it's the sort of thing he might do. But I wonder how he got the picture? And why the doctor?'

Paget began to shuffle papers on his desk. 'What about this girl-friend Palmer is supposed to have followed here?' he said. 'Anyone know anything about her?'

Tregalles slowly shook his head. 'I don't think there ever was a girl-friend,' he said. 'I think it was just something Palmer made up when he called Lucas, pretending to be Dennison.'

'But we can't be sure of that,' said Paget. 'Better look into it.' He pulled a file towards him and opened it. When Tregalles didn't move, the chief inspector looked up and said: 'Well?'

The sergeant scrambled to his feet. 'Sorry,' he said. 'I thought we still had…' He shrugged. 'I'll get on it,' he said. He took what remained of his coffee and left the office.

What the hell was the matter with Paget? he wondered. This girl-friend story was something Palmer had made up to account for his being in the area; Tregalles was sure of it, and he was sure Paget knew it as well. Palmer had never mentioned a girl-friend to anyone at Glenacres, apart from Lucas, and apparently he'd hardly ever left the stables since he'd been there, so why was Paget suddenly interested in having him spend his time on a task they both knew to be pointless?

At his desk, Paget pushed aside the file and sat back in his chair. He was allowing his emotions to cloud his judgement, he told himself. There had been no need to snap at Tregalles. The man was only trying to do his job.

There was no doubt in his mind that Palmer had been threatening Andrea that day he'd seen them at Glenacres. The look on her face was more than proof of that. But with what? Something to do with Sarah as Tregalles had suggested? The thought of someone like Palmer with the child made his blood run cold. The trouble was he couldn't get over the fact that Andrea had lied to him. Or if not lied, she had certainly withheld the truth. Was it because she felt she couldn't trust him? Or was it, perhaps, because he was a policeman?

Someone had waited in the barn for Palmer. Someone who hated him so much that they had rammed a pitchfork into his chest…

Paget closed his eyes against the picture in his mind.

EIGHTEEN

Sunday, 3 January

SUNDAY WAS A FRUSTRATING DAY. Both Paget and Tregalles spent time in the incident room with Cooper, but between the holiday weekend, three people off with flu, and almost everything they needed for support being shut down or on skeleton staff, they were making no progress at all. The mobile incident room had been put in place at Glenacres, but no telephones or data lines had been hooked up; neither would there be anyone out there to man the mobile unit until Monday. Tomorrow, no doubt, activity would resume, but until then there was little they could do.

At eleven o'clock, Paget sent Tregalles home. Paget remained there for another hour then packed it in himself.

Monday, 4 January

'I HATE THIS TIME OF YEAR.'

Superintendent Alcott stood before the window, staring out across the rain-swept playing field behind the building. 'Dark when you come to work; dark when you go home. Day after day of rain.' He turned away and lit a cigarette. 'They should outlaw bloody January in this country,' he said as he sat down. Paget and Tregalles sat down and faced him across the desk.

'Well, it's not that bad, sir,' Tregalles said cheerfully. 'What is it, now? A couple of weeks before you and your wife leave for sunny Florida?' Alcott had talked of almost nothing else but his forthcoming visit to America for months, it seemed.

'My younger brother, Arnold, you know,' he was fond of telling anyone who'd listen. 'Done very well for himself out there. Invited us for a month. Just look at those beaches.' The superintendent had a stack of holiday brochures depicting bikini-clad Amazons lounging in provocative poses on golden sands, with palms and endless surf serving as a backdrop.

Alcott glowered at him. 'No, we don't leave for bloody Florida,' he said curtly. 'My sister-in-law rang us from Miami last night. It seems she and Arnold are getting a divorce. Just like that. Married fifteen years; two kids, and now he's gone off with some woman he met at work. Bloody idiot.'

He drew heavily on his cigarette. 'But that's enough of that. What have we got on this Prescott killing?'

'Palmer,' Paget corrected. 'Victor Palmer. Child molester. Got five years for it and served his full time. No parole. He was released November fifth. Got a job at Glenacres a month later, using the name of Prescott, after he was supposedly recommended by a man named Dennison who owns a stable down south. But Dennison claims he never heard of the man.' The chief inspector went on to summarize what they had learned so far, including their finding of the photograph of Dr McMillan and her daughter.

'Palmer's file should be here this morning,' he ended, 'and I'm hoping that will give us a clue. Dr McMillan has been away, but she should be back at work this morning, so I shall talk to her as soon as possible. Also, I spoke to Dr Starkie a few minutes ago, and he tells me that Palmer died between nine and eleven Friday night, and the cause of death was undoubtedly the pitchfork. One tine went right through the heart. The thrust was almost straight on, like a bayonet thrust, and Starkie sees that as unusual. He said it would have seemed more natural to him if the thrust had been slightly upward—unless, of course, the killer was much taller than Palmer, but Palmer himself was close to six feet, so that's not too likely. One of the outer tines struck and broke a lower rib, but that didn't even slow it down. Starkie said it would take a lot of power to do that.'

'Motive?' said Alcott.

Paget shook his head. 'I'm afraid we haven't got one at the moment, sir,' he said bluntly. 'My feeling is that Palmer got a job at Glenacres for a particular reason, but I have no idea what that reason was as yet. I'm having backgrounds checked out to see if anyone working at Glenacres has crossed paths with Palmer before, and as I said, there may be something in Palmer's file.'

Alcott grunted. 'Let's hope so,' he said. 'Make sure you keep me posted.' With a curt nod, the superintendent swung round in his chair to face the window, effectively dismissing them.

Rain rattled against the glass. 'Bloody weather,' he muttered. He swung back to face the desk and crushed out his cigarette with such violence that butts and ash went flying from the ashtray.

As the door closed behind the two detectives, he picked up the travel folders and spread them like a fan. 'Sod you, Arnold,' he said beneath his breath. 'Why the hell couldn't you have waited till we'd had our holiday?'

PAGET GLANCED AT THE TIME. Ten thirty. He stood up and looked outside as he shrugged into his coat. It seemed the rain had settled in for the day.

Tregalles appeared in the open doorway. He was carrying a bulky file. 'This came in by courier from Exeter about fifteen minutes ago,' he said. He sounded strangely subdued. 'It's the file on Palmer.'

'Anything interesting in it?' Paget was sure that the sergeant would have skimmed it already.

'Let's just say that if you're on your way to the hospital to see Dr McMillan, I'd suggest you look at it before you go. You might try page three for a start.'

PAGET TRACKED ANDREA DOWN on the fourth floor of the hospital where she was just finishing her rounds. He waited until she'd finished issuing instructions to one of the nurses behind the desk then said: 'Is there somewhere private we can talk?'

It was significant that she didn't ask him why he was there, but simply led the way to a small consulting room. 'We won't be disturbed here,' she said as she closed the door. She stood there leaning against it, hands thrust deep inside the pockets of her white coat, watching him with those calm eyes of hers as he walked over to the window and turned to face her.

She looked tired. Bone weary would be closer to the mark. Even make-up couldn't hide the dark smudges beneath her eyes, and the lines seemed etched more deeply in her face.

In a quiet voice she asked: 'What is it, Neil?'

'Don't you know why I'm here?' he said.

Andrea McMillan walked over to a chair beside the desk and sat down. She waved a listless hand towards the only other chair and thrust it back into her pocket again. 'I'd rather you told me,' she said.

Paget searched her face as he lowered himself into the seat opposite her, but he saw nothing there but weariness.

'You've seen the morning papers?' he said.

There was a momentary flicker in her eyes. She nodded but remained silent.

'So you know that Victor Palmer is dead?'

Andrea McMillan turned her head and looked into the distance. 'Yes,' she said almost inaudibly.

'You were once married to him?'

She closed her eyes. 'Yes.'

'When did you last see him?'

There was a slight frown on her face as she turned back to face him. 'Five years ago in court,' she said.

Her answer stopped him dead. He hadn't been expecting it. He hadn't expected her to lie. Perhaps, he rationalized, she didn't realize how important it was.

'This is important, Andrea,' he said earnestly. 'Are you quite sure you haven't seen him since?'

Her eyes met his squarely. 'Quite sure,' she said calmly.

'You didn't know he was working at Glenacres?' he persisted.

'No—at least not until I read it in the papers.'

'I see.' So that was that, he thought resignedly. He'd given her the opportunity to change her story, but she had chosen not to take it.

'Tell me where were you last Friday evening?'

'I went down to see my daughter, Sarah, at my mother's place in Devon.'

'What time did you leave Broadminster?'

She thought. 'About eight thirty, I think it was,' she said.

'And your mother lives where, exactly?'

'Not far from Newton Abbot.' She gave him the address.

'And what time did you arrive there?'

'Just after eleven. Sarah had gone to bed, of course, but Mother was up. I usually try to get down there before Sarah goes to bed, but I was running late that night.'

'Any particular reason?'

'No. I was late getting away from the hospital, and that put me behind all evening.' Andrea looked faintly puzzled. 'Look, Neil, is all this really necessary?' she said. 'It's true I was once married to Victor, but that was years ago. To be truthful, I can't say I'm sorry he's dead. I assume, since you know about me, that you know why he went to prison?'

'We have a copy of his record,' said Paget.

'Then you will understand why I feel the way I do,' she said. 'He tried to kill me, Neil. And those children…' She shuddered.

'I saw you talking to him at Glenacres on Boxing Day,' he said softly. 'I was there, Andrea.'

It jolted her. He could see it in her face. She had looked pale before, but now her skin was almost grey. Slowly, she stood up and walked over to the window, standing with her back to him as she looked out across the town with unseeing eyes.

'You're right, of course,' she said quietly, still with her back to him. 'I did see him there on Boxing Day. I had no idea that he was there until he suddenly appeared. It shook me up, I can tell you.'

'What did he want?'

'Want?' Andrea turned away from the window and came back to her chair. She was frowning as she sat down. 'I don't know,' she said. 'He *said* he just wanted to say how sorry he was for all the trouble he'd caused. He *said* he had changed; that he'd had therapy. He kept saying he was sorry.'

'Did he threaten you?'

'No.'

Her answer was swift and unequivocal, but he didn't believe her. 'Why is Sarah living with her grandmother when she used to live here with you?' he asked.

'She is just visiting, that's all. They get along well together, and my mother enjoys having her. She'll be coming home soon.'

'Now that Victor's dead, you mean?'

Colour rushed into Andrea's cheeks. Her lips compressed into a thin line and her mouth set stubbornly.

Paget leaned forward and spoke earnestly. 'Look, Andrea, I need to know the truth. After reading Palmer's file, I don't think it is a coincidence that you sent your daughter away shortly after he came out of prison. I think you were afraid he might trace you here, and you wanted her out of harm's way if there was any trouble. You had changed back to your maiden name of McMillan after divorcing Palmer, and you'd moved up here to Broadminster, but I think you were still afraid that he might find you. Now, for your own good, please tell me the truth. If you had nothing to do with Palmer's death, you have nothing to fear.'

Andrea McMillan remained silent for a long time. Her face might have been made of stone, and her eyes were as blank as shutters. At last she sighed and gave a tiny shrug of resignation. 'All right,' she said. 'What is it you want to know?'

'I've read the file, but not the transcript of the trial, so I'd like you to go back to the beginning, when all this began.'

She grimaced. 'Is that really necessary, Neil? It's a part of my life I've tried very hard to put behind me. It's not something I like to talk about, especially with you.'

'It may help me understand,' he said gently.

'But Neil...' Her eyes pleaded with him, and he longed to go to her. He wanted to put his arms around her and hold her close, and tell her that everything was going to be all right.

But he had a job to do. And, dammit, she had lied to him. Several times. Deliberately, he got up and walked over to the window and turned to face her. 'I'm sorry, Andrea,' he said stiffly, 'but I have to know. I can read the transcript, but I'd rather you told me in your own words.'

Andrea sensed his withdrawal. The distance between them in the room was a mere few feet, but the gulf between them had suddenly become immeasurable. Why, of all the police in this town, did it have to be Neil? For years she had kept the world at bay; kept people at arm's length, especially men. She didn't need them; didn't need anyone. Not after Victor. She would never allow any man to get close enough to hurt her ever again.

But Neil... There was something different about him. Something solid; something safe. Perhaps it was the feeling that he, too, had been hurt, but in a different way. Not that he ever dwelt on it, but it was there in his eyes and in his voice when he spoke of his dead wife, and she felt a kinship with him that she'd never felt before.

More than kinship. Much more. She'd allowed herself to feel again. And to dream.

Until last week. Until Victor had appeared to smash her life to pieces once again.

Rage welled up inside her, and a cold fury gripped her. She held her breathing steady for fear that Neil would notice when she spoke.

'Very well,' she said. 'It seems I have no choice.'

Paget felt the barb, and winced inwardly. He should have sent Tregalles. He was breaking his own rule about emotional involvement, and yet he couldn't bear the thought of anyone else questioning Andrea like this.

She was speaking, and he forced himself to listen—as a policeman.

As he had learned from Palmer's file, Andrea McMillan had been married to Palmer at the time of his arrest. They'd lived, she said, not far from Taunton where Victor had a small stable he was trying to build up. Both he and Andrea had married relatively late; he was thirty-two, and she was twenty-eight. The stable was barely paying its way, but with Andrea working full time they were managing quite nicely. They had, she said, a normal marriage, and as far as she was concerned, a healthy relationship.

They had been married less than two years when everything blew up in her face.

'I was upstairs,' she said, not looking at Paget now. 'I was trying to clear a space in the box-room so I could set up my typewriter there, and I went to move this old suitcase of Victor's. I don't know what prompted me to do it, but I opened it.'

She stopped. Her eyes were fixed on the floor. She was breathing deeply, steadying herself before continuing.

'There was bloodstained clothing in the case. Children's clothing. And there was a mask; a clown's mask.' Andrea McMillan spoke mechanically. It was as if she'd learned the piece by heart. There was no inflection; no emotion.

'I knew immediately what it meant, but I couldn't bring myself to believe it.' She looked directly at him as she continued. He could see the pain. 'You see, there'd been a series of attacks on young children in the area by a man who lured them into his car using a clown mask and the promise of chocolate and ice cream. He would take them deep into the local woods and...' She brushed a hand across her face. 'Later, the children would be found dazed and hurt and wandering on some remote road where he'd pushed them out of the car. Some of them...' She choked on the words and had to stop until she could regain her composure.

'The police did everything they could, of course, but they couldn't find a single clue to the man's identity.'

She was still there in the attic in a state of shock when Victor came home. She tackled him about it, and it was clear from his face that he was guilty. At first, he'd tried to reason with her, pleading with her to say nothing; promising to stop if she would just give her another chance. But the attacks, of late, had become more frequent and more violent, and the police had warned that there might come a day when a child would be killed.

She had refused to listen to him, and told him she was going to ring the police. 'He went berserk,' she said. 'He came at me like a madman; he hit me with his fists and knocked me down. He started choking me, but I managed to fight him off and started down the stairs. But he caught me and had me by the throat...' Her voice dried up and died. Her eyes were blank and fixed as she relived the horror.

'If the local vet hadn't come up to the house from the barn where he'd been treating one of the horses, I'm sure Victor would have killed me,' she concluded.

Thirteen attacks on children had taken place over a two-year period, and the police were convinced that Palmer was responsible for all of them. But he was only charged with two, and was sentenced to five years without the option of parole.

'You said he tried to kill you, but there was nothing about that in the file. Wasn't he charged?'

'No.' Andrea passed a hand across her face. 'There was some problem with the evidence; the vet said he couldn't swear that Victor was choking me. Anyway, the lawyers said it wouldn't make much difference to how much time he spent in prison, and it would only muddy the waters.' She shrugged. 'The charge was dropped.'

'It was three months before he came to trial,' Andrea went on after a moment, 'and I know this must sound strange, but it wasn't until then that I realized I was pregnant.' Her mouth twisted into a wry smile. 'Some doctor, I was. But I was in such a state of physical and emotional shock that I failed completely to recognize the signs.

'After the trial, I gave up my job and went to stay with a friend. Divorce proceedings were already under way, but Sarah was born before the decree was granted. Other than my friend with whom I was staying, only my mother knew that I'd had a baby. I went back to using my maiden name, and eventually landed a job here in Broadminster.'

'You're saying that your husband never knew that you'd had a child?'

Andrea McMillan closed her eyes. 'Please, Neil, don't ever call him my husband,' she said huskily. 'I start to shake every time I think of the time we were together.' She opened her eyes and looked at him. 'But that's right. He never knew, and I was foolish enough to think that I could hide and keep it from him.

'When he got out he went to visit my mother, asking about me. She sent him packing, of course, but that night he broke into the house and went through it. He found a photograph of Sarah and me. I'm sure that's the first he ever knew of Sarah, but I can imagine how it must have pleased him. He'd sworn he'd come after me, and now, knowing that I'd had a child, *his* child…

'I don't know how he traced me here. I suppose it wouldn't be too hard, but I thought that after five years…' She brushed the thought aside. 'I took some basic precautions, but I thought we'd be safe, Sarah and I. I was stunned when my mother phoned to tell me about him breaking into the house and taking the photograph. I took Sarah away. It was hard, but I had to keep her out of danger. If he found me, that was one thing, but Sarah—I swore to myself that I would see him dead before I'd let him near her.'

Did she realize, Paget wondered, what she'd said? He saw the set of her jaw, the determination in her face, and he had no doubt she meant every word.

Paget looked at the floor. 'You never mentioned Sarah to me,' he said. 'Why was that?'

Andrea shrugged. 'I don't know, exactly,' she said slowly. 'Just natural caution, I suppose. It wasn't long after we first started going out together that my mother rang to tell me about Victor. I hadn't mentioned Sarah to you be fore, so I said nothing. I didn't want to have to explain her absence.'

'And that's why you always met me outside your door—and didn't invite me in.'

'Yes. I... Perhaps I'm an over-protective mother.'

'So you took Sarah away,' he said. 'But not to your mother's, obviously. Where is she, Andrea?'

Andrea had the grace to look guilty. 'I'm sorry, Neil, but you see I had to tell people *something* when I took Sarah away, and it seemed best to tell them she was visiting her grandmother. As it was, Mrs Ansell thought me a very strange mother. She practically accused me of abandoning my daughter, but then, she is very fond of Sarah. Unfortunately, once you start a lie like that, you're forced to tell everyone the same thing, and I'm afraid that's what I did with you just now.'

'Where is Sarah now?'

'With a very good friend.'

'Not in Devon, I take it?'

Andrea shook her head.

'And that's where you went on Friday night?'

'Yes.'

'You didn't go out to Glenacres?'

'No.'

'Where were you between the hours of nine and eleven last Friday night?'

'Driving down to my friend's place.'

'Did you stop anywhere? See anyone you knew?'

'No.'

Paget drew in a long breath and let it out again. It didn't look good. It didn't look good at all. Andrea had lied to him. She'd lied about seeing Palmer, and she'd lied about Sarah. And it appeared that she had no alibi for the time of the murder.

'I'll need your friend's name and address,' he said. 'And I'm afraid you're going to have to come with me.'

THE COACH AND HORSES was a long, low, modern-looking pub with a garden at the back. The garden overlooked the river, and on good days patrons could sit out there beneath the trees and pretend they were in the country. But on days such as this one, with the rain bucketing down outside, they gathered in the bar to take advantage of the radiant warmth of an artificial log fire.

Not that there were many there this Monday lunch-time. A handful of office workers who'd come down for a pint and a hot meat pie; four corporation workers who had the dominoes out and looked as if they were settling in for the afternoon; and a young couple who sat in the farthest corner of the room, oblivious to everything except each other.

Tregalles stood at the end of the bar and finished his drink. He caught the eye of the woman behind the bar; a heavily made-up blonde of about fifty, and the landlord's wife according to the photographs that adorned the wall behind the bar. She raised an eyebrow and he nodded. 'Same again, please, luv,' he said. 'And have something for yourself.'

'Thank you. I'll have a small port, if that's all right?' she said. 'You've not been in before, then?'

'No. Been meaning to. A chap I know keeps telling me I should. He comes here to play darts.'

The woman slid his drink across the bar, along with his change. 'Who's that, then?' she asked.

'Chap by the name of Lucas. Jack Lucas. Runs a stable.'

'Jack? Oh yes. He's down here regular. On the team. Do you play?'

Tregalles shrugged modestly. 'A bit. Not in Jack's league, of course.' He sipped his drink. 'I was supposed to have come down Friday night to meet him, but it was late when I got home. I could have come, I suppose, but it was getting on for ten.'

'Good job you didn't, then,' the woman told him. 'Jack's team got itself knocked out in the first round. They were all finished by eight or thereabouts. I was busy, but my husband, Tom, said he'd never seen Jack play so bad. Went off home in a right old huff, too, he said.'

'What, straightaway? That's not like Jack. I'd have thought he'd have stayed on to drown his sorrows.'

The woman eyed him speculatively. 'You did say you were a friend of his, didn't you?'

Tregalles shrugged. 'Well, I knew him,' he said. 'Do a bit of business with him now and then, but we're not close friends. Why?'

The woman looked up and down the bar, and lowered her voice. 'Well, if you knew him better, you'd know Jack doesn't like to lose. Not in anything. Gets right snarky, sometimes, and if he's had a pint or two too many, he gets proper nasty.'

'Does he, now? Thanks for the warning.' Tregalles took another pull at his beer, and cast around for another subject before the woman became suspicious.

'Make your own pies?' he asked. 'They smell good.'

The woman beamed. 'Fresh this morning,' she assured him. 'I make them myself.'

Tregalles sniffed appreciatively. 'I'll have one of those, then, luv,' he said. 'On second thoughts, make it two.'

NINETEEN

'DR MCMILLAN IS DOWNSTAIRS now,' said Paget. 'They're taking her statement.' He was in Alcott's office, having just given the superintendent a summary of the interview with Andrea. Alcott, with his ever-present cigarette burning its way towards his fingers, sat hunched over his desk.

'I don't give a damn what she says,' the superintendent growled. 'Palmer went to a lot of trouble to find her, and it wasn't just to say how sorry he was for what he'd done. He threatened her; you can bet on it, and knowing what he was like with kids—' Alcott grimaced at the thought '—you can also bet that she would do anything to protect her daughter. Including murder. Which makes her prime suspect for his murder.'

'She claims to have been driving down to see her daughter at the time we believe Palmer was killed,' said Paget neutrally.

Alcott grunted. 'Not much of an alibi,' he said. 'Get rid of that and we have motive, opportunity, and a doctor who would know exactly where to strike.'

Grudgingly, Paget had to admit that Alcott was probably right. They couldn't prove that Palmer had threatened Andrea, but he himself had witnessed their encounter on Boxing Day, and he had seen the look on Andrea's face. Try as he might, he could not rid himself of the vision of Andrea, hand raised to strike and Palmer standing there looking smug and insolent. Could that same hand have been behind the savage thrust that ended Palmer's life?

'We're working on it,' Paget said cautiously. 'But if she is telling the truth, then were back to square one. According to the doctor, she left here somewhere between eight thirty and nine. Her first story was that she went to her mother's place near Newton Abbot, but now she says Sarah is with a friend just outside Bath, and that's where she went, arriving there about ten thirty. If that's true, she wouldn't have had time to get out to the stables, kill Palmer, then get down to Bath by ten thirty. I'm sending Tregalles down to check that out, and to make sure that Sarah is in fact where the doctor says she is.'

Alcott squinted at him through a haze of smoke. 'She's guilty, Paget,' he said softly. 'Times can be manipulated as you well know. All we need is a doubtful fifteen minutes and she won't have a leg to stand on.' He swung his chair around to face the window and stared off into the distance. 'Now get out there and tear that alibi to shreds.'

IT WAS THE MIDDLE OF the afternoon by the time Paget climbed inside the mobile incident room set up behind the stables. It was an old unit, a lash-up of scrounged desks and chairs and office equipment considered obsolete by other departments, and destined for the scrap heap. Paget edged his way past two WPCs thumping away on typewriters that looked as if they'd come out of the ark, and made his way to the back where Sergeant Ormside was seated at a desk.

'Afternoon, sir,' said Ormside, swivelling in his chair to face the chief inspector.

'Hello, Len. Good to see you in charge out here.'

Len Ormside was a tall, thin, sharp-featured man with hooded eyes that gave him the appearance of being half asleep. But the sergeant had thirty years of experience behind him, and when it came to co-ordinating an investigation, there was no one who could touch him.

Ormside hooked his toe under a chair and slid it towards

Paget. 'Have a seat,' he invited, 'but watch it; there's a wheel off.'

Gingerly, Paget sat down. 'What have we got?' he asked the sergeant.

'Considering what we've go to work with—' Ormside cast his eye around the room at the array of decrepit equipment '—we're doing all right,' he said. 'We've taken all the statements, and they're being typed up now. I've looked them over, but apart from one or two things that don't quite add up, I don't see too much wrong with them. I'll have a better idea when they're plotted out and cross-referenced on a chart.

'We've had damn-all back from Forensic, so far. Charlie's men have picked up a few odd bits and pieces, but it's too early to tell whether they mean anything or not.'

'What sort of things?'

'Well for a start, it looks as if someone's been parking his car part-way up the bridle-path across the road. Charlie's men did a sweep of the area, and they found fresh tyre impressions along the track that goes off through the woods. Comes out by Malford, so they tell me. I asked that fellow, Blake, about it, and he said it's a regular bridle-path. They use it all the time.'

'Sounds like a bit of a lovers' lane to me,' said Paget. 'I can't see it having any bearing on our murder.'

'That's what I thought,' Ormside said in his unhurried way. 'But Charlie has a different idea, and he may be right. The area is still cordoned off if you'd like to take a look for yourself.'

'I shall,' Paget assured him. 'Anything else?'

'There was one thing,' Ormside said slowly, 'but I don't know if it means anything. I was taking Sally Pritchard's statement down when she happened to mention that it was Blake's turn to do rounds last Friday. When I asked her about it, she said people often swapped between themselves, and nobody minded as long as someone did the rounds. I haven't spoken to Blake about it yet, but she was right; his name was on the rota. I thought you might like to have a word yourself.'

'I would, indeed,' said Paget. 'He made no mention of it to me when I spoke to him on Saturday.'

'Nor to me this morning,' said Ormside. He picked up a handful of forms. 'These are the statements we have from people living in the area, but we still have a few to go.' Paget riffled through them, stopping as a name caught his eye.

'Miss Crowther?' he said, surprised. 'What's she doing in here?'

'Sally Pritchard, again,' said Ormside. 'She mentioned that Miss Crowther often does a circular walk in the evening. She walks round here by road, then cuts through the stable yard and goes back to the school across the fields. Not that Miss Crowther turned out to be much help. She said she was over this way Friday evening, but it was earlier, about eight, she thought it was, and she didn't notice anything unusual.'

Paget scanned the sheet, but there was nothing more to be learned from it. 'Right, then,' he said. 'I'll be on my way.'

'There is one thing you might look into,' he said as he rose to go. 'Lucas said he had a call from a man named Dennison the day before Palmer arrived looking for a job, but Dennison says he never made the call. I think that call was made by Palmer. Find out where he was staying then, and see if there's a record of it.'

'I'll have someone on it right away,' said Ormside.

Paget walked back down the drive to the road, crossed it, and found a well-worn track leading into the woods. Fifty paces took him into deep cover—and brought him to the spot Ormside had mentioned. Two men were taking down the tapes that had cordoned off a small area.

'Afternoon, sir,' said one, recognizing Paget. 'Come to have a look, have you?'

'That's right. What have you found?'

The man showed Paget the tyre tracks; pointed to where the car had sat for some time, and to several markers within a few feet of each other where he said someone had tossed cigarettes into the long grass. 'If you stand here in the middle of the track, which is roughly where someone would be if they were sitting in a car facing the road, you can see both gates,' he explained. 'The one leads to the stables; the other to the house. Charlie—Inspector Dobbs—reckons somebody's been watching those two entrances for weeks.'

'It could have been some young couple who wanted a bit of privacy,' Paget suggested, but the man shook his head emphatically.

'If that was their game, they'd have gone farther up the lane beyond that bend,' he said, pointing. 'There'd have been no chance of being seen up there. No, sir, he was watching the road, all right.'

The man was very likely right. But why? Why would anyone want to sit here night after night watching the entrances? 'You keep saying "he". Do you know that for certain, or is that just a figure of speech?'

The man pointed to a tree some little distance from the track. It too, had been marked, and a slice of the trunk had been cut away. 'That's where he got out to take a piss,' he said. 'We stripped the bark and it's gone into the lab as well. And we have a partial footprint. A man's boot by the look of it.'

As he walked back to the driveway leading to the stables, Paget was passed by a Cavalier Estate driven by a woman. In the seat beside her was James. The boy spotted him and waved as the car turned into the driveway leading to the house. The woman, he assumed from Tregalles's description, was Georgie Lucas. He waved back.

Paget entered the barn and was making his way to the office when he heard voices.

'I'm sorry, Sally. I didn't mean to upset you,' he heard Jane Wolsey say. There was a quaver in her voice; she sounded hurt—or petulant; it was hard to tell which. 'I was just out for my walk and I thought I'd pop in to see...' He heard the scrape of a chair as it was pushed back.'

'No. Jane, I'm sorry.' Sally sounded contrite, and yet Paget thought he detected an edge to her voice. 'I didn't mean to be short with you, but as you can see...'

They both caught sight of him at once as he approached the open door.

The housemistress was on her feet, making for the door, and Sally stood behind the desk. Jane Wolsey looked far from well; her face was gaunt, her hair in disarray, and she looked to be on the verge of tears. As for Sally, the look on her face was strained as she reached out in a futile gesture to halt her friend's departure.

'Chief Inspector,' said Miss Wolsey as she sidled round him. She bobbed her head in an old-fashioned way and scuttled out of the door.

Sally, whose arm had remained extended, dropped it to her side. 'Poor Jane,' she said. 'She seems so lost.' There were tears in her eyes. 'She still blames herself for Monica's death, you know. I just wish...' Whatever Sally wished was lost in a deep sigh as she brushed the tears from her face.

Her hands, he saw, were trembling. Something had upset the girl; something more than the recent murder, he was sure of it. 'Has something else happened?' he asked. 'You seem upset.'

Sally Pritchard put her hands to her head and closed her eyes. 'No,' she said wearily. 'It's just...I'm tired, that's all.'

He didn't believe her.

She dropped her hands and returned to her seat behind the desk. 'I'm sorry,' she apologized, 'but I'm afraid all this is getting me down. I haven't been sleeping too well, lately. What was it you wanted?'

'I want to make quite sure that nothing was taken from the office, now that you've had time to have a good look round,' he said. 'I know you said you keep nothing of value in here, but have you come across anything at all that struck you as odd?'

'No. And I did go through everything as you asked. Nothing seems to be missing, that is unless you count a ball of twine.' She forced a smile to indicate she wasn't serious.

But Paget asked her what she meant.

'Well, you did ask if anything was missing,' she said, 'and there was a ball of twine here in the office. It usually sits up there on the shelf.' She pointed to a shelf level with his head.

'When I went to get it this morning, it had gone. I asked everyone if they'd seen it, but no one admitted taking it.'

'This morning was the first time you missed it?'

'Yes.'

'When did you see it last?'

Sally thought for a moment. 'Last Thursday, I think it was,' she said. 'Yes, it would be last Thursday.'

The barn door banged open, and they heard the sound of running feet. James Lucas appeared in the office door-way, and he stopped dead when he saw Paget. 'Hello,' he said, and turned to Sally. 'Can I have my swing down, please, Sally?' he asked.

'The chief inspector and I were talking,' Sally told him sternly. 'You know better than to interrupt, James.'

'Sorry,' he said perfunctorily. 'But can I, Sally? Please?'

She looked at Paget. 'Inspector Dobbs said they were

finished in here,' she said. 'Can James have his swing down now?'

'I don't see why not,' said Paget.

'Oh, good!' The boy turned to go, but Sally caught him back. 'James, you haven't changed into your old clothes since you got home from school,' she said sternly. 'Does your mother know you're down here?'

'She didn't say I had to,' the boy countered.

'That's probably because you were gone before she could,' said Sally. 'I'll get the swing down. You're sure to get your clothes dirty if you climb up there, and your mother won't be pleased about that.'

All three left the office. The swing had been pulled up out of the way beneath the open rafters by means of a long cord looped over a beam, and tied to a large nail hammered into one of the posts.

'Here, let me,' said Paget as Sally went to climb up on a broken piece of farm machinery to undo the cord. He reached up quickly.

'Watch out for that...' Sally began, but her warming came too late.

The jagged edge of what looked like part of an old mechanical grass-cutter caught the side of his hand and made it bleed. It was not serious, and he undid the cord and let it out to allow the swing to come down.

'I'm sorry,' Sally said as he climbed down. 'I should have warned you sooner. Is it bad?'

'Just a scratch,' he said, dabbing at it with a handkerchief.

James unhooked the cord and climbed aboard the swing. 'Will you give me a push to get me started?' he asked, but Sally told him she had better things to do, and not to be such a nuisance.

'Come on,' she said to Paget, 'I'll put something on that cut. It could turn septic.' She began to move towards the office, but Paget called her back. He reached down behind the machine, stretched and came up with something in his hand.

'Is that what you were looking for?' he asked her, holding up a ball of twine.

Sally looked puzzled. 'How did that get over there?' she said. 'James? Did you have the twine?' The boy shook his head emphatically. 'Well, I don't know,' she said mystified, as she led the way to the office.

Paget stood frowning at the ball of twine in his hands. 'Do you mind if I take this with me?' he asked.

Sally Pritchard shot him a quizzical look, but said, no, she didn't mind; there was lots of twine about the place. She clucked her tongue as she brushed at the sleeve of his coat. 'That's a rust mark on your coat,' she told him, 'and I don't think it's going to come out. Now, let's have a look at that hand.'

Despite his protests that it was nothing, she brought out the first aid kit and began to clean the jagged cut. 'You can't be too careful with that rusty old metal,' she told him sternly. 'I remember when Monica cut her leg…' She trailed off into silence and seemed suddenly intent upon what she was doing.

'You were saying?' he prompted gently.

'Nothing. It was nothing. I don't know why I even mentioned it.' She began to put things back into the first aid kit. Her hands were shaking, and she wouldn't look at him.

'You said that Monica cut her leg,' he persisted. 'What happened?'

Sally Pritchard shook her head impatiently as if annoyed with herself for bringing the subject up. 'It was nothing,' she repeated. 'She cut her leg on one of those old machines out there.' Her words were clipped, grudging. 'She refused to let me treat it and it turned septic, that's all. It took a month for it to heal. She was like that; impulsive; she would never listen to... Oh, God!' Her hand flew to her mouth, as she stared wide-eyed beyond him. 'Oh, God!' she said again.

Paget whirled to see what she was staring at. A figure stood in the office doorway; dark-haired, pale-faced, and wearing a long blue coat. The late-afternoon light had almost gone from the room, and the figure was silhouetted against the overhead lights in the main body of the barn.

'Sorry to interrupt,' said Sylvia Gray, 'but can I have the keys to the shed? I can't seem to find mine.' She stepped inside the office. 'Is anything wrong, Sally?'

Sally Pritchard took a deep breath to steady her shaking voice. 'No. No, of course not, Sylvia,' she said. 'You just gave me a start, that's all.' She passed a hand across her brow and began to rummage in the desk. She found the keys and tossed them to the girl. The young groom thanked her, apologized again, and went on her way. As the outer door closed behind her, the only sound that could be heard in the otherwise silent office was the monotonous creaking of the swing.

Sally Pritchard sank into her chair. 'I'm sorry,' she said in a shaky voice. 'For a moment I thought...' She shook her head as if to rid herself of a bad dream.

'You thought it was Monica,' he guessed.

She nodded slowly. 'The hair, the face, the coat—she was on my mind at the time, I suppose, and when I saw...' She forced a nervous laugh. 'Silly of me, wasn't it? Would you mind turning on the light?'

PAGET FOUND MAURICE BLAKE talking quietly to a fresh-faced young woman in the tack room. They were standing close together. His right arm was draped loosely around her shoulders, and her hand was on his arm. Paget judged her to be no more than eighteen, if that, and she was hanging on Blake's every word.

When Paget spoke, she jumped nervously and she moved away from Blake, and colour flooded into her young face.

'Th-thank you, Maurice,' she said breathlessly as she turned to leave. 'I—I'll see you tomorrow, then?'

Blake looked amused. 'Ten o'clock,' he said. 'I shall look forward to it, Cynthia. You won't be late, will you?'

'Oh, no!' She sounded shocked at the very suggestion. She brushed past Paget with barely a glance.

Blake followed her with his eyes. 'That girl shows a lot of promise,' he said, and left it to Paget to guess his meaning. 'What can I do for you, Chief Inspector?'

Paget asked him about Friday evening. 'I'm told it was your turn to do the rounds that night. Who asked for the change? You or Palmer?'

'So his name *was* Palmer,' said Blake. 'I thought they'd got it wrong in the paper this morning. Anyway, whatever his name was, he offered to do it, so I let him. I can always find better ways of spending my time than doing evening rounds.'

'Like watching television and going to bed early?' Paget said.

Blake eyed him levelly. 'If there's nothing better to do, yes,' he said.

'Did Palmer offer any explanation? Did he say why he wanted to do rounds that particular night?'

Blake shrugged. 'Not that I recall,' he said. 'He said perhaps I'd return the favour sometime if he needed time off. I assumed he must have something coming up when he would need someone to cover for him.'

'Had he ever done that before?'

'No. In fact this was the first time he'd done the evening round. He'd only been here a week or two, so I was going to give him another week before putting him on the rota.'

'Why didn't you mention that you'd swapped with Palmer when I spoke to you on Saturday?' he asked.

Blake thrust his hands deep into his pockets. 'I didn't think it was important,' he said.

'Didn't think it was important? Or were you afraid that the pitchfork was intended for you?'

Blake stared at him. 'Why would anyone want to do that to me?' he countered.

Why, indeed? Paget had no answer. But the question refused to go away, and it was still with him as he left Glenacres for the day. What if Blake *had* been the intended victim? It would shift the focus of the investigation entirely.

And wasn't that exactly what he wanted? Wasn't he looking for something—anything—that would help Andrea McMillan's cause?

As he passed the entrance to the driveway leading to Sally Pritchard's cottage, he glanced in. The rusting green Fiesta was still at the stables; he had seen it as he left, but there was another car parked beside the cottage. He recognized it as one he'd seen before. It was the same Range Rover he'd seen outside the school; the one belonging to Lady Tyndall.

It reminded him of the missing picture, and he wondered whether Miss Crowther had solved the mystery of its disappearance.

His thoughts switched to Sally Pritchard, and the way she'd looked when she saw Sylvia Gray standing in the doorway. She looked as if she'd seen a ghost, and had said as much. There was something about that scene that bothered him, and it kept niggling away at the back of his mind. Sally Pritchard knew something; something to do with Monica Shaw's death; he was sure of it. He had sensed it when he first talked to her on Christmas Day.

And why, he wondered, did he keep coming back to the idea that the death of Monica Shaw was in some way connected with the death of Victor Palmer?

TWENTY

'PAGET. JUST THE MAN I want to see.' Inspector Tom Cooper came out from behind his desk in the incident room. He was a stocky, balding man with a round, pockmarked face. His expression, as always, was earnest.

'Forensic have identified three sets of prints on the pitchfork handle,' he said. 'Palmer's were there. He must have grabbed at it when he was struck because they were near the ferrule and reversed as you might expect. Sally Pritchard's prints were also on there, and so were Bob Tillman's, but they both say they use the pitchfork all the time, so that may not mean much. There were other prints on there as well, but they were too smudged to identify. And there were several fibres caught in a section of rough grain in the wood. They're looking at them now, but I'm not exactly holding my breath for the results. Fibres on a pitchfork in a barn could come from anywhere.' He shrugged. 'Sorry, Neil, but that's all they've got so far.'

Paget nodded, his face a mask. At least Andrea's prints weren't on the weapon that had killed Palmer. Thank God for that. 'Can't be helped,' he said. 'Thanks, Tom. And keep after them, will you? We don't have a hell of a lot to go on, and Alcott is not going to be happy with those results.'

The telephone rang on Cooper's desk, and he picked it up.

'That was DI Martin,' he told Paget when he hung up. 'He says they have a match between the tyres on the stolen motor bike that Palmer was using and the impressions they took at the Craddock murder scene, so it looks as if you were right. Palmer could have killed Craddock to get in at Glenacres.' He grimaced. 'He must have been a cold-blooded bastard. No wonder Dr McMillan wanted to keep him away from her daughter. Pity she had to use a pitchfork to do it, though.'

'You believe she killed him?' said Paget. Cooper had taken Andrea's statement himself.

Tom Cooper looked surprised that Paget should even pose the question. 'No doubt about it in my mind,' he said firmly.

'What about her claim that she was driving down to her friend's place on the other side of Bath?' Paget persisted.

Cooper dismissed that with a shake of the head. 'That time of night?' he said. 'New Year's Day when there'd be almost nothing on the road? Piece of cake. She had more than enough time to get out to the stables, kill Palmer, then get down to Bath more or less by the time she says she did. Don't you worry. When Tregalles gets back, we'll have it locked up.'

TRAFFIC WAS LIGHT, and Tregalles made good time until he got down as far as the M4 and the Severn Bridge. He lost a good ten minutes there, but traffic thinned out again after he took the Bath exit on to the A46. From there he made his way across country to the village of Wickston, which lay somewhat closer to Chippenham than Bath.

He had to stop and ask directions twice, and on the second try an old man tending a bonfire said he would find the place he was looking for about a quarter of a mile down the lane.

To have called it a farm would have been an exaggeration, but there were pigs and goats and chickens, at least one cow, and a couple of enormous dogs that met him at the gate and kept him there. Their furious barking brought a response in the form of a tall, wiry-looking woman dressed in a leather jacket, jeans, and unlaced boots.

'Storm! Lady! Quiet!' The stentorian command almost rattled the gate.

The two dogs paused, then each gave a final bark before turning and trotting back towards the woman. She strode across the muddy yard and came to a halt on the other side of the gate, but she made no move to open it.

Tregalles said: 'Good morning. Miss Ferris? My name is Tregalles; Detective Sergeant Tregalles from Broadminster.'

'May I see some identification?' The pleasant tones and diction spoke more of Oxford than of the woman's present rough surroundings.

Tregalles showed her his warrant card.

'I'm Kate Ferris,' she said. 'And you're here to ask me about Andrea.'

'Partly,' he said.

Kate Ferris eyed him calmly. She had a strong face; weathered and creased, but when it wasn't being stern, as it was now, Tregalles suspected it would be a pleasant face.

'Ah, yes, I see,' she said. 'You want to make sure that Sarah is actually here. Otherwise all this could have been done by telephone.'

'Something like that,' said Tregalles.

'I hope you didn't come with the idea of taking Sarah back with you,' she said. There was a warning in her words she made no attempt to conceal.

'Nothing like that,' he assured her, 'but I would like to ask you about last Friday night.'

'You'd better come inside then.' Kate Ferris glanced down at his feet and smiled faintly. 'Andrea must have warned you,' she said. 'I see you came prepared.'

She was right, of course. Tregalles had put on welling-tons before getting out of the car.

As they walked across the yard, the two dogs insinuated themselves between Tregalles and their mistress. 'Good guard dogs,' he observed. 'I shouldn't think you'd have much to worry about with them around.'

'They do their job,' she said cryptically.

They went in the back way, through a porch where Kate Ferris kicked off her boots. Tregalles did the same before stepping into a large, warm and pleasant room. The sun had broken through the clouds and was casting patterned shadows from the windows across the polished floor. It was a comfortable room, with bookshelves lining two sides, four big armchairs, and a dining-table and chairs set off to one side.

Sarah McMillan knelt on one of the chairs at the table, surrounded by colouring books and crayons. There was no doubt she was the same girl that Tregalles had seen in the photograph they'd found in Palmer's room.

'I've finished the house, Aunt Kate,' she said. 'I'm going to do the garden next.'

'That's good,' said Kate. 'Say hello to Mr Tregalles, Sarah.'

Th girl eyed him solemnly. 'Hello,' she said.

'Hello, Sarah. Did Father Christmas bring you that book?'

Sarah shook her head. 'No, Mummy brought it, didn't she, Aunt Kate?'

'That's right,' said Kate Ferris.

'Would you like to colour with me?' Sarah asked Tregalles.

'Mr Tregalles and I have to talk first,' said Kate, then surprised Tregalles by asking: 'Have you had lunch?'

He admitted he hadn't, but said he thought he might stop in the village on the way back.

'You're welcome to have something with us,' she said, 'if it's not too early for you. You see, we have breakfast just after six, so I was about to make lunch.'

'Thank you. To tell you the truth, I am a bit hungry, but don't go to any trouble. Can I help?'

She shook her head. Sarah, who had been watching them, said: 'He can help me colour, then, can't he, Aunt Kate?'

'Do you mind?' said Kate.

'Not a bit,' Tregalles said. 'I have two children of my own at home.' He shrugged out of his coat and sat down at the table.

'But no questions, mind,' Kate warned him. 'I'll not have you asking her a lot of questions. Understood?'

'Understood,' he said. 'Now, Sarah, do you want to do the big flowers or the small ones?'

'ANDREA AND I WERE AT SCHOOL together,' Kate explained. 'We've known each other for a long time.'

Lunch, consisting of several good-sized sandwiches, herb tea, and a mixture of fruit and nuts, was over, and they were sitting facing one another in the big armchairs. Relaxed, Kate Ferris was a good-looking woman, and she positively glowed with health.

'When Andrea learned from her mother that Victor had taken the photograph of her and Sarah, she brought Sarah here to me to keep her out of harm's way. Sarah was born here, you know, and I was only too happy to have her. I shall miss her very much when she's gone.'

Kate had given Sarah a basket and sent her out to look for eggs. 'She'll be all right,' she said. 'The dogs will look after her.'

Tregalles didn't doubt it.

'Dr McMillan has been visiting her here since November?' Tregalles asked.

'Yes. She comes down whenever she can, but her hours at the hospital make it difficult.'

'But she did come down on Friday night? The night of New Year's Day.'

'Yes.'

'Do you remember what time it was when she arrived?'

Kate Ferris pursed her lips and regarded him levelly. 'She was here by eleven; I know that,' she said. 'Exactly how long before, I'm afraid I can't say.'

'You're sure it couldn't have been later than that?'

'Quite sure.'

It had taken Tregalles two hours and seven minutes to cover the distance from Dr McMillan's flat to Kate Ferris's gate. Take ten minutes off for the Severn Bridge, and five minutes more while he sought directions in the village, and he was left with one hour and fifty-two minutes. And he'd driven fast. Even at night, with less traffic, he doubted whether the doctor could have done it in much less.

Which meant that she had no more than eight minutes to get out to Glenacres, meet Palmer, kill him, then come back through town and head south. And that was assuming that Palmer had been killed at nine, which was the very earliest he could have died, according to Starkie. There was no way she could have done all that in eight minutes.

Assuming, of course that both the doctor and Kate Ferris were telling the truth.

TWENTY-ONE

'NOTHING,' SAID ORMSIDE disgustedly. 'They're a proper dozy lot out here. No one saw anything, went anywhere, or did anything the night after New Year's Eve. Too thick-headed after the night before, most likely.'

Paget skimmed through the reports, but Ormside was right. It seemed that hardly anyone had been abroad that night. And no one could be found who had seen a car being driven into or out of the trees across the road from the entrance to the stables.

He tossed the reports back to Ormside. 'It's early days, yet,' he said. 'Give it time.'

Ormside grunted something unintelligible. 'There was one other thing, but I don't know if you're still interested. Forensic sent over a report on the Shaw girl, and a copy of it came out here. Isn't that case closed?'

'That's right, it is,' said Paget. 'Why? Is there anything of interest in the report?'

The sergeant shrugged. 'Hard for me to say, sir,' he said, 'not having worked on it. Shall I send it in to Records?'

'No, I'll take it,' Paget said. 'I'd like to look it over before it goes back. Which reminds me; I have a couple of questions I'd like to ask Miss Wolsey. I think I'll take a walk over to the school before I talk to Lucas.'

Ormside cocked an enquiring eye at the chief inspector, but no explanation was forthcoming.

Paget followed the path that began behind the red barn. It went along the back of the horse stalls, past the end of the schooling ring, and down the hill to a small bridge. The snow was melting fast, and tiny rivulets criss-crossed the hillside as they made their way to the stream below. The sun was warm against his face, and he found himself squinting against the ever-shifting light reflecting off the water and surrounding snow.

He paused at the bridge to listen to the sound of rushing water and the raucous squabbling of far-off crows. There was the illusion of spring in the air, but a glance towards the west, where clouds were banked beyond the hills, reminded him that winter was still far from over.

Paget climbed the slope on the other side of the bridge to a gate in the fence marking the boundary of the school grounds and went inside. From there he followed the path through a narrow band of trees and came out beside the green houses.

'Chief Inspector.'

He'd thought himself alone, and the voice surprised him. He turned to find Jane Wolsey watching him from the doorway of one of the greenhouses. She wore an old brown parka over a heavy pullover and long brown skirt. Her feet were encased in wellingtons, and she wore thin cotton gardening gloves.

She didn't look well at all. Her eyes were bleak, and her face looked pinched and grey. But at least, he thought, she had come out of that dreadful little room of hers and was getting some fresh air.

'I was on my way to see you,' he said. 'Getting ready for spring, are you?'

She glanced down at the tray of seedlings in her hands. 'Yes. I simply couldn't resist coming out here on such a lovely day. Will you come inside while I see to these?'

Paget followed her into the green house. It was an old iron-framed building, probably dating back to when the school itself was built, and it was in desperate need of repair. Jane Wolsey correctly judged his appraising glance.

'Pity to see the old place falling apart like this,' she said, 'but there's no money for repairs these days, I'm afraid. I don't know where it's all going to end.' She set the seedling down and pulled off her gloves. The left one, covering her deformed hand, came off easily, but removing the glove from her right hand was more difficult. It was an awkward manoeuvre that involved tucking the hand beneath her arm and more or less wriggling it out of the tight-fitting glove. In the process, the glove fell to the floor, and Paget quickly bent to retrieve it.

'Thank you,' she said as he handed it to her. She pushed hair out of her eyes and wiped her brow. 'It's quite warm in here, isn't it? Surprising what a little sun and glass will do even in January.' She shrugged out of the parka and set it aside, folding it neatly and placing the gloves just so on top of it.

Paget watched, fascinated by the care she took of such obviously well-worn clothes. The collar of the parka was frayed; both sleeves were almost threadbare, and one was badly stained. And the gloves. Just ordinary, well-used gardening gloves worth no more than a pound or two at most, yet the one he'd picked up had been mended carefully. But then, he reminded himself, a pound might mean a lot to Miss Wolsey; she probably wasn't paid all that much, especially living in as she did.

'You said you were on your way to see me, Chief Inspector,' she said. 'What was it about?'

'It has to do with something you mentioned when I spoke to you shortly after Monica died,' he said. 'I wanted to be sure I had it right.'

'Monica?' Jane Wolsey caught her breath. She looked surprised. 'But you said that the investigation was closed. Has something happened to open it again?' She picked up some geranium cuttings and began to trim them.

She was remarkably adept, considering the fact that her left hand was devoid of proper fingers. The index finger ended at the first joint, while the rest, including the thumb, were merely stubs, yet she managed to grasp the plants in the V formed between the forefinger and thumb and hold them while she trimmed.

'No,' he said, 'but I can't help wondering why Monica got dressed and went out again that evening. It puzzles me. And, since I happened to be out here investigating the death of Victor Palmer—you may have know him as Prescott—over at Glenacres, I thought I'd just check a couple of points with you.'

Jane Wolsey made a grimace of distaste. 'Yes,' she said, 'there were a couple of policemen round asking if we'd seen or heard anything unusual that night, but of course no one had. I believe they even asked the head to give some sort of statement.'

The housemistress looked up from what she was doing. 'But you wanted to know something about Monica. What was it, Chief Inspector?'

'You mentioned that Monica wore a white anorak to the party Christmas Eve,' he said. 'She spilled wine on it, and you took it to your room to try to do something about the stain. Is that correct?'

'Yes.' She looked puzzled.

'And the coat we found on the floor at the foot of the bed; you said it was new. In fact I believe you said it had never been worn before.'

'Yes, that's right.'

'You're quite sure about that? Could Monica have shown it to someone? Someone who came to see her at the school, for example?'

The housemistress looked mystified, but she shook her head. 'No. You see, it only arrived that morning. I was with Monica when she bought it—it must have been a good two weeks before Christmas—and it had to be altered. They promised to send it out to the school within the week, but it still hadn't come by the Tuesday before Christmas, so Monica rang them and said if it wasn't there by Thursday morning at the latest, they could keep the coat, alterations and all.' Miss Wolsey shot Paget an apologetic look. 'I'm afraid she wasn't very polite about it, either,' she confessed, 'but they brought it out just before noon on Thursday.'

'How did she get to Glenacres that day? Did anyone pick her up?'

'No. She walked over. Why? Is it important?'

'I'm not sure,' he said, 'but I think it might be. Thank you, Miss Wolsey.' He paused. 'I must admit I'm curious,' he said, nodding in the direction of the cuttings. 'What is it you are doing with those cuttings?'

Jane Wolsey brushed her hair away from her face with the back of her hand. Her features softened and the worry lines all but disappeared as she glanced around the greenhouse. For a moment it made her look years younger, and he realized it was the first time he had seen the housemistress really smile. 'Actually, I'm committing a crime,' she confided. 'It's one of the few times the gardeners are away, so I come in here, steal some of their cuttings, and pot them up for myself and some of the staff. If I don't do it now, they'll all end up in the flower beds, and we'll have no plants inside at all. Is that a crime, Chief Inspector?'

'Indeed it is,' he told her with mock gravity. 'You could be in serious trouble, Miss Wolsey.'

The housemistress looked down at the cutting she was holding in her hand, and the worry lines creased her face once more. 'Yes,' she said absently as if her mind had gone on to something else. 'I suppose I could, couldn't I?'

RETURNING TO THE STABLES, Paget met Jack Lucas in the yard, and tackled him about the time he'd left the Coach and Horses Friday evening.

Lucas shrugged it off. 'It seemed the simplest thing to

say at the time,' he said blithely. 'I wasn't out here at the time you say Prescott, or whatever his name was, was killed, so what does it matter where I was?'

'I think you know better than that, Mr Lucas,' said Paget. 'Especially as you may be asked to swear to what you said under oath. According to our information, your darts match finished about eight o'clock, and you left shortly after that.'

Lucas scowled. 'So, you've been grubbing around, then, have you?' he said. 'I should have thought you'd have better things to do with your time.' Paget remained silent, waiting. Lucas gave an elaborate sigh of resignation. 'All right, so I left,' he said. 'I let the side down. I wasn't going to hang about after that, so I left the Coach and went up to the George and had a few drinks there. Got talking and stayed there till chucking out time, then came home. That's it.'

'This person you were talking to. Friend of yours?'

'Never saw him before,' said Lucas. His eyes challenged Paget to dispute it.

'So you met no one who can verify your story?'

'Story? I'm telling you it's what I did. Are you calling me a liar?'

Paget eyed him. 'You lied before,' he said. 'Why should I believe you now, Mr Lucas?'

PAGET CALLED IN TO SEE Ormside before leaving for home, recounting for the record the story Lucas had told him.

'I'll lay odds that no one at the George remembers him,' said Ormside.

'Have someone check it out, anyway,' said Paget. 'I don't believe him either, but we'd better make sure.'

He was about to leave when there was a knock on the door. One of the WPCs opened it and there was a brief exchange of words. She turned to Ormside with a grin on her face.

'There's a young gentleman here to see you, sir,' she said. Behind her, James Lucas poked his head through the door. 'He wants to know if he can come in.'

'Does he, now?' said Ormside, heavily. He cocked an enquiring eye at Paget, and the chief inspector grinned and nodded. 'All right, then,' Ormside said. 'Tell him he can come in if he behaves himself.'

James scrambled up the steps and stood looking round, wide-eyed and breathless. He didn't speak for a moment, then advanced towards the two men. 'Hello,' he said to Paget, then looked at Ormside, imposing in his uniform behind the desk. 'I'm James Lucas,' he said, and thrust out his hand. Paget smothered a grin. The boy might not look like his father, but the mannerisms were the same—except the boy was more polite.

Ormside half rose in his seat and took the outstretched hand and shook it. 'Pleased to meet you, Jamie,' he said solemnly. 'My name is Sergeant Ormside.'

'If you don't mind, sir, it's James, not Jamie.'

Ormside's mouth twitched. 'Sorry,' he said as he sat down again. 'James.' He looked sternly at the boy. 'Now then, lad, what can I do for you?'

James looked down at the floor. 'Sally said I wasn't to bother you, but I just wanted to have a look inside so I could tell the other boys at school.' He looked up. 'I thought you would ask me questions like you asked Sally and Penny and Mummy, because I live here, too, but you didn't.'

'Ah, well, you see,' said Ormside, 'that's because what happened was late at night, and you'd be in your bed by then. Besides, I don't think this sort of thing is something that…'

'I wasn't.'

Ormside frowned. 'You wasn't—weren't what, James?'

'I wasn't in bed.'

The sergeant leaned back in his chair and eyed the boy. 'What time did you go to bed, then?' he asked.

'Nine o'clock. I always go to bed at nine, except when it's Christmas or my birthday or special things like that.'

'Well, there you are, then. You were in your bed like I said.'

James was shaking his head vigorously. 'I wasn't in bed,' he said. 'I sat up at the window for ever such a long time.'

Ormside caught Paget's eye. Questioning a child without one of his parents being present was a dicey thing. 'Did you now?' she said. 'And what can you see from your window?'

'Not much,' James said candidly. 'Just the back gate and the sheds and trees and things.'

'You can't see the stables?'

'No.'

'Did you *hear* anything?' Ormside persisted.

The boy furrowed his brow in concentration. 'Like what?' he said at last.

'Did you hear any cars coming up the drive or over by the stables? Or people talking—anything at all?'

The boy slowly shook his head, and Ormside settled back in his chair again. For a moment he had thought the boy might have seen or heard something, but if his room over-looked the back of the house he would be facing away from the stables. He was about to send the boy on his way when Paget spoke up.

'James,' he said, 'why were you sitting up beside the window when you should have been in bed?'

The boy half turned to face him, and for the first time since he'd entered the mobile unit, he appeared to be at a loss. 'I—I like looking out of the window,' he said, but he wouldn't look directly at the chief inspector.

'In the dark, James?'

Colour rose in the boy's face. 'The moon...' he began, but his mouth dried up and the words were lost.

'When Sergeant Ormside asked you what you could see from the back window, you said you could see the back gate. Who were you expecting to see at the back gate?'

The colour deepened in the boy's face, and his eyes darted around the room as if seeking a way out.

Paget leaned forward and took the boy's hand. 'Do you know why we are here?' he asked.

James nodded but his eyes were guarded.

'Tell me so that I know you understand.'

'You're here to find out who killed Victor.'

'That's right. And we don't want that person to get away, do we? So, if you saw someone that night, I'd like you to tell me who it was. It could be very important.'

'But it wasn't—wasn't anybody like that,' the boy protested. 'I didn't see anybody.'

'Then why were you watching the gate?'

James looked down at the floor. 'I was waiting,' he mumbled. 'But I went to sleep in the chair.'

'Waiting for...?'

'Mummy to come home,' said the boy miserably.

LATER THAT EVENING, Paget settled down to read the forensic report on Monica Shaw. Its pedantic style made heavy reading; there seemed to be nothing in it that he hadn't heard already from either Starkie or Charlie Dobbs, and his eyes began to close. In fact he was half asleep when something he'd just read brought him awake again.

'...shards of glass ranging in length from 2mm to 8mm.' It went on to describe the type of glass, listing a range of uses—including that commonly used in picture frames.

He was fully awake now. He carried on reading but the only other thing he found of interest was a comment regarding the cotton wool found in the wastepaper basket.

The cotton wool, it said, contained a concentration of lipstick that matched both the tube of lipstick found on the
dressing-table and that worn by Monica at the time of her
death.

MIDNIGHT. The clock in the living-room chimed the hour
softly.

Sally Pritchard heard it; heard it as she'd heard every
other sound since she'd gone to bed at ten. The sleep she
sought so desperately eluded her as it had since she'd
learned of Monica's death more than a week ago. She'd
taken a sleeping pill, but she might as well have saved
herself the trouble. It wasn't working, and she was afraid
to take another. 'Be careful,' her doctor had warned her.
'They may seem harmless, but they can become addictive.'

She lay there staring at the ceiling. What *was* she going
to do? What was she going to *do*? The question went round
and round inside her head until she thought it would ex-
plode. It was her fault. No matter what anyone said it was
her fault! She was the one who had started the chain reaction, but she'd never dreamed it would come to this.

'Oh, God!' she breathed aloud. 'Help me. Please help
me.' She buried her face in the pillow already wet with
tears.

TWENTY-TWO

Wednesday, 6 January

PENNY WAKEFIELD SHIVERED and pulled the bedclothes tighter around her shoulders. Outside, the wind was getting up and it was cold in the tiny room she shared with Sylvia Gray. Beneath her, she could hear Sunday's Girl shifting restlessly in her stall, while from across the yard she heard the rattle of one of the box-stall doors. Number 14, probably. Shalimar's stall. That one always rattled in the wind. She began to drift off to sleep again.

Outside, the night was black, the moon obscured by cloud. The high pressure system that had kept the clouds at bay throughout the day had moved off to the east, and the forecast was for gusting winds with showers overnight and scattered showers on Thursday.

A spattering of rain swept across the yard before the wind and dashed itself against the red barn, rattling the door. Inside, the dark figure beside the bench froze, snapped off the torch and stood poised for flight. The wind rattled the door again. There was an audible release of breath as the listener recognized the cause of the sound. The pale circle of light reappeared and the task was resumed.

Penny Wakefield came awake and started up in bed. She was cold, yet her face was bathed in sweat. She'd been dreaming, but for the life of her she couldn't remember what the dream had been about. There'd been a noise...

A rasping sound came out of the darkness. Syl must be

lying on her back again, snoring. That must have been what woke her. And yet...

The cot beneath her shook as Sunday's Girl screamed and crashed heavily into the side of the stall below.

IT WAS TWENTY MINUTES TO SIX, according to the digital clock beside his bed, when Paget was roused from a deep sleep to be told by the duty sergeant that there had been a fire at Glenacres.

'Anyone hurt?' he asked, still blinking sleep from his eyes. He had visions of the barn and perhaps the stalls going up in flames. 'The horses...?'

'One person dead sir. Didn't stand a chance according to the firemen. A chap by the name of Blake. Maurice Blake. It was his caravan that burned. Completely destroyed. They reckon the fire was set.'

Paget was fully awake now. 'I'm on my way,' he told the sergeant. 'Better ring Sergeant Tregalles and tell him I'll meet him out there.'

By the time Paget arrived, the caravan was nothing more than smoking embers, stirred every now and then by gusting winds. Tregalles, who didn't have as far to come, was already there, and Charlie's people were busy setting up their lights.

Starkie arrived a few minutes later. Blake's body had been pulled out by firemen, and now lay on the grass, charred, still smoking, and quite unrecognizable. Against all his better instincts, Paget forced himself to look, and gave silent thanks that he'd not had time to stop for breakfast. He turned away. The sight was bad enough, but the smell was something else.

'Petrol,' said one of the firemen. 'You can still smell it. And with this wind the whole thing went up like a torch.' He moved towards the stables. 'Good thing the wind was

blowing away from them,' he said grimly, 'or we'd have
had a right mess on our hands.'

Paget spoke to one of the constables who had been first
on the scene, a man by the name of Bell. 'It was a Miss
Wakefield who rang for the fire brigade,' he told the chief
inspector. 'She says the horses started acting up, and when
she went to see to them she saw the fire. She said it was
well alight by then and she couldn't get near, so she ran
down to the barn to phone. It's that big red barn over...'

'Yes, I know the one she means,' said Paget. 'I don't
suppose she saw anyone else?'

'No, sir. She said she ran back to the stables and got
everybody else up. She sent one of the lads up to the house
to tell the owner, a Mr Lucas, while she and the others
went back to see if there was anything they could do. But
there's no water back here. Apparently this chap, Blake,
got his water from a tap at the back of the stables. Even if
there had been, she said the heat was so bad they couldn't
get near. She said all they could do was wait for the fire
brigade.'

'Sounds as if she kept her wits about her,' Paget observed.

'Yes, sir. Not like the other one.' The constable consulted his notebook. 'A Miss Gray. She was so upset they
sent for the doctor. Went to pieces good and proper.
Screaming, she was.' The constable nodded towards the
still smouldering body of Blake, and grimaced. 'Not that
you could blame her,' he said. 'It's not a pretty sight.'

Paget thanked the man, then he and Tregalles took another look round while they waited for Starkie to finish his
examination. Not that there was much to see; virtually everything that was not made of metal had been destroyed.

'You might be interested in this, sir,' said one of Charlie's men. He used an instrument resembling a large pair

of forceps to lift something from the still smouldering debris, and held it up for Paget's inspection.

It was part of the door handle of the caravan, and it was joined to a larger, similarly shaped handle by several strands of heavy wire. The second handle had been mounted beside the door as an aid to getting in and out of the caravan. Paget remembered grasping it himself as he'd climbed the steps.

'Somebody wanted to make damned sure he stayed inside,' the man observed. 'They wired the door shut. Nice people.'

Starkie finished his examination and came over to them. 'I can't tell you much at all until we get him on the table,' the pathologist said as he stripped off his gloves. 'I wouldn't even want to try to estimate the time of death, and I can't say for certain whether he was alive or dead before the fire started. Sorry, Paget, but you'll have to wait for this one, I'm afraid.'

Starkie fell silent as he watched the activity around the site. 'Is it true the door was wired shut?' he asked abruptly. 'I heard someone say…'

'That's what it looks like,' Paget said.

Starkie slowly shook his head. 'I just hope you find this bastard soon. I'm assuming it's the same person who stuck the fork into Palmer. I'd hate to think there are two of them running around out here.'

'So would I,' said Paget fervently. The thought was chilling.

But, even as he spoke, it occurred to him that this latest killing could have nothing to do with Andrea. In fact, it was beginning to look as if Blake had been the intended victim all along, and Palmer had simply been in the wrong place at the wrong time. The thought cheered him, but he wasn't allowed time to dwell on it.

The site of the caravan was behind the stables, and the

path leading to it ran through a dense grove of birch and poplar. Now, emerging from the trees was a constable, one hand firmly grasping the arm of Sally Pritchard as he pushed her forward none too gently.

'I found this young woman down by the barn,' he said as he stopped in front of them. 'She says she works here, sir. She was about to get rid of these.' He displayed a bundle of dirty rags. 'They're soaked in petrol, sir.'

'I wasn't trying to get rid of anything!' Sally protested. 'I didn't even know what this man was talking about when he stopped me.' Although she was speaking to Paget, she couldn't seem to tear her eyes away from the smouldering caravan. Starkie excused himself and went over to direct two men who had begun to move the body and carry it to a waiting van.

'Maurice?' she said, wide-eyed, and Page nodded. 'What happened?'

'I'd like you to tell me what you were doing with those rags, first,' he said.

She stared at him, and then at the remains of the caravan, and an expression of horror crossed her face. 'Are you saying someone *set* the fire? You can't think that I...' She buried her face in her hands. 'Oh, God!'

If it was an act, it was a damned good one, Paget thought. He pulled the collar of his mac up against the wind. It seemed to be getting stronger as daylight forced its way across the cloudfilled sky. 'Let's hear your side of it, then, Miss Pritchard,' he said quietly.

Sally Pritchard lifted her head defiantly. 'I used those rags to mop up the mess on the bench in the barn,' she said. 'I was going to take them out and burn them when your man grabbed me and started asking questions.'

'From the beginning, please,' said Paget patiently. 'What time did you get to work this morning?'

Sally looked at her watch. 'Just a few minutes ago,' she

said. 'I was a bit late this morning because I had no water. The pump from the well packed up again, so I had to get it going before I left.

'There was no one about when I got here, and I couldn't understand it. I went into the barn and there was this smell of petrol; it hit me as soon as I opened the door. I turned on the light and I could see someone had been messing about with the petrol on the bench. So I set about cleaning it up, and when I went to take the rags out, this police-man...'

'Are you saying you knew nothing of the fire?' Paget looked at her in disbelief.

Sally shook her head. 'How could I?' she countered. 'You can't see this place from the yard.'

She was quite right, of course. Not only were the build-ings in the way, but there was a knoll between the stables and the caravan. With the wind blowing the smoke away from the stables, it was just possible that she wouldn't have known.

'You didn't hear the fire engine earlier on?' he said. 'It must have gone right past your house.'

Again she shook her head. 'I took a sleeping pill last night. I didn't hear a thing.'

'What about the petrol? You keep it in the barn?'

Sally nodded. 'Two five-gallon tins,' she said, and he remembered seeing them there. 'It's for emergencies—for when someone forgets to fill the tractor; things like that. And one of the tins is missing.'

Paget turned to Tregalles. 'Better give these to Charlie,' he said, indicating the rags, 'and tell him about the bench so he can have his men go over it. And get a search or-ganized for the missing petrol tin. Chances are it's not too far away.'

'On my way,' Tregalles said.

Paget turned back to Sally. 'How well did you know Maurice Blake?'

The girl shrugged. 'As well as I know most of the people I work with,' she said. 'We weren't friends, if that's what you mean, and to be honest, I can't say that we always got along, but this... It's horrible!' She hugged herself and shivered.

He saw little point in detaining her further, especially standing out there in the biting wind. What he needed to do now was to talk to the others as soon as possible. 'Take Miss Pritchard down to the mobile unit and have someone there take her statement,' he told the constable.

'And see if there's a cup of good hot coffee going. I think Miss Pritchard could use one.'

Sergeant Ormside, who had arrived there not long after Paget, came over to talk to him as Sally Pritchard left with the constable. 'My people are taking statements from the grooms,' he said, 'and we should have them in some sort of order by mid-morning. But I haven't had a chance to talk to anyone at the house, yet, nor Sylvia Gray because the doctor's with her.'

'I'm going over to the house myself in a few minutes,' Paget told him, 'but you might see what you can find out from the doctor before he leaves, then talk to Sylvia if she's all right.'

Ormside grunted. 'Right,' he said. 'But there's something else you should know if you're going to see Lucas. There was a report on the fax machine when I came in this morning. They've identified the impressions they took from the bridle-path as matching the tyres fitted on the new Mercedes line. Lucas owns a new Mercedes. I'm having casts taken to see if they match, but I'm betting they will.'

'Watching his own stables?' Paget mused. 'I'll have to see what he has to say about that.'

'there was something else, too,' said Ormside. 'You sent a ball of twine over to Forensic the other day?'

'That's right.'

'Ah! Well, they say the fibres from that match those found on the handle of the pitchfork, whatever that may mean.'

'I'm not sure myself, yet,' said Paget. 'But thanks. I'll work on it.'

LUCAS APPEARED TO BE genuinely shaken by Blake's death. 'He was a good man,' he said. He lit a cigarette and inhaled deeply. 'Good with horses and good with women, and that's damned important in this business, Paget. God knows what we're going to do around here now he's gone.'

Lucas looked grim as he swung slowly back and forth in his swivel chair beside the desk.

Paget looked round. 'Is Mrs Lucas about?' he asked. 'I'd like to talk to her as well.'

'What for? She can't tell you anything. Anyway, she's upstairs looking after the boy; keeping him out of the way.'

'I'll speak to her as soon as we're finished here, then,' said Paget. He had no intention of being fobbed off by Lucas. 'Now, then, Mr Lucas, what can you tell me about Maurice Blake?'

Blake, Lucas told him, had been at Glenacres a little over four years. He was divorced. His ex-wife, who had remarried, and his two children, now lived in Hull. As far as Lucas knew, the divorce had been by mutual consent, and Blake had been in the habit of visiting his children every four to six weeks. Blake's parents were both teachers living in Dublin. He'd never heard Blake speak of any brothers or sisters.

'How did he get on with the staff, here?' Paget asked.

'He was well respected. He knew his job.'

'But was he liked?'

Lucas's eyes narrowed. 'You've been listening to young Penny, haven't you?' he accused. 'She never did get on with him. Said as much when she handed in her notice the other day.'

'Do you know why she didn't like him?'

Lucas shrugged. 'She said she didn't like the way he chatted up the women,' he said. 'Thought it degrading or some such thing. More like jealousy on her part, I should think.'

Paget shifted ground. 'You went over there to the fire, I believe,' he said.

Lucas gave a curt nod. 'Penny came and got me. I went over but there was nothing I could do. Nothing anyone could do. The fire had too good a hold. You couldn't get near it. If there'd been any way to get Maurice out...' He shook his head and butted his cigarette.

'You must have smelt the petrol,' said Paget quietly.

Lucas shot him a glance from beneath his heavy brows, but he didn't answer.

'Someone wanted Maurice Blake dead, Mr Lucas. Someone who wired the door shut, then doused the caravan in petrol before setting it alight. Do you have any idea who that might be?'

Lucas lit another cigarette and squinted at Paget through the smoke. 'I hope you're not suggesting it was me,' he said thinly.

'Where were you when Penny came to tell you about the fire?'

'Where the hell do you think I was?' Lucas snapped. 'I was here, in bed, with my wife. If you don't believe me, you can ask her.'

'And you didn't leave the house at any time during the night?'

Lucas jabbed a finger at Paget. 'I don't think I like your

tone, Mr Paget,' he said. 'I'll not have you come into my house and accuse me of...'

'Of what, Mr Lucas?' Paget broke in. He sat forward in his chair. 'Someone killed Maurice Blake. Someone killed Victor Palmer. Both of them worked here, and I'm going to be asking everyone the same questions, so let's not play games, Mr Lucas. Did you or did you not leave the house between, say, midnight and when Penny came to get you?'

'No, I did not,' said Lucas shortly.

'Good. Now, perhaps you will tell me where you were last Friday night after you left the Coach and Horses?'

Lucas's eyes blazed. 'I *told* you what I did,' he snapped. 'I'll not be badgered by you or anyone else.'

'I'm well aware of what you told me,' Paget said, 'and I'm also aware that it was a lie.' Lucas looked thunderous, but Paget continued on. 'Someone has been watching the entrances to the driveways leading to this house and the stables. We found tyre tracks up the bridle-path in the wood across the road. We also found cigarette butts and other evidence. Those tracks were made by tyres supplied with this year's Mercedes, Mr Lucas, and there are not a lot of them about. I think the casts we took will match the tyres on your car, and I think that you are the one who has been watching the entrances.'

Lucas pulled deeply on his cigarette. He sat there eyeing Paget, weighing up his options as he rocked gently back and forth in his swivel chair.

'So I was watching,' he said. 'What does that prove?'

'Nothing in itself,' said Paget. 'But it does make me wonder why you lied about where you were when Palmer was murdered.'

Lucas shook his head impatiently. 'It had nothing to do with him,' he said. 'In fact, it had nothing to do with any of this, and it's none of your damned business.'

'I'll be the one to decide what is or is not my business,'

Paget told him sharply. 'What were you doing there that night?'

The silence between them lengthened. Finally, Lucas waved an impatient hand. 'Watching for thieves,' he said.

Paget looked sceptical.

'They come in after dark and take things,' Lucas said. 'Anything lying about that will fetch a few quid.' He wasn't looking at Paget now.

'You reported these thefts to the police, of course?'

Lucas shrugged. 'What could they do?' he countered. 'They're not interested in this petty pilfering. They're not likely to send someone out to watch, are they?'

'So you didn't report the losses?'

'It would have been a waste of time,' said Lucas shortly. 'The local man couldn't find a bloody haystack, let alone a needle.'

'What sort of things were stolen?'

'I haven't got a list,' snapped Lucas irritably. 'Tack, brushes, odds and ends. Small stuff but expensive when you add it up.'

'Expensive enough for you to sit out there night after night in the hopes of catching someone?'

'As I said, it adds up.'

'Strange,' said Paget.

'What's so strange about it?' Lucas growled. 'If you lot were on your toes we wouldn't have to worry about things like that.'

'I meant it strikes me as strange that you would only watch for so short a time,' said Paget.

'Eh? I don't follow you.'

'You left the Coach and Horses just after eight, so we can assume that you would be out here by eight thirty or quarter to nine at the latest. Yet you were home by eleven. It's been my experience that most thieves wait until people have gone to bed.'

Lucas glowered at him but said nothing. It was obvious the man was lying, but if he insisted on sticking to his story there were other ways to get at the truth.

'Tell me, Mr Lucas, did you see anyone while you were watching? It could be very important.'

The man didn't answer immediately. Paget waited.

Finally, Lucas spoke. 'Yes,' he said, 'I did see someone, as it happens.' He seemed preoccupied with tapping non-existent ash into the ashtray, and didn't look at Paget. 'Looking back, it might well have been your murderer. I didn't think it possible at the time, which is why I didn't mention it before, but now...'

'You mean that if you'd mentioned it, you would have had to admit that you were there yourself,' said Paget bluntly.

Lucas shrugged. 'Have it your way,' he said as he crushed the cigarette. 'But I did see a car arrive. It pulled up between the two driveways on that wide strip of grass verge. The driver got out and disappeared. So I went down the bridle-path to investigate. That's when I heard someone running down the road. I could tell by the way she ran it was a woman, but I couldn't see her properly. It was too dark, but I thought I might get a look at her when she got into the car. You know, the light comes on when you open the door. But she got into the car so fast I didn't get a good look at her. She was in and had the car started all in a couple of seconds, and then she took off from there as if all the demons in hell were after her.'

'Do you have any idea who she was?'

'No. But the car was a light-coloured Peugeot.' Lucas reached into an inside pocket and brought out a heavy note-book. 'I wrote the number down when I got back to my car. Yes, here it is.'

Andrea McMillan drove a Peugeot. Even before Lucas read it out, Paget knew the number would match the plate on Andrea's car.

TWENTY-THREE

PAGET'S FACE WAS BLEAK as he walked slowly through the stable yard and thought about what Lucas had told him. Regardless of what he thought of the man himself, Lucas couldn't have made up the story about seeing Andrea's car. He felt angry; angry with Andrea for lying to him, and angry with himself for believing her. He would have to bring her in; there was no getting around it. And yet... What if Blake had been the intended target all along? He was supposed to be making rounds that night when he switched with Palmer. And Blake was dead, killed by the same person, presumably.

So what motive would Andrea have for killing Blake? None that he could think of. It was Palmer who had threatened her, not Blake. If he could only find the motive for Blake's murder there might be a chance that Andrea was innocent. But she'd been there when Palmer was killed. At least...her car had been there, but that didn't necessarily mean that she'd been there.

But even he had to admit he was clutching at straws to believe that. Andrea had lied to him. There was no getting around it. And he had believed her because he had wanted to believe her.

He reached the mobile unit and went inside. Ormside and Tregalles had their heads together, going over statements. Tregalles saw the scowl on Paget's face.

'Something wrong?' he asked.

'That man, Lucas, is beginning to get to me,' Paget growled as he took the proffered mug of coffee from Ormside. 'The man has lied from start to finish. And his wife skipped out of the back door with the boy while I was busy with him. Lucas explained *that* away by saying she had to take the boy to school.'

'She does take James to school and bring him home,' Tregalles pointed out, but Paget merely glowered over the rim of the mug, and the sergeant wisely refrained from saying more. Something had got up Paget's nose, and it wasn't just Lucas.

Paget sipped his coffee. 'He tried to give me some cock and bull story about sitting out there watching for whoever has been pilfering stuff from the stables, but I don't believe a word of it.' He sat down on the chair with a wheel missing, and almost toppled over, sloshing coffee all over his hand. 'For God's sake, Len, can't you do something about this bloody chair?' he burst out.

The sergeant exchanged glances with Tregalles. 'Sorry, sir,' he said stiffly. 'I'll have it seen to.'

Paget grunted and set the dripping mug aside and wiped his hand. 'Now, what about this fire? Anything new on that?'

'Everyone claims to have been fast asleep when Penny raised the alarm,' said Ormside. 'We found the empty petrol tin in the long grass at the edge of the trees, and it's been taken in for examination. Sally Pritchard identified it as the tin missing from the barn, and she said almost anyone could have known they kept petrol there.'

Ormside slid into his own chair. 'I had a word with the doctor about Sylvia Gray, and he tells me there is nothing seriously wrong with her. Just nerves, was how he described it. But she was in quite a state, so he gave her something to settle her down. I've asked young Penny to give me a shout when she's a bit calmer.'

Paget nodded absently as he turned to Tregalles. The sergeant had propped himself up beside a filing cabinet, and was on his second mug of coffee. 'What about you, Tregalles?' he asked. 'What did you find out yesterday?'

Tregalles looked down at the mug in his hand. 'I found out that Dr McMillan has a very good friend in Kate Ferris,' he said quietly. 'She assured me that the doctor arrived there before eleven o'clock last Friday night, which made it impossible for her to have been out here between nine and ten. Unfortunately for her, I stopped to talk to an old chap who lives down the lane—he'd given me directions on the way there—and he told me that it was well after twelve when the doctor arrived. Not only that, but she was in a state of panic when she did arrive.'

'I see.' Paget's voice sounded oddly strained. 'Go on,' he said tightly.

'He says he never goes to bed until close to midnight,' Tregalles explained, 'and even then he has trouble getting to sleep. He lives on the corner of the lane leading to the Ferris place, and the headlights of any car turning into the lane shine right into his bedroom. He's met the doctor, and he knows the sound of her car. It's a diesel. He said he'd know that sound anywhere.

'Anyway, he heard her go down the lane, but he knew she'd find no one at home because Kate Ferris and Sarah had left that evening to go to Kate's mother's in Melisham. He told me that Mrs Ferris has these mini-strokes; she can tell when they're coming on, so she phones for her daughter to come over. When that happens, Kate leaves the key with the old man and he looks after the place till she gets back. He said she's never gone for more than a couple of days.'

'So Dr McMillan arrived to find an empty house?'

'Right. But she knew that Kate left the key with the old man whenever she had to leave the place, so she came back to ask him if he knew where Kate was. He says she was in a terrible state, and she didn't calm down until he gave her the key to the Ferris place and she went back there to telephone Kate at her mother's. See, he doesn't have a phone himself. Anyway, a bit later, she brought the key back and drove off again. He didn't see her or anyone else until Sunday morning when Kate and Sarah came back, and the doctor was with them. He assumed that she'd driven down to Kate's mother's when she left him about one thirty Saturday morning.'

Paget stared down at the floor, not daring for the moment to lift his eyes. He felt numb. There was no getting around it. Tregalles had just driven the final nail into Andrea's coffin.

'Lucas claims to have seen the doctor's car here Friday night,' he said. 'He says it was well after ten before it left.'

'Did he see Dr McMillan?'

'No, but he did say the driver was a woman. And he took down the number of the car. It checks out.' Paget felt like a traitor as he uttered the words. 'According to Lucas, the driver left the car for some time, then came running back from the direction of the stables. She had driven off before he could get a good look at her.'

Tregalles shook his head sadly. 'I must admit I hoped we were wrong about her,' he said. 'I've always rather liked her.'

Paget rested his head against the wall and closed his eyes. 'You saw the little girl, Sarah?'

'Yes. She's a nice kid; looks a lot like her mother. I'd say she's in good hands with Kate Ferris, but God knows what will happen to her if it turns out her mother did kill Palmer.'

Paget didn't want to think about that.

'But where does Blake fit in?' Tregalles said. 'Who killed him? And why?' He looked at Ormside. 'What about the background checks? Has anything turned up to suggest that Palmer and Blake might have known each other in the past?'

'Nothing so far,' the sergeant said, 'but I can't help remembering what Sally Pritchard said about it being Blake's turn to do rounds the night Palmer was killed. I've been thinking about that. If someone was waiting inside the barn, expecting Blake to come through the door, all they would see would be a silhouette in the doorway. Blake and Palmer were roughly the same height, and we know that Palmer couldn't have taken more than a step inside the barn before he was struck. The killer might not have realized his mistake until too late. When he did, he had another go at Blake—and got him.'

Ormside's reasoning was identical to Paget's, and the chief inspector would have liked nothing better than to embrace it. But the evidence against Andrea McMillan was overwhelming, and if it could be proved that she knew that Palmer had swapped with Blake...

But if that were the case, why had Blake been killed?

'I think I'll go and see if Charlie's people have come up with anything,' Tregalles said. 'And while I'm at it, I'm going to take another look around the barn.' He waited, but there was no response from Paget.

As he stepped out of the mobile unit, he saw Penny Wakefield coming towards him. She waved, and he stopped and waited for her. 'Is the chief inspector in there?' she asked.

'Yes. Did you want to speak to him?'

The girl nodded. 'But not in there. Do you think I could have a word with him in private?'

'IT'S ABOUT SYL,' said Penny as she and Paget walked slowly down the driveway towards the road. 'I don't want somebody questioning her when she wakes up. She was fast asleep no more than three feet away from me when that fire broke out, so she can't help you find out who it was who...' Her voice dried up and cracked.

'God! What a horrible way to die!' she said. 'I didn't care much for Maurice, but to set fire to his caravan when he was in it...' She shuddered.

'But why are you so concerned about Sylvia Gray?' asked Paget. 'And I must warn you that I cannot promise to keep what you tell me confidential if I think it may help the investigation.'

'But that's just the point. It's nothing to do with it, really. It's just that Syl... Well, I don't know what it would do to her if she was pushed too hard.' The girl fell silent as they came to the road. They turned as if by mutual consent, and began walking back up the drive again.

'I spoke to Sally before I came to you,' she said at last, 'and she said she thought you would understand, once I'd explained.'

Paget remained silent. It had to be Penny's decision.

'Oh, what the hell,' the girl said roughly as if to herself. 'I can't make it any worse for her if I tell you.' She stopped beside a gate leading into the field between the stables and the road, and Paget stopped beside her.

'See, it was Syl in that shed with Maurice on Christmas Eve,' she burst out. 'She'd had a bit too much to drink and she's not used to it. I know you're not supposed to speak ill of the dead, but Maurice was a randy bastard, and he got her in there. It wasn't rape or anything like that, but it was Syl's first time, and she's petrified that she's going to have a baby.'

Paget stared at her. 'But that was less than two weeks ago,' he said. 'How can she possibly...'

But Penny was shaking her head. 'I *know*,' she said. 'That's what I keep telling her, but she's very—what do you call it?—naïve, is Syl. She just won't listen when I try to tell her she'll probably be all right. See, she's Catholic, and her parents are ever so strict. She had to fight tooth and nail to get them to agree to let her come here, and I sort of promised I'd look out for her.'

Penny leaned on the gate and stared off into the distance. 'Poor old Syl,' she said. 'She kept talking about how Maurice would have to marry her. It was the only way, she said.' Penny sighed. 'Fat chance there was of that, but you couldn't tell her that. Then, this morning, when she realized Maurice was inside that caravan, she just went to pieces.'

'I see. Then Monica…'

'…heard them at it, then made that story up to get back at Sally,' said Penny. 'Least, that's what I think. It's the sort of thing she'd do.'

Which would account for the evidence Starkie had found, thought Paget. Monica's own skin and blood beneath her fingernails.

They resumed their walk up the drive toward the stables. 'If that's all there was to it,' Paget said, 'then I see no need for any of it to become public knowledge, and I'll bear in mind what you've told me if it should become necessary to question her.'

Penny heaved a sigh of relief. 'Thank you,' she said. 'Sal was right. She said you'd understand.'

WHEN PAGET RETURNED to the mobile unit, he found Charlie there.

'Pillowcase,' said Charlie, pointing an accusing finger at Paget. 'That's what I've been meaning to talk to you about.'

Paget stared at him, mystified.

'I stopped off at the school yesterday with all the stuff from the lab,' he said. 'You know, the stuff we took from the Shaw girl's room. It was all there; the sheets, the blankets, and all the odds and ends, and two pillows and one pillowcase. Miss Wolsey insisted on checking everything— she told me she'd catch hell from Miss Crowther if she didn't, or words to that effect—and she said that there was a pillowcase missing. I told her we only took one pillowcase because that's all there was. But she insisted that there were two. She said she was quite sure both pillows had pillowcases on them when she left Monica in bed on Christmas Eve.'

Charlie sniffed. 'I don't know whether she thinks we pinched the damned thing or what, but do you remember seeing a second pillowcase?'

Paget closed his eyes, concentrating, recalling a picture of Monica Shaw's room. 'I saw two pillows,' he said. 'One, the top one, had a pillowcase on it, but the bottom pillow didn't. I'm afraid I didn't think much about it at the time. Mind you, there could have been another pillowcase in a cupboard or somewhere for all I know.'

Charlie shook his head. 'There wasn't. I checked the inventory myself. Besides, Miss Wolsey swears both pillows were covered when she left the room that night. So where did the other pillowcase go? What's more to the point is, does it matter?'

Paget was wondering the same thing. It seemed like such a trivial thing, and yet it might have meaning if only he could think what that meaning was. Somewhere in the back of his mind still lurked the idea that the death of Monica Shaw was somehow linked with what had happened here at Glenacres. But if there was a connection, it eluded him at the moment.

'Sorry, Charlie. I'm afraid I can't help you,' he said. 'But there is something I'd like you to do for me. Would you have those bits of glass you found on top of Monica's dressing-table checked against the glass in the photographs of the board of governors in the entrance hall? Or with the photographer who supplied the pictures and frames. See if you can get a match.'

The inspector looked doubtful. 'They've probably

chucked it out by now,' he said, 'but I'll see what I can do.'

'Thanks, Charlie.'

TREGALLES STUCK HIS HEAD in the door. 'Mrs Lucas is back,' he announced. 'Just saw her come in, and Lucas has taken off somewhere in his car.'

'Right,' said Paget. 'Let's go and have a word with her. I think she has some explaining to do.'

According to the information Ormside had on Georgie Lucas, she had been a model and part-time actress before marrying Lucas a few months before James was born. Gossip around the stables was that it had been an unsuitable match from the start. Jack Lucas lived and breathed horses; Georgie couldn't stand them. Jack was at least twenty years her senior, down to earth, and jealous. Georgie was a dreamer, a romantic, and inclined to stray from time to time.

Ormside went on to say that the word around the stables was that Georgie had had an affair with someone in town; a married man. The story went that when Jack found out, he said nothing to Georgie, but a few weeks later he caught the man on his way home one night and hammered him into the ground.

'We spoke to the man in question,' said Ormside. 'He was beaten all right; bad enough to be sent to hospital, but he swore he had no idea who did it to him. Insisted there were two of them, but he couldn't give a description of either. Nothing was stolen, so it was assumed that whoever did it was frightened off before they could finish the job. It's still on the books, as a matter of fact, but the investigation was dropped long ago.'

Despite Tregalles's glowing description of Georgie Lucas's charms, Paget was taken by surprise when she answered the door. Until now, he had only caught a glimpse of her in the car as she'd driven by, but seeing her face to face, he had to agree with the assessment of his sergeant. Tregalles was right. She was indeed beautiful, and he wouldn't find it hard to believe the gossip Ormside had picked up.

'I'm afraid Jack's not here,' she said, perhaps hoping they would go away.

'Actually, it is you we wish to talk to,' Paget told her. 'May we come in?'

Georgie just stood there for a moment, her eyes blank as if she hadn't heard. Then, without a word, she turned and led the way inside. She waved in an offhanded way at chairs and sat down herself. Her short skirt slid well above her knees, but she made no attempt to pull it down. Beside her was a tumbler half full of amber liquid, and now she picked it up and swirled it around in the glass before drinking.

It *could* have been iced tea, but Paget didn't think so.

It was hard to tell that she was drunk. The hand that held the glass was steady. It was only when he looked closely at her eyes that he could see the puffiness there, and she seemed to be having trouble focusing as she looked from one to the other enquiringly.

'Well?' she prompted languidly.

The word caught Paget by surprise. He realized he'd been staring, and he felt his face go warm as he settled himself in his seat.

He explained why they were there, then said: 'Would you tell us where you were around four o'clock this morning, Mrs Lucas?'

Her eyes clouded, and she frowned as if she felt the need to concentrate on the question. 'I was in bed,' she said carefully. 'Jack will tell you.' She looked directly at him and Paget felt the full impact of her eyes. 'In fact, I dare say he has,' she said, and giggled suddenly. She brought herself up short. 'Sorry,' she apologized. 'It's been... It's nerves, that's all. You must think...'

She broke off and gulped down half her drink.

'How well did you know Maurice Blake?'

Georgie stared into the glass and gave an elaborate shrug. 'Since he came here a few years ago, I suppose,' she said.

'I'm sorry. Perhaps you misunderstood me, Mrs Lucas. I asked how *well* you knew Maurice Blake; not how long.'

'Oh! Sorry.' She pulled herself upright in the chair as if determined to make an effort and pay attention. 'I didn't know him well at all,' she said, but her eyes slid away to her glass as she spoke. 'I don't have much to do with the stables. That's Jack's department.'

'I'd like you to think very carefully about your answers to these questions, Mrs Lucas,' Paget said. 'Maurice Blake was murdered, you know. The fire was not an accident.'

Georgie's mouth quivered, and suddenly her eyes were moist. 'I know,' she breathed almost inaudibly.

'Tell me, where were you the night Victor Palmer was murdered?' Paget said. 'The man you knew as Prescott.'

The woman averted her eyes, then looked at Tregalles. 'I told you I was here—didn't I?' She stopped, looked confused, and passed a hand across her face. 'At least I *thought* I did.'

'But you weren't here, were you?' said Paget gently but firmly. 'Where were you, Mrs Lucas?'

Georgie shook her head in denial. 'I *was* here,' she insisted. 'I was. I was.' Her face began to crumple.

'You left the house by the back door,' Paget went on. 'Went out of the garden by the back gate and returned the same way. You left just after nine after seeing young James off to bed, didn't you? And you were gone for some time.'

'I...' Georgie finished off her drink and began to get up, empty glass in hand.

'Please sit down, Mrs Lucas,' Paget said. 'I'd prefer you to answer my questions before you have another drink.'

Her eyes flared, and she seemed about to protest, but the fight went out of her as she met his implacable gaze. She sat down again and set the glass down very carefully on the table beside her.

'Where were you, Mrs Lucas?' he asked again.

'I went out for a walk,' she said sullenly.

'Where did you go?'

'I went down the drive, then walked as far as the cross-roads and back, that's all. What's wrong with that?'

'Nothing, if that is what you did,' said Paget. 'But in order to do that you would have had to either leave by the front door or go around the house if you left by the back door. And we know you left and returned via the back gate. I ask you again: where did you go, Mrs Lucas?'

Her mouth set in a stubborn line. 'I told you...' she began, but Paget cut her off.

'Did you know that your husband was sitting in his car across the road watching both driveways that night?' he asked harshly.

'Jack was...?' Her hand flew to her mouth. Pretence vanished as pent-up tears flowed down her face. She buried her face in her hands and rocked back and forth. 'Oh, God,' she moaned. 'Oh, God! He'll kill me if he ever finds out.' She lifted a tear-stained face. 'You don't have to tell him— do you?' she whispered. 'Please...'

'SHE SAYS SHE WAS WITH BLAKE the night Palmer was killed,' said Paget. They were back in the mobile unit, talking to Ormside.

'And she swears she didn't know that Lucas was watching the house,' Tregalles put in. 'She was sure she was safe because of the darts match. Apparently Lucas never twigged she was having it off with Blake right under his nose. She said Blake wouldn't have lasted five minutes if Lucas had even suspected there was anything between them. It seems he thought she was sneaking off to see someone in town again. That's why he waited where he did.'

'But she didn't dare try that again. Your information was right, Len. Lucas did find out about her and the man she was seeing in town, and he beat the poor sod half to death.'

'But why would she play the game at all,' said Ormside, 'knowing what her husband is like?'

'I don't think she can help herself,' said Tregalles. He looked at Paget for confirmation. 'At least, that's the way I read it. She told us straight out that she only married Lucas because of James and what he could do for the baby. She had no money, and Lucas was well fixed so she agreed to marry him. But since they've been married, Lucas hasn't been all that interested, so she's gone looking elsewhere. Not that she'd have to look far,' he added, half enviously. 'You haven't met her, have you, Len?'

Ormside grunted. 'I think you'd better watch yourself, my lad,' he said heavily. 'I wouldn't like to have to scrape you up off the floor after Lucas has had a go at you.'

'I was just saying…' Tregalles began, then wisely closed his mouth.

'If Lucas *did* know what was going on, between his wife and Blake, it gives him a hell of a good motive for murder,' Ormside said.

'I'm sure that's what his wife thought at first,' said Tregalles. 'But she insisted that Lucas never moved after he came to bed around midnight.'

'If she's drinking that heavily, there's a good chance she wouldn't even know if he did,' said Ormside.

'Or she's too scared of him to say,' Tregalles added.

'It would tie the two murders together,' said Paget thoughtfully. 'If Lucas knew about Blake and was waiting for him to come through the door that night, he may have struck before he realized his mistake. But he's not the sort who would give up easily. All he had to do was wait until his wife was sound asleep, leave the house, set fire to the caravan, and slip back into bed. She wouldn't even be aware of it.'

It made sense. What's more, it held the added attraction of letting Andrea off the hook—at least as far as killing Palmer went. But she still had some explaining to do; a lot of explaining.

'But we need proof,' he went on. 'There is nothing to show that Lucas knew about Blake. In fact, the evidence we do have tends to show that he didn't know. We have nothing to connect him directly to the fire unless the lab comes up with something.'

He turned to Ormside. 'Len, it's up to you and your people to do some digging,' he said. 'Talk to anyone and everyone. See if they can find anything to indicate that Lucas might have known about his wife and Blake. Talk to Penny Wakefield; she seems to know as much as anyone about what goes on around here. And, speaking of Penny, I'd like you to have a WPC talk to Sylvia Gray when she's feeling a bit better.' He went on to tell Ormside what Penny Wakefield had told him.

'If that's all there is to it, I don't want to upset the kid any more than she is already,' he said. 'Mind you, if your WPC suspects that Sylvia isn't being truthful, she has my permission to come down on her like a ton of bricks.'

TWENTY-FOUR

PERHAPS IT WOULD HAVE BEEN better for both of them if he'd sent Tregalles to talk to Andrea, but Paget felt he'd be shirking his responsibilities if he sent the sergeant to do a job he was unwilling to do himself. But now, sitting no more than four feet way from her in one of the hospital consulting rooms, he wished he could be anywhere but here.

He should have had Andrea brought in to Charter Lane for further questioning after hearing what Lucas and Tregalles had had to say that morning. There could no longer be any doubt that Andrea had lied about where she was the night of Palmer's murder. She'd signed a statement she knew to be false, and she of all people still had the best motive of anyone for killing her ex-husband.

But he couldn't bring himself to do it—not without first giving her the opportunity to tell him why she'd lied. As he sat there now, so close and yet so very far away, he knew the impossible had happened. He had thought there could never be anyone for him after Jill. When she died, something in him had died as well. But, almost against his will, Andrea had stirred in him long-forgotten feelings, and he'd dared to hope that she might feel the same.

Which was why, despite all the evidence to the contrary, he had searched so desperately for a less sinister explanation for Andrea's presence at Glenacres on the night of Palmer's murder. To no avail.

Now, quietly, dispassionately, he told her what Tregalles had found out; told her there was a witness who had seen her at Glenacres the night that Victor was killed.

She'd listened calmly, eyes down and hooded, nodding gently every so often, as if confirming what he'd said. Her manner puzzled him. She was too calm.

He stopped speaking, and there was silence in the room. Andrea lifted her head and looked at him.

'He wanted money,' she said. She spoke the words so softly that Paget almost failed to catch them. 'At least, that's what he said and I believed him, fool that I was. I believed him because I wanted to. I told myself he'd go away; that he would leave us alone, but…' She dropped her gaze and sighed. 'But I knew. I knew he would never be satisfied until he'd taken his revenge.'

'You say Palmer wanted money?'

She lifted her head and brushed a lock of hair away from her face.

'It was Boxing Day,' she said. Her voice was normal now, crisp and clear and businesslike. 'The day you saw me at the Glenacres. I told you the truth about that except for the money. He said he had a chance to get back into business in the south. His old stables were sold to pay for his defence, so he had nothing to fall back on. All he needed was a start. He said he needed two thousand pounds. I told him he could go to hell; he'd get no money from me.'

Andrea looked down at her hands. 'That's when he said he thought two thousand pounds was little enough compensation for giving up his daughter.'

Andrea McMillan pushed herself up and out of the chair. She walked over to the window and stood looking out.

'You agreed to pay him the money?'

She didn't answer for some time; just stood there looking out across the town, massaging her arms as if she were cold. 'Yes,' she said at last. 'I agreed to pay him the money. It was all I could do to scrape it up, but I managed it, and I took it with me on Friday. I remember thinking all the

way out there that I was being silly; it would never stop.
And yet another part of me said perhaps he was telling the
truth. Perhaps there was a job for him down south. Perhaps
he had changed. Dear God, how I wanted to believe that.'

She sighed wearily. 'He refused to come into town for
the money. He insisted that I meet him at the entrance to
the stables at ten o'clock on Friday night. Something about
him having to do rounds that night—he didn't explain. I
waited, but he never came. I even went part-way up the
drive with some idea of finding him, but it was about then
that it suddenly occurred to me that he wasn't coming because he'd found out where Sarah was and had gone to get
her. The more I thought about it the more I became convinced that he'd planned it that way. I thought maybe he'd
known about Sarah all along. Maybe he'd been planning
all this in prison just to get back at me. I panicked. I jumped
in the car and drove into the village and tried to telephone
Kate to tell her to get Sarah out of there; to just pick her
up and go!

'But she wasn't there! I rang the number again in case
I'd got it wrong, but no one answered. Someone should
have been there and they weren't! I got back in the car and
drove like a maniac through the night. I had to find out
whether Sarah was all right. I hardly remember anything of
the drive. I was so scared. When I got there and found that
both of them were gone, I nearly went mad with worry.'

'But you remembered that the old man who lives on the
corner might know where they'd gone,' said Paget.

'Yes. Kate had tried to reach me by telephone to let me
know, he said, but I must have left for Glenacres by then.
But I knew I wouldn't be satisfied until I'd seen Sarah for
myself, so I carried on down to Kate's mother's. Of course,
everything was all right, and I needn't have worried, but I
didn't know that until I got there.'

'You say you went part-way up the drive,' Paget said. 'Did you go up as far as the red barn?'

Andrea shook her head firmly. 'No. I only went a few steps up there when, as I said, it occurred to me that Victor might have gone after Sarah.'

'But you are familiar with the barn? You do stable your horse out there, and I imagine you've been inside to the yard office?'

'Of course. I've been in there a number of times.'

'But you say you didn't go there that night?'

Irritation crept into her voice as she said: 'I told you, no, Neil.'

'And you didn't see Victor that night?'

'No.'

'Alive or dead?'

Anger flared in her eyes. 'No,' she said curtly.

Paget drew in a breath and let it out again slowly. 'Andrea, did you see anyone while you were out there who might corroborate your story? Did you stop anywhere? Talk to anyone?' He realized he was almost pleading with her now, for what she had told him could do her nothing but harm. Andrea McMillan had admitted earlier that she would have done anything to keep Victor Palmer away from her daughter. She had now admitted being at the stables at the time the pathologist said Palmer was killed. She knew her way around the inside of the barn. She'd probably seen the pitchfork there...

She was shaking her head slowly from side to side. 'The only place I stopped was in the village when I tried to phone Kate,' she said, 'and I don't recall seeing a soul. Sorry.'

Sorry. It wasn't good enough.

'Where were you between the hours of two and six this morning?' he asked.

She frowned. 'This morning? In bed, of course. Why, for heaven's sake?'

'Tell me, how well did you know Maurice Blake?'

Her eyes narrowed. 'My goodness, we are jumping about, aren't we,' she said in a mocking voice. 'What on earth has...? Did you say ''did'' know Maurice Blake?'

Paget nodded. 'He died this morning.'

The shock in her eyes seemed genuine. 'How?'

'Someone set fire to his caravan after making sure he couldn't get out,' Paget said bluntly.

'Oh, my God!' She stared at him for what seemed like a long time. 'But you can't think that I... Good God, why, Neil? Why would I want to kill someone like Maurice? I hardly knew the man.'

'But you did know him?'

'Well, yes, I knew him in the sense that I've spoken to him a few times, but that's all. Sally Pritchard handles Busker, so my contact with him was minimal.'

Andrea began to pace. 'I can understand why you would think that I might have killed Victor,' she said. 'I know I lied to you about where I was, but I was scared to death that you would think exactly that if I told the truth. Dammit, Neil, why would I kill Maurice? As I said, I hardly knew the man.'

Why, indeed. 'You might if he saw you out there on the night that Palmer was killed,' he said quietly. 'Was he blackmailing you?'

Andrea stopped in front of him. All colour had drained from her face. She was trembling. Not with fear, but with anger.

'I refuse to say any more until I've spoken to my solicitor,' she said coldly, and turned away.

Paget rose slowly from his chair. 'I think you're very wise,' he said sadly. 'Very wise indeed.'

THE WIND BUFFETED THE CAR as it climbed out of the valley and left the lights of the town behind. It was trying to snow again, wet, heavy flakes mixed with rain. Paget muttered beneath his breath and switched on the wipers. Perhaps Alcott had a point, he thought; with weather like this, January should be banned.

It had been touch and go with the superintendent this afternoon. Alcott was a man who saw the world in black and white; he had little time for shades of grey. As far as he was concerned, the case against Andrea McMillan was cut and dried, and he couldn't understand Paget's reluctance to charge her.

'Dammit, man, she had motive, means, and opportunity. And you said yourself that she admits to being there when Palmer was killed. What more do you want?' he'd said, not unreasonably.

'But everything is circumstantial,' Paget had argued. 'We don't have one piece of physical evidence that ties her to either crime, and in the case of Blake we have nothing. We can't prove that she was anywhere but where she says she was, and we have no motive. A better case can be made against Lucas when it comes right down to it. We know he wasn't sitting out there night after night watching for thieves; even his own staff say nothing of any real value has disappeared around there. I'm quite sure he was waiting to find out who his wife was seeing whenever he went out. But we only have his word for it that he was waiting in the lane that night. If we assume that he'd found out about Blake, then it's not too hard to imagine him lying in wait for Blake inside the barn, and not sitting in his car as he says.

'When he realized he'd got the wrong man, he went after Blake in his caravan.'

'But we also know that the doctor was out there. She

admitted it herself,' Alcott reminded him. 'And Lucas saw her car.'

Paget had countered by pointing out that Dr McMillan had said she was out there to give Palmer money; to buy him off, in effect, and her bank manager had confirmed that she had withdrawn two thousand pounds two days before.

Alcott had brushed that aside. 'That could have been a blind,' he said. 'Or she might have changed her mind. Blackmail seldom ends with one payment, and she's certainly right enough to realize that.'

'Then where does Blake fit into the picture?'

Alcott sucked on his cigarette until it glowed bright red, then stubbed it out. 'Damned if I know,' he said irritably. 'Perhaps he saw her...'

He stopped, recognizing the futility of going on. 'This is getting us nowhere,' he growled. 'See what the lab has to say. And there must be something that will tie the doctor to both Blake and Palmer. Stir Ormside up, and check with the patrol cars. If she did kill Blake, and I believe she did, she had to get out to the stables one way or another. Someone must have seen her.'

'We're checking with everyone who was on duty that night,' Paget has assured him, 'and Sergeant Ormside has men talking to virtually everyone in the immediate area. If anyone saw her, he'll find them.'

It wasn't just because it was Andrea that he wasn't prepared to take the circumstantial evidence at face value, Paget told himself. Much as he didn't want to believe her guilty, he knew better than to dismiss the possibility. She had a powerful motive in trying to protect her daughter.

But there was more to it than that, he was sure of it. He felt it in his bones. Every time he went out to Glenacres he could feel it. It was there in Lucas's behaviour; it was there in Sally Pritchard's eyes.

He thought of Sally now. She'd been hiding something

ever since that first day; Christmas Day. Something to do with the death of Monica Shaw. Had Sally really been ill that morning? Or had she simply feigned illness so that she wouldn't have to go over to the school?

It was only one of several questions he would put to her tomorrow.

As he entered Ashton Prior, his thoughts went back to the day that Andrea had asked him if he would like to go with her to the local theatre. A grateful patient had given her two tickets, she said. Would he care to go?

She had been very matter-of-fact about it. They were having coffee together late one evening in the hospital cafeteria, talking about a man he was sure was feigning illness to avoid questioning, when she'd put the question.

It had surprised him. He'd only spoken to her a few times prior to that, and the relationship between them was purely professional. For a moment, he was at a loss for words.

Andrea had laughed self-consciously. 'I'm sorry, Chief Inspector,' she apologized. 'I can see I've embarrassed you. It was—' she shrugged helplessly, embarrassed now herself '—a spur of the moment thing. Believe me, I don't make a habit of this sort of thing. It was presumptuous of me. Please, just forget I asked.'

He found his voice. 'I must admit you did take me by surprise,' he said ruefully, 'but I'm flattered. Please don't apologize, because I *would* like to go. In fact, Doctor, I shall look forward to it with a great deal of pleasure.'

She regarded him with solemn eyes, and he remembered thinking that he'd never really looked at her before. Not really *looked*. Even here beneath the unflattering fluorescent lights, and tired after a long, exhausting day, she looked lovely, and he wondered why he'd never noticed that before.

'That's very chivalrous, Chief Inspector,' she said, 'but really, you don't have to...'

'No. I mean it,' he said earnestly.

Thinking of it now, he remembered how it had suddenly become important that she believe him. 'I really do mean it, Doctor,' he'd said again.

A slow, half-embarrassed smile crept across her face. 'Then, perhaps,' she said, thrusting out her hand across the table, 'we should stop calling one another "Doctor" and "Chief Inspector". My name is Andrea.'

'And mine is Neil.'

Now, as vividly as the moment itself, he recalled the inexplicable rush of pleasure he had felt as he'd grasped the slender hand.

As far as he was concerned, the evening had been a great success. The calibre of acting had surprised him, and he had enjoyed himself in a way he hadn't done in years. Asking Andrea to go out again had seemed the natural thing to do.

But now, as he drove up the hill towards the house, he wondered bitterly whether it might have been better if he'd said no instead of yes that day in the cafeteria.

TWENTY-FIVE

Thursday, 7 January

CHARLIE TELEPHONED just after ten the following day to say that he'd been successful in persuading Miss Crowther to part with a picture of one of the governors, and had sent it on to the lab for comparison with the glass they'd found in Monica's room.

'I've given the information to Cooper,' he said, 'but I thought I'd better give you a ring as well. Mind you, it may be a few days before you get the results back. They're really busy with the back-up from the holidays, and the same goes for the stuff we sent in from the fire yesterday.'

That wouldn't sit well with Alcott. The local papers were full of the most recent developments out there at Glenacres, and now the national press had picked it up. The sooner there was an arrest, the happier he would be.

'Thanks for letting me know, Charlie,' he said. He hung up and sat there drumming fingers on his desk. What if Forensic came up empty? They were good, but if the evidence wasn't there to begin with…

He picked up the phone and asked Tregalles to come up.

Tregalles appeared, coffee mug in hand. 'I just had a look at the information we have so far on Blake,' he said as he sat down. 'Apart from a liking for the ladies—which was why his wife divorced him, by the way—he has no form. The references he gave from the last place he worked stand up. In fact, he was very good at his job, by all accounts.'

'No prior connection with Palmer?'

'Nothing so far.'

'Or with any of the others at Glenacres?'

'No.'

Paget hunched over the desk. 'So,' he said softly, 'we have a problem, Sergeant. The way things stand, both killings could have been done by either Dr McMillan or Lucas. We need to examine everything again, starting at the very beginning.'

Tregalles eyed Paget over the rim of the mug as he sipped his coffee. 'Fair enough,' he said. 'So we start with Palmer's murder, do we?'

Paget shook his head. 'No, we start with the death of Monica Shaw. We find out exactly what happened on Christmas Eve; we find out where she went, and we find out why she tried to kill herself when she returned.'

Tregalles looked sceptical. 'I don't see how her death can have anything to do with the other two,' he objected. 'I know they came close together, but from all accounts she was a high-strung kid who had been heading for trouble for a long time. Something just tipped her over the edge that night. But the Palmer killing was cold-blooded murder, and so was Blake's. Anyway, we've been over that ground already. I don't see…'

'That's just it,' Paget interrupted. 'We haven't. The investigation was dropped because it was decided that there wouldn't be an inquest. Starkie recommended one, but the coroner chose to ignore his recommendation. That in itself is unusual, and I asked myself why. So I checked with Starkie. He tells me it is the first time that's happened. Normally, the coroner relies heavily on the judgement of the pathologist, and follows his advice. Someone has been putting the pressure on.'

'But even Starkie said that the cause of death was an aneurysm; that it could have happened to anyone,' Tregalles objected. 'Wouldn't the coroner take that into account? I mean, when it comes right down to it, she did die of natural causes.'

Paget sat forward in his seat, elbows on the desk, shoulders hunched as he made his point. 'There was nothing natural about the way that girl died,' he growled. 'My guess is that someone had a quiet word with the coroner. Nothing heavy; just a suggestion, but it would be enough.'

'So, where do we start? Tackle the coroner?' Tregalles grimaced at the thought.

'That would get us nowhere,' Paget said. 'No, we start with someone who has been lying to us from the very beginning. Someone who knows a lot more than she's told us. We start with Sally Pritchard.'

LIVING AS SHE DID JUST DOWN the road from the stables, Sally Pritchard usually went home for lunch, and today was no exception. She'd just finished her second cup of coffee when she heard a car come up the drive and stop. Frowning, she went to the window and looked out.

The car outside was a police car, and getting out of it were Sergeant Tregalles and a policewoman. Their movements, it seemed to her, were deliberate and businesslike. Neither of them looked particularly friendly.

The cup she still held in her hand began to shake, and the fears she had thought suppressed came rushing back. She moved away from the window before they saw her, and set the cup down. She stood there for a moment, forcing herself to remain calm. It was silly to get all upset, she told herself. It would just be more questions about Maurice or Victor.

Even so, she jumped when the heavy knock came on the door.

She took a deep breath and opened it. 'Miss Pritchard?' said Tregalles as if they'd never met before. His face was grave.

'Yes?'

'The chief inspector would like to see you at headquarters regarding a serious matter concerning the death of Monica Shaw.'

Sally fought the rising panic. How could they know? It wasn't possible. Her mouth went dry. 'Now?' she said. It came out as a croak.

'Yes, miss.'

Sally looked beyond Tregalles to where the policewoman stood behind him. The policewoman regarded her with stony eyes. 'But I have to get back to work.'

'It is important, miss. The chief inspector is waiting.'

There must be something she could say. Something she could do, but her mind refused to function. All she could think about was that if she refused they would simply handcuff her and take her anyway. 'I must ring the stables,' she said abstractedly, and began to turn away.

She didn't know quite what happened, but somehow the policewoman was there beside her with a hand on her arm.

'You can do that from headquarters,' the woman said. 'This *is* an urgent matter, Miss Pritchard.'

Sally looked down at the policewoman's hand. It simply lay there, flat, fingers extended, resting lightly on her arm. She was surprised to see how small the hand was; how neat the manicured nails. Yet she felt she had only to move and the fingers would close like a vice around her arm.

She swallowed hard. 'Very well. May I get my coat?'

The policewoman smiled. It transformed her face. 'Of course,' she said pleasantly. 'You'll need it. It's quite cold again today.'

Sally shivered. Even with her coat on, she found she was still shaking as she locked the door and went with them to the car.

THE INTERVIEW ROOM WAS WARM but Sally kept her coat on. For all their seeming hurry to get her there, she'd now been sitting on a wooden chair beside the table for almost half an hour. Any attempt to engage the policewoman—not the same one—in conversation had been met with stony silence.

The only thing on the table was a large, old-fashioned tape recorder, yet it seemed to dominate the room. Her eyes kept coming back to it. Her palms were hot and sweaty; her throat was dry. She would have liked to take her coat off but she was afraid it might be taken as a sign of nervousness, so she kept it on. Besides, she felt just a little safer with it wrapped around her.

Silly, she told herself as she grew even warmer. But still she kept it on.

Paget entered the room, followed closely by Tregalles. The chief inspector was carrying a thick folder which he sat before him on the table as he took his seat opposite her. His smile was perfunctory; he seemed preoccupied.

Tregalles slid into a chair at the end of the table.

Paget said: 'Thank you for coming in, Miss Pritchard.' As if she'd had a choice. 'This will be a recorded interview.' He snapped the tape recorder switch to On, gave the date, time, and location, and who was present in the room. 'Now, then, Miss Pritchard,' he said, 'the questions I am about to ask you relate to the death of Monica Shaw on or about the morning of December twenty-fifth of last year. They arise from certain discrepancies discovered in the statement you gave to the police later that same day, and during subsequent interviews with me and Sergeant Tregalles.'

He paused. 'If you wish to make a statement at this point, or change your previous statement, you have the opportunity to do so now, Miss Pritchard.'

It seemed to Sally that she had been holding her breath ever since the chief inspector had entered the room, and now she let it out in a long, drawn-out sigh that sounded more like a whimper. This couldn't be happening to her. The reels of the tape recorder ground slowly on. Round and round. One of them made a scraping sound on every revolution, and she found herself waiting for it. She coughed, and the needle jumped and fell back, waiting for her words. She took a deep breath.

'May I have a glass of water, please?' she said in a voice so low the needle barely moved.

'Of course,' said Paget, nodding to the policewoman behind her, 'but would you say that a little louder for the tape, please, Miss Pritchard?'

She cleared her throat and repeated her request.

The policewoman opened the door and spoke to someone outside. She didn't leave the room, but a jug of water and several paper cups appeared in a remarkably short space of time. The policewoman set them on the table and filled a cup for Sally. Throughout the whole procedure, no one spoke a word. She gulped the water down, spilling some down the front of her coat.

'You must be warm,' said Paget. 'Would you like to take your coat off?'

Stubbornly, illogically, she shook her head.

'What do you want?' she asked him as she filled the cup again.

'The truth, Miss Pritchard. That's all.'

'But I thought…that is…' She stopped, not knowing what to say.

'That the investigation into Miss Shaw's death was closed?'

She nodded. Paget's eyes flicked towards the tape recorder. Sally cleared her throat again and said: 'Yes.'

'It was,' he said candidly. 'That is until I realized that it was you Monica went to see that night after she was supposed to have gone to bed. And it was you who followed her back to the school; followed her upstairs and…'

'No!' Sally Pritchard looked as if she were about to faint. 'No,' she said again. She closed her eyes and put her hands to her face. 'I didn't follow her. But I am to blame. It was my fault. I didn't mean to…' She groaned. 'If only she hadn't come that night. She'd be alive. Monica would be alive.'

Paget exchanged glances with Tregalles.

Sally dropped her hands. Her face was wet with tears.

'I think you'd better tell me about it,' said Paget quietly. 'From the beginning, please. Would you like to take your coat off now, Miss Pritchard? You must be sweltering.'

Slowly, she took the offending garment off. Her shirt clung to her upper arms; it was soaked with perspiration, but it didn't matter now. Nothing mattered now.

It had begun, Sally said, at the party Christmas Eve. 'Although, in fact, it began long before that. It's just that Monica hadn't realized it,' she said. 'I knew what was happening, but I hoped that somehow she would—oh, I don't know. I'm not sure now what I thought,' she said distractedly.

Sally said she'd felt guilty about sending Monica off the way she did in the middle of the Christmas party, so she went looking for her. 'That part was true,' she told Paget earnestly. 'And, as I said, I found her up there by the shed. She was sobbing her heart out, and I really thought someone had dragged her inside the shed and tried to rape her. It was only after Penny told me that it was Sylvia in there with Maurice that I realized Monica had been having me on all the time. She must have seen me coming and decided to punish me by saying she'd been attacked.' Sally leaned back in her chair and stared up at the ceiling. She ran her hands through her short hair. 'God! If I'd only known that at the time,' she groaned.

'But I didn't. I felt sorry for her. I felt it was all my fault.
I tried to comfort her. I held her, soothed her, and…and…'
She seemed to be having trouble getting the words out.
'…and I kissed her.'

Sally avoided his eyes.

'I felt the shock go through her,' she said quietly. 'I'd
known for months that Monica was in love with me, but
she had no idea what was happening to her. I told you she
was very naïve. It was as if she'd been struck by light-
ning. She went rigid and held on to me. She dug her nails
into me, and she kissed me back. Hard. So fiercely that I
couldn't breathe.

'I said the first thing that came to mind. I had to try to
convince her that nothing had happened. That everything
was as it had been. I said: ''You're drunk, Monica,'' and
shook her off. I practically had to drag her down the yard
to the car. I bundled her inside and she was all over me. I
could hardly drive for fending her off. And questions! I
kept telling her she was drunk and finally she moved over
against the door and went into a sulk. I kept telling her that
she mustn't say anything to anyone, especially Jane Wolsey, or she would be barred from ever coming over to the
stables again.'

Sally shook her head as if in wonder at herself. 'I don't
know what I said,' she went on. 'I just kept talking…' She
looked down at her hands. 'You see, no one knew about
me. I've managed to keep it secret all the time I worked at
Glenacres. I even went out on the odd date with a man just
to…well, you know. Everyone at work just assumed my
only passion was horses, and I encouraged them to think
that.'

'But Monica wouldn't let it go, would she?'

'No. But then again, I was so stupid. As I said, Monica
sat there sulking, and I began to feel guilty again. You see,
at that time I still thought she was telling the truth when

she said she'd been attacked. By the time we got to Thornton Hill, I felt perhaps I'd been too rough on her, so as I took her into the school, I gave her a little hug just to show her I wasn't angry with her.'

Sally sighed. 'But being Monica, she read more into it than was meant. She was smart enough to realize that she couldn't say anything to Jane Wolsey about what had happened. Poor Jane wouldn't have been able to cope with anything like that. She'd probably have had hysterics on the spot, and God only knows what she would have done to me. You see, awkward and obstinate as Monica was, Jane was very fond of her. I think she saw something of herself in her, and she tried her best to protect and defend her.

'It must have been a terrible shock to Jane when she found Monica the next morning.'

Sally lowered her eyes and looked down at her hands. Paget couldn't see her hands below the table, but he could see the tremor in her arms. She was coming to the crucial part of her story, and was finding it difficult to go on.

'After Miss Wolsey left her that night, Monica got up, got dressed and came to see you, didn't she?' he prompted.

'Yes.' The word was like a sigh; there was unutterable sadness in the sound. 'But...' Sally frowned. 'How did you know that? No one knew except...' Colour touched her face and she looked away.

'You told me that day in the barn when Sylvia came in looking for the key to the shed,' he said. 'In the dusk, you saw her silhouetted in the doorway and you mistook her for Monica. You said yourself there was the hair, the face, and the coat. Sylvia was wearing a long blue coat. In that light it looked much like the new coat of Monica's. But Monica had never worn that coat until she went out late that night. She was wearing a white jacket when you were supposed to have seen her last. She'd spilled wine on the jacket, and Miss Wolsey had taken it to have it cleaned, so she wore her new coat.

'Besides,' he continued, 'she wanted to look her best for you, didn't she?'

Sally slowly shook her head and closed her eyes as if in pain. 'Don't,' she whispered. 'My God, don't you think I feel bad enough?'

Paget couldn't help but feel some pity for Sally Pritchard. After all, she had asked for none of this, but he could not afford to ease the pressure on her. Not yet, at least.

'Tell me what happened,' he said. He filled her cup with water and she took it gratefully.

'It was after midnight,' she said. 'We—I was in bed. Suddenly there was this banging on the door, and I could hear someone calling out. I thought there must be some sort of trouble; an accident or something. I ran to the door, but as I got there I could hear this person outside. She was singing at the top of her voice. I thought at first it was some drunken caroller playing the fool, but it was Monica. She was singing ''Joy to the World'' just the first line over and over again like a broken record.'

Sally took another sip of water. 'As soon as I opened the door, she burst inside, grabbed me and hugged me until I thought I'd suffocate. She was happy, exuberant. I'd never seen her like that before. And she kept talking; chattering away like a magpie. She kept saying how wonderful it was to be there on Christmas Day with someone who loved her. I tried to talk to her, to calm her down, but she kept flitting around the room, chattering away… And then she flung open the bedroom door and saw…'

The words caught in her throat and her lips trembled. Her eyes implored him to understand; to ask her no more questions, but he couldn't allow her to stop now.

'She saw your lover there,' he finished for her.

Something in Sally's eyes seemed to die. She looked

away, but it was answer enough. 'What happened next?' he asked gently.

It was a long time before Sally answered. 'She just stopped,' she said. 'Monica just stood there. It was as if she were frozen. The look on her face as she looked at me...' Sally buried her face in her hands. 'I shall never forget it as long as I live,' she whispered.

'Then she ran out. I ran after her. I could hear her sobbing as she ran, but she was gone. She ran like the wind. There was nothing I could do.'

'Nothing?'

Sally Pritchard raised a haggard face. 'I—I don't understand,' she said.

'You didn't follow her to the school? Go in the back door? Go up to her room? You would know the way, wouldn't you, Miss Pritchard? You were once a pupil there.'

'No. No, I didn't. I—stayed up all night trying to think what to do. I couldn't forget the pain on Monica's face. She'd been rejected all her life, and now, when she thought she'd finally found someone...'

Sally took a deep breath. 'I couldn't face her and Jane in the morning. I simply couldn't. That's why I phoned and told Sylvia that I was ill, and asked her to take them to church. Then, when she telephoned to say that Monica had committed suicide, I didn't know what to do. I knew I'd killed her just as surely as if I'd stabbed her through the heart.'

'And you still say you didn't go out again that night?'

'I *told* you...'

'Someone did,' he said roughly. 'Someone went to Monica's room.'

She flinched as if he'd struck her. 'It wasn't me,' she said shakily.

'Then there is only one other person it could have been,'

Paget went on relentlessly. 'Someone who feared exposure; someone who was there with you that night; there in your bed when Monica came bursting in. Someone who knew about the unlocked back door at the school; someone…' Sally began to shake. She put her hands to her ears to block the words. 'Stop!' she cried. 'Stop! Please stop. Please…'

TWENTY-SIX

THE PALE WINTER SUN SLIPPED behind the western hills as they drove the now familiar road. The forecast was for more settled weather, and Paget hoped they were right for once. He was tired of the rain.

Behind him, Sally Pritchard stared out of the window with dull, unseeing eyes. Her body swayed with the motion of the car but she felt nothing. Nothing, that is, except an overwhelming sense of guilt. She wanted to cry out; to take back what she'd said or say it wasn't true.

But it was true.

A tear slowly trickled down her face.

'Miss Pritchard?'

She became aware that the car had stopped. The door was open and the policewoman was holding out her hand. Sally Pritchard undid her seat-belt and got out of the car, ignoring the proffered help.

The chief inspector and sergeant stood to one side, waiting.

The car had stopped opposite the front door, but Sally set off around the side of the cottage with the others following in single file. As she passed a lean-to beside the back door, she reached in and grasped a spade and continued on.

She led them down a brick-lined path and came to a halt beside a raised vegetable garden, now covered in snow. Without a word being spoken, she began to dig.

There was no frost in the ground. The heavy rains had seen to that. The spade went deep beneath her foot, and she grunted as she lifted the sodden clay. Tregalles stepped

forward to take the spade from her, but she pulled away
and jammed it even deeper into the ground.

She continued to dig; the mound beside her grew, and
water began to trickle into the hole. Abruptly, she dropped
the spade and reached down into the mud. She pulled at
what appeared to be a sodden rag and dragged it clear of
the hole, dumping it unceremoniously at Paget's feet.

The missing pillowcase.

Paget stooped and opened it to reveal a broken picture
frame and shards of glass. He peered into the bag. There
was something else in the bottom. He coaxed it out until it
lay revealed. He looked up at Sally, but she had turned
away, blinking hard to hold back the tears.

'Right, that's it, then,' he said quietly. 'Once we have it
we'll be on our way.' He turned to the policewoman. 'I'd
like you to remain here in the house with Miss Pritchard
until we return,' he told her. 'You will answer any incom-
ing phone calls yourself, and it goes without saying that
Miss Pritchard will not be calling anyone.'

'I understand, sir.'

Sally Pritchard spoke for the first time. Her voice was
flat, without expression. 'Am I under arrest?'

'For the moment, no,' said Paget. 'But charges may be
laid when I return. It all depends on how truthful you have
been, Miss Pritchard.'

THE LIGHT WAS FADING FAST by the time they reached the
open gates of Warrendale Hall. The driveway was flanked
by ancient oaks, their leafless branches meeting overhead
to form a vaulted canopy against the darkening sky.

The house was not as large as Paget had thought it would
be. From the size of the estate, he'd imagined something
much more grand, and certainly of stone. But Warrendale
Hall was on a smaller scale, and the better for it, Paget
thought. Gabled and half-timbered in Tudor style, it looked

as if it had grown there, so well did it blend with its surroundings.

'Looks as if it has been there for ever, doesn't it?' Tregalles said as they got out of the car. 'But it hasn't. Len
Ormside's great-grandfather helped build this house. The
first one burned down, and they had it rebuilt exactly the
way it was originally. It's less than a hundred years old,
according to Len. Hard to believe, isn't it?'

Paget stood looking at the house. It was beautifully pro-
portioned, and he looked forward to seeing the interior.

But it was not to be. Lady Tyndall, they were informed
by the maid who answered the door, was in the conservatory. She picked up a house telephone, punched in two
numbers and spoke briefly to someone at the other end.

'Lady Tyndall will see you,' she said, putting the phone
down. 'Please follow me.'

She led them down an exterior passageway that bypassed
the main house. Long, leaded windows looked out over the
grounds, but it was becoming too dark to see much of the
parklike setting. At the end of the passage was a glass door.
The maid opened it and stood to one side, allowing the two
men to enter the conservatory. The door closed quietly behind them.

Like the house, the conservatory was not overly large,
but it was well stocked with plants of every description.
Warm, moist air wrapped itself around them, and Paget
found himself loosening his coat.

'Chief Inspector Paget?' Lady Tyndall appeared from behind a bench containing row upon row of potted plants.

She was younger than he'd thought, but then he'd only
seen her at a distance before today. Mid-thirties, perhaps;
not much older than Sally Pritchard, in fact. Today, she
wore a black, turtle-neck pullover and a pair of light grey
trousers protected by a full-length apron tied at the waist.
Her jet-black hair was pulled back hard against her head,

and held in place by an ornamental silver comb. The style, combined with her olive-coloured skin and facial structure, made him think of warmer climes.

'And Sergeant Tregalles, Lady Tyndall,' Paget said.

'Sergeant.' A faint inclination of the head in Tregalles's direction. 'How may I help you?'

Paget came straight to the point. 'We have received certain information concerning the death of Monica Shaw,' he said quietly. 'Specifically, we have a sworn statement accusing you of causing the death of Monica Shaw, and I must caution you that you are not obliged to say anything unless you wish to do so, but...'

'Thank you, Chief Inspector, but I hardly think that is necessary,' Lady Tyndall broke in. She didn't seem at all surprised, but there came into her eyes a look of weary resignation. She turned and began to fiddle with one of the plants, nipping out leaves with thumbnail and finger. 'I was rather afraid Sally would do something foolish like this,' she said softly. 'But she's wrong, you know. I had nothing to do with Monica's death.' She paused, head on one side as if considering what she had just said. 'Oh, I suppose I did in a sense,' she amended, 'but that was hardly my fault.'

Lady Tyndall turned to face Paget. 'I assume that Sally has told you...everything?'

'Concerning your relationship with her? Yes, she has,' said Paget.

'Hmm.' A flicker of annoyance crossed her face. 'I suppose it was inevitable, but it was quite unnecessary. Poor Sally. I tried to tell her, you know, but she wouldn't listen.'

'Then, perhaps you would tell us what *did* happen that night,' Paget prompted her.

She flicked a glance at him and pursed her lips in a speculative way. 'Yes,' she said as if talking to herself. 'I suppose that would be best.'

DRIVING HOME THAT NIGHT, Paget went over Lady Tyndall's story in his mind. Once she'd agreed to talk to them, she had been remarkably frank.

Her marriage to Lord Tyndall some ten years earlier had been one of convenience for both of them, she said. He was twenty years her senior, and a good friend of the family, so she had known him ever since she was a child. Despite the difference in their ages, they were remarkably well matched intellectually, and they had enjoyed each other's company for years before they married.

Tyndall, like so many descendants of the old aristocracy, was going ever deeper into debt just to keep up the estate. Maria Carrera, on the other hand, although born and raised in England, came from an extremely wealthy South American family, and so a deal was struck.

'Richard needed the money and I wanted the title,' she said. 'And I was prepared to pay for it. It was as simple as that. And we have both been well satisfied with the bargain.'

Tyndall, though not a homosexual, had virtually no interest in a sexual relationship with her, and he had recognized long before they agreed to marry that she was not interested in men. In every other way, they were good friends and well matched, and if Maria wished to indulge in a discreet affair from time to time, he had no objection.

'It's an unusual arrangement, I agree,' said Lady Tyndall. 'But it is a sensible one. We both have what we want, and we enjoy each other's company.'

On Christmas Eve, she said, her husband had been detained in London, and had telephoned to say he would stay in their Knightsbridge flat overnight and try to get back by lunch-time Christmas Day. She telephoned Sally, then went over to the cottage to spend the night with her.

Her version of what happened when Monica burst into the cottage tallied closely with that of Sally Pritchard. She said she thought Sally would be able to calm Monica down and get her out, but suddenly the door flew open and there stood Monica.

'I'll never forget the look on her face.' Lady Tyndall shivered despite the fact that she was surrounded by warm, humid air. 'I've never seen such despair, such utter desolation as was on that child's face that night.'

She went on to say that she and Sally had talked and talked about what they should do. Wondering what Monica would do. They both knew how unpredictable the girl could be, but it never occurred to either of them that she might kill herself.

Sally was in such a state that it was Lady Tyndall who finally took matters into her own hands. She took the Range Rover and drove over to the school. She had, she insisted, no plan in mind. She just wanted to talk to Monica, to try to persuade her to say nothing.

'If it was a matter of money, I was prepared to pay her,' she said flatly.

Having attended Thornton Hill herself, she knew all about the back way into the school. She went up the back stairs and had no trouble finding Monica's room.

Lady Tyndall had raised her head at this point and looked Paget directly in the eye. 'She was dead when I entered the room,' she said. 'In fact, she was already cold. It wasn't hard to see what had happened. The syringes were there—and then, of course, there was the picture.'

Paget pulled a rolled polythene bag from his pocket. 'This picture?' he asked her.

She glanced at what once had been a photograph of herself, disfigured now beyond recognition. Savage scars crisscrossed the face, leaving it in shreds. Lady Tyndall shuddered and turned away.

'She must have gone straight into the hall and taken the picture up to her room when she came in,' she said. 'She'd smashed the frame, and stuck the picture on her mirror with Sellotape, and she'd scrawled words across it in lipstick. Obscene, horrible words. I can't repeat them. I'm sorry.'

Lady Tyndall drew in a deep breath. 'There was nothing I could do for her. Absolutely nothing. So, I pulled what was left of the picture off the mirror, cleaned the lipstick off, and swept all the bits and pieces into the pillowcase.

'Then I left. I drove back to Sally's and told her what happened. I asked her to get rid of the pillowcase and its contents because I thought it would be easier for her to get rid of it than it would for me.'

'But Sally didn't believe you, did she?' Paget had said.

'No. She went to pieces. She was sure I'd killed Monica to keep her quiet. I tried to tell her the girl had committed suicide, but it was useless. Finally, I just had to leave her. I've tried several times since then to talk to her, but...'

'Do you have any idea what time it was when you went up to Monica's room?' Paget had asked her.

Lady Tyndall frowned in concentration. 'I'm sure Sally and I talked for at least a couple of hours before I went over there,' she said. 'Sally was in such a state that I didn't want to leave her before that. I'd say it was somewhere between three and four o'clock. I know it was almost five when I got back home.'

Which tallied closely to what Sally had told them. Unless there was a much deeper collusion between the two of them than he believed to be the case, then Lady Tyndall was probably telling the truth. Monica had been dead for some time before she got there.

Was there anyone other than Sally Pritchard who could confirm any of this? he'd asked her. Had she passed anyone on the road, for example?

Of course, the answer had been no.

At least her story dovetailed neatly with the evidence. Perhaps he had been wrong. Perhaps Monica's death had

nothing to do with the murders that followed. Perhaps it
was simply a matter of coincidence.

Perhaps.

SALLY PRITCHARD SAT HUDDLED in a chair beside the dy-
ing fire. It was almost midnight, but she made no move to
go to bed, her thoughts too chaotic to even think of sleep.

The chief inspector had said that Monica had died no
later than two on Christmas morning, so Maria couldn't
have been responsible for her death. Sally closed her eyes.
Maria had been telling the truth all along. Why hadn't she
believed her? She had accused Maria of killing Monica to
save her reputation. She'd been so *certain*.

And now she'd ruined everything. Destroyed the love,
the trust, the passion because of her suspicion. It could
never be the same again between them. It was over. Finished. There was nothing she could do to change that. She
choked back a sob. Oh, why had she not believed Maria?
Why? Why? Why?

At least there was *one* thing she could do. It wouldn't
bring Maria back to her, and it wouldn't bring Monica
back, but it had to be done, painful as that might be. In
fact it *must* be done. She must set things right.

TWENTY-SEVEN

Friday, 8 January

BETWEEN WRITING UP their respective reports, and a lengthy discussion with Alcott and Cooper that took up the rest of the morning, Paget and Tregalles didn't get out to Glenacres until after lunch. They had gone over and over the statements made by the two women the day before, but as Alcott had pointed out with such acerbity, there was nothing to tie what had taken place early Christmas morning to the killing of Palmer or Blake.

They were back, it seemed, to two suspects: Andrea McMillan and Jack Lucas. But which one?

'We'll go over the ground again,' said Paget. 'Go back to Glenacres and see if there is anything we've missed.'

Tregalles groaned. 'We've been over everything out there with a microscope already,' he complained. But it was token resistance at best. There was no other choice, and he knew it.

They had just missed Sally, according to Penny Wakefield. She hadn't come in to work until after lunch, and she'd just left again, saying there was something she must do over at the school. She said Lucas had just been in looking for Sally, and he was anything but pleased when she told him Sally wasn't there.

'He went straight up the wall,' said Penny. 'What with being so short-handed, and everything to get ready for the weekend riders tomorrow, I'm not sure what we'll do. At least the girls at Thornton Hill won't be back until next week, so we'll have a bit of a breather there.' She grinned wryly. 'Mr Lucas even offered me a rise if I'd stay on.'

'Will you?'

She shook her head. 'No. Too much aggro around here. I'll be much better off where I'm going.'

'How was Sally?' Paget asked.

Penny shook her head. 'I don't know why she didn't stay home in bed,' she said. 'She looked ill. She looked like death warmed over. Whatever it is she's got, I hope it isn't catching. That's all we need around here right now.'

They left her to her work in the office, and went out into the body of the barn where they went over every detail of the Palmer killing, item by item. They searched the barn again but found nothing new.

They were on the point of leaving when the door opened and James came in. Tregalles looked at him in surprise.

'Hello?' he said. 'And why aren't you in school today, young James?'

'We're going away,' the boy said solemnly. 'Mummy said I could come down here for a swing before we go.' He climbed aboard the swing, stood up and began to pump.

'Going away, are you?' said Tregalles. 'Just you and your mum?'

'Yes. We're going to my grandma's to live. She says we might be there for ever such a long time. I don't like staying at grandma's house.'

'Oh, why's that, James?'

'It's all houses and shops stuck together,' said the boy. 'There aren't any fields, and she doesn't have a swing.'

The boy had allowed the swing to slow down until it had almost stopped. It was as if all the pleasure had gone out of it. But suddenly he seized the ropes and began to swing from side to side instead of back and forth. His mouth was set determinedly, but he looked very close to tears. His thin legs bent like twigs as he forced the swing to go higher. It paused at the top of the arc above the bench, then swung back again, gathering speed...

The barn door opened suddenly and Bob Tillman stood there in the doorway, peering in. The swing flashed across the barn—and stopped within inches of the startled stableman as it reached its apogee. If he hadn't paused before stepping over the sill, the swing would have slammed into Tillman's chest.

'Look out!' Tregalles shouted, far too late. He darted forward and grabbed the boy on the downward arc as Tillman stood their frozen. The sergeant lifted the boy bodily from the swing and set him on the ground. James backed away, his eyes large and round, fearful of what might come.

But Tregalles wasn't looking at the boy at all. He and Paget were looking at each other as understanding dawned.

'I'm sorry,' said James fearfully as Tillman, now recovered from his initial fright, stepped inside. The stableman wagged a warning finger at the boy.

'You damned near had me that time, boy,' he said goodnaturedly, and with a nod towards the two detectives he moved off towards the office.

Penny, having heard Tregalles's shouted warning, came running out. 'What happened?' she wanted to know, looking from one to the other.

'It's all right,' Paget assured her. 'The swing got away on James, that's all. No damage done.'

He turned to the boy. 'I think you'd better go back to the house, now, James, don't you?'

James didn't hesitate. Relief flooded into the small face as he realized he wasn't going to be scolded. He shot out of the door and was gone. Penny, still looking faintly puzzled, looked at both of them in turn, then returned to the office to see what Tillman wanted.

Paget moved over to the door and closed it. He ran his

fingers over the inside surface about chest height. Tregalles joined him and they inspected the door together.

'There they are,' the sergeant said. He pointed to several marks where something had dug into the wood. They were all but lost among the scars and pock-mocks that had accumulated over the years, but now they knew what to look for, they were plain enough to see.

'We'll have to get the pitchfork back,' said Paget, 'but I don't think there can be much doubt the tines will match the holes. Someone has been practising.'

He moved over to the swing, lifting the seat to examine it more closely. It consisted of a single piece of wood, ten or twelve inches wide by a couple of feet long. It was thick and sturdy and worn smooth by constant use.

But his keen eyes sought and found what they were looking for. Marks in two places on the edges of the wood where something had been bound beneath the seat. With twine, no doubt. He could see the score marks where it had been pulled tight.

'No wonder the pitchfork damned nearly went right through Palmer,' said Tregalles soberly.

Paget nodded. 'The pitchfork was tied along the bottom of the swing, with the tines pointing towards the door. All the killer would have to do was pull the swing sideways, climb up on the chairs to the bench, hold it there and wait. When Palmer came through the door he or she just let it go—or gave it an extra shove. The weight of the thing alone would carry it down. If they gave it a push...'

'Lucas?' said Tregalles. 'He'd have the opportunity to test it out. I doubt if the doctor would have the same opportunity.'

But Paget didn't appear to be listening. Instead he went over to the place where the swing was normally tied up out of the way. He ran his hand gently over the jagged edge of metal on which he'd cut his hand, then peered down behind it to where he'd found the missing ball of twine. Tregalles watched, curious, as Paget removed his coat, examined it closely, then put it on again.

'Staring me in the face,' he said as he turned back to Tregalles. 'Dammit, I should have known. The answer was literally staring me in the face and I didn't see it.'

SALLY WENT IN THE BACK WAY. She wasn't anxious to run into Miss Crowther. She mounted the long flight of narrow stairs and stepped out into the corridor. With only two small windows to illuminate its entire length, it was a gloomy place smelling faintly of disinfectant. There was no one about. The girls wouldn't be back until the beginning of next week, so there was no need to worry on that score. She made her way down the corridor and knocked gently on Jane Wolsey's door.

The housemistress opened the door. 'Why, Sally, what a nice surprise,' she said. Unconsciously she pulled the sleeve of her cardigan down over her left hand. The smile of welcome faded as she looked closer at Sally's face. 'Is there anything wrong?' she asked anxiously.

'I must talk to you,' the young woman said. She sounded nervous; ill at ease. Jane had never seen her like this before.

Jane Wolsey opened the door wider. 'You'd better come in and tell me about it, then,' she said. 'I'll make a cup of tea.'

PAGET GAVE A PEREMPTORY KNOCK on the open door as he stuck his head inside the office. 'Sorry to interrupt,' he told Penny, 'but did you say Sally had gone over to the school?'

'That's right.'

'Did she say why? Did she say who it was she was going to see? It's important.'

The girl caught his sense of urgency. 'She said something about seeing Miss Wolsey to set things straight.'

'Did she walk or take her car?'

'She took the car.'

'Thanks,' he said and was gone.

The light was fading as the school came into view. 'I don't see her car,' said Paget. 'Drop me here, and I'll go round the back. You go in the front. Try Miss Wolsey's room first.'

Paget was out of the car before it had stopped. He slammed the door and began to run down the side of Braden Hall.

Tregalles shot forward and brought the car to a halt outside the main entrance.

He dashed up the steps and across the main hall towards the stairs.

'Sergeant Tregalles!'

Tregalles swung round. 'Miss Crowther. Have you seen Sally Pritchard or Miss Wolsey?'

The headmistress ignored the question. 'Just what do you think you are doing?' she demanded. 'Dashing in here like that. I will not tolerate such behaviour, especially from the police. You should be setting an example instead of...'

Tregalles cut her off. 'Have-you-seen-Sally-Pritchard-or-Miss-Wolsey?' he said brusquely.

Miss Crowther bristled. 'No, I have not, and I don't know...'

'Thank you,' he called back as he took the marble stairs three at a time. Behind him, he was conscious of Miss Crowther saying: 'Really!'

He reached the top and crossed the corridor to Miss Wolsey's room. His hand was raised to knock when he caught movement out of the corner of his eye.

Far down the corridor.

He turned to see the door leading to the back stairs slowly closing. He opened his mouth to shout, but knew no one would hear him through the heavy door. He raced the length of the corridor.

Paget came round the corner of the building and saw Sally Pritchard's car. So she had gone in the back. He made his way to the back door, found it open, and went inside. The corridor ahead was deserted.

There was a sound. The heavy thud of a door closing somewhere above him. He moved swiftly to the bottom of the back stairs and looked up.

Sally Pritchard and Miss Wolsey stood on the landing at the top of the long flight of narrow stairs. Sally had her foot out over the first step. Behind her, he saw Jane Wolsey's arm come up; reach out…

'Sally! Behind you!' he bellowed as loud and hard as he could.

The girl half turned, but not soon enough to avoid the violent thrust of a hand between her shoulder blades. She left the top step and hung suspended in space for what seemed like an eternity. Her hand flew out, grabbing frantically for the metal rail that served as a banister. Her fingers touched; curled around…

Behind her, her face contorted with frustrated rage, Jane Wolsey reached out to thrust again.

The door behind her crashed open. Off balance, she half turned, lost her footing, and fell…

She hurtled past Sally, now lying head downward on the stairs, and clinging with all her strength to the rail. The small body turned over in the air and crashed with sickening force half-way down. Slowly, as in slow motion, it tumbled over and over again until it landed at Paget's feet.

Paget dropped to his knees. Jane Wolsey's eyes were open. She stared up at him. 'I think—I think my back is broken,' she said faintly, and closed her eyes.

Above him, Tregalles was pulling Sally Pritchard to her feet.

TWENTY-EIGHT

THEY SAT IN ONE OF THE HOSPITAL day rooms, Paget, Tregalles and Sally Pritchard. Sally's right arm was bandaged and taped from wrist to elbow, but she was able to use her fingers. She shifted uncomfortably in the chair. Her back was bruised and sore, but she had been lucky. No bones were broken, but she'd pulled most of the ligaments in her arm. It would be painful for a few days, the doctor had told her.

'If you're not feeling up to it, we can let this wait until morning,' said Paget, but Sally shook her head.

'I'd rather get it over with now,' she said. 'Then I can go home and not have to think about it any more.'

Not think about it any more. How could she not think about it? she wondered. Jane, of all people, trying to kill her? The very idea was insane. Yet even now the surgeons were working feverishly to save her life right here in the hospital. In spite of everything, Sally couldn't help but feel sorry for her.

'Poor Jane,' she said.

'If ''poor Jane'' had had her way, you wouldn't be talking to us now,' Tregalles pointed out.

Sally shook her head sadly. 'You're right, of course,' she said. 'It's just that it's so hard to think of her as being capable of doing something like that. And yet…'

'And yet?' Paget prompted gently.

Sally looked at him for a long moment. 'Jane's had a rotten life,' she said. 'It didn't seem to matter how hard she tried; how much she did for the girls. They always looked down on her; made fun of her behind her back. Schoolgirls can be very nasty little creatures, you know, especially when they think they're superior to someone else.

'But I liked her. I suppose I felt sorry for her, too. Perhaps it was because I came from a poor background myself. I was a day girl, and I can't say I had too good a time of it at school. My mother didn't have much, but she was determined to give me an education, and she did. Unfortunately, she didn't live to see me finish.' Sally took a deep breath and let it out again. 'But that's got nothing to do with Jane, has it?'

She flinched as she moved her arm. 'It was during my last year at Thornton Hill when one of the girls found out about Jane. I'm not sure how, exactly—I think her family knew Miss Crowther and found out that way. Not that it matters now.

'You see, Jane came from a very strict, religious family—at least that was how they saw themselves—and when Jane was born with the deformed arm and hand, they saw it as a sign that God regarded her as wicked. As a consequence, they took it upon themselves to punish her for her wickedness. She was beaten repeatedly, starved, shut up in cupboards...' Despite the warmth of the room, Sally shivered.

'She was five years old before anyone found out about it. Her parents stood trial, and she was taken away from them. Perhaps because of her deformity, she was never adopted, but shunted from one set of foster-parents to another. I don't know all the details, but she ended up living with Miss Crowther's elder sister. I know the sister died young, and Miss Crowther felt obliged to give Jane a job. At least, that's what this girl told us. She put the story all round the school, and, naturally, Jane heard about it as I'm sure she was meant to. You can imagine how she must have felt.

Sally fell silent, easing herself into a more comfortable

position before going on. 'I tell you this', she said to Paget, 'so that you might better understand why she acted the way she did. I know it was wrong; I know that what she did was terrible, but I think I understand why.

'You see, she was inordinately fond of Monica. I think she saw in her the rejected little girl that she had been herself. She doted on her; went out of her way to protect her. But the more Jane tried to do for her, the more Monica resented it. It must have hurt poor Jane.'

'Why did you go to see her this afternoon?' Paget asked. 'And what did you say to her that made her attack you?'

'I went to tell her the truth,' said Sally. 'I felt that I was responsible, at least in part, for Monica's death, and I wanted to tell Jane that. I thought Jane was blaming herself; punishing herself. She looked so ill.'

'Please go on.'

'Well, when I got there, she invited me in and made a cup of tea. We sat and chatted for a few minutes, then I simply plunged right in and told her about—well, what happened at the party, and how Monica had come to me that night. I told her everything—well, almost everything. I didn't tell her who was there.'

'How did she react?'

Sally shrugged and promptly winced. 'She didn't say anything for a long time,' she said. 'I wasn't quite sure what to do, so finally I got up and started to leave. But she got up, too, and walked with me to the door and out into the corridor. She began to talk. It was almost as if I wasn't there at first. It was strange.'

'What did she talk about, Miss Pritchard?'

Sally frowned. 'It was a bit hard to follow, but she said that she was worried about the way Monica had looked when she left her in bed on Christmas Eve, so she went back later to check up on her. She said she found her out of bed, flushed, excited. Jane said she was very cross with her and made Monica get back in bed. I'm not sure I've got it right, but I think Jane must have badgered Monica about what happened over at the stables, and Monica, probably in desperation—or perhaps maliciously—told her the same story she'd told me. She even showed Jane her bruises, and said Maurice had done that to her.' Sally was silent for a moment. 'I suppose Monica just wanted to get rid of Jane in any way she could so that she could slip out of school to come and see—' the word stuck in her throat as she swallowed hard '—me.'

And that was the crux of the matter, thought Paget. The lie that was to leave behind a legacy of death for Maurice Blake and, unfortunately for him, Victor Palmer.

'We were walking down the corridor,' Sally went on. 'Jane was holding on to my arm. Her fingers were like iron, digging into my flesh. She kept stopping, talking right at me as if she wanted to make sure I understood. Then she'd walk on a few paces and stop again.'

Sally's voice shook as she ran trembling fingers through her hair. 'She started talking about people having to pay for what they'd done. Frankly, I thought she was rambling. We had just reached the door on the landing of the back stairs when she said something about being sorry about Victor, but he shouldn't have been there. It was only as we went through the door that I realized what she was saying. And then she said: "But it was you all the time! You were the one. You killed Monica. Not Maurice."

'I heard you shout just as she pushed me.' Sally caught her breath. 'If it hadn't been for you, Chief Inspector...' She glanced up at Tregalles. 'And you, Sergeant. I'm sorry, I haven't even thanked you for saving my life.'

'We're just thankful we arrived in time,' said Paget.

'But, how *did* you know?' she asked. 'I've been wondering about that.'

'We didn't until just a few minutes before,' said Paget.

He explained about their findings in the barn. 'The twine was used to tie the pitchfork to the swing,' he said. 'Then, all Miss Wolsey had to do was pull the swing sideways, climb up on the bench with it, and wait. When Palmer— or Blake, as she thought—came through the door, she just let it go, or gave it a push for good measure. Its own weight was more than enough to carry it down. Either the twine broke when he fell, or Miss Wolsey cut the pitchfork loose herself, then pulled the swing up out of the way so we couldn't connect it to the killing. It was only when I looked at that old machine that I remembered cutting myself on it and getting those rust marks on my coat when I retrieved the twine.

'Identical marks were on Miss Wolsey's coat when I went over to talk to her the next day. I saw them, but they didn't register. She'd tried to retrieve the ball of twine just as I had, but she couldn't reach it so she had to leave it there. Also, one of her gardening gloves had been mended. The tear was in exactly the same place as where I cut my hand when I undid the cord to let the swing down.'

'But her hand…?' Sally shook her head as if she couldn't believe what she was hearing. 'How could she have tied the pitchfork to the swing?'

'She's a lot more adept with that hand than you might think,' said Paget. 'I wondered about that, too, until I recalled the first time I met her on Christmas Day. I couldn't help but notice the gift she'd bought for Monica. It was beautifully wrapped and finished off with ribbons and bows. She told me she had wrapped it herself, and I wondered then how she had managed it. It must have been very difficult for her, but knowing what I do now, I suspect she would have seen it as a labour of love.'

Tregalles nodded. 'Unfortunately, the way in which Palmer was killed led us to believe that the killer had to be fairly strong. It wasn't until we saw young James swing sideways and nearly knock Bob Tillman down that we twigged it. Once we had the idea, then it wasn't hard to see where the twine had been used to tie the pitchfork to the swing. Blake was lucky that night. He'd changed shifts with Palmer, but when Miss Wolsey realized that she'd killed the wrong man, she went after Blake again, and this time she got him.'

Sally shuddered. 'No wonder she looked ill, poor soul,' she said half to herself. 'She must have been out of her mind.'

'I wouldn't feel too sorry for her if I were you,' Tregalles said. 'Remember, once you told her about your part in all this, she tried to kill you, too.'

'We'll need a formal statement from you,' Paget said, 'but that can be done later. I'll have a driver take you home if you feel up to it.'

'There's no need for that.'

Their heads turned in unison. Lady Tyndall stood there just inside the door. 'I'll take her home,' she said.

'Maria!' Tears filled Sally's eyes and spilled down her cheeks.

Lady Tyndall crossed swiftly to her side. Gently, very gently, she put an arm around Sally's shoulders. 'Miss Crowther rang to tell me what had happened,' she said. 'As one of the governors, she thought I ought to know. I came as quickly as I could. Come on, let's get you home.'

ANDREA MCMILLAN LOOKED TIRED as she stood there in the doorway.

'May I come in?' he said.

She lifted an eyebrow in faint enquiry, but didn't speak.

'We have the person who killed Palmer in custody,' he said. 'I thought you ought to know.'

Still she didn't speak; just turned and led the way into the living-room, leaving him to follow. She reached the middle of the room and turned to face him. 'Does this mean I am no longer under suspicion?' she said.

He nodded. 'Yes. It appears that Victor Palmer was killed by mistake. The person who killed him was after Blake. She was expecting him to come through the door that night, but unknown to her, Blake had switched with Palmer.'

'You said "she"...?'

'A Miss Wolsey. She's a housemistress at Thornton Hill School. One of her girls died on Christmas Day as a result of a suicide attempt, and Miss Wolsey believed—mistakenly as it turned out—that it was because Blake had attempted to rape her. Miss Wolsey was very much attached to Monica. Too much so, I'm afraid. She also attempted to kill Sally Pritchard. Fortunately, she failed.'

Concern flooded across her face. 'Sally? Is she all right?'

'She has a sprained arm and a sore back, but she'll be all right,' Paget said. 'Miss Wolsey tried to push her down the stairs, but went down herself instead. She broke her back in the fall.'

'But she's still alive? You said she was in custody.'

'Yes. She's still alive, but the surgeon told me that even if she does recover, she'll never walk again.'

Professional interest took over. 'Was that Hepworth?'

'That's right.'

She nodded. 'He's good,' she said. 'How bad is the injury? Did he say?'

'He said he could only do so much for her here. He mentioned Birmingham.'

'Then it is bad,' she concluded.

Paget looked at her. For a moment, standing there, brow furrowed with concern for someone else, she reminded him of the first time they'd met. She was consoling a young nurse who had been attacked by a patient under guard, and she'd looked exactly the way she looked now.

'Andrea…' he began.

Her expression changed. 'Thank you for letting me know,' she said. She hesitated; looked away. 'I've already given notice at the hospital. It didn't seem fair, somehow, to remain on staff. Not when it's obvious to everyone that you are suspected of murder.' A bitter smile touched her lips. 'People like to have confidence in their doctor, and—' she shrugged '—as I said, it didn't seem fair. Now that I'm free to go, I shall go down and join Sarah and stay with Kate for a while. She could do with some help, and I think a bit if manual labour might do me the world of good. It will give me time to think; get things sorted out.'

He nodded. There was so much he wanted to say, but it was too late. Much too late. He turned and walked to the door. It seemed a very long way.

He turned to look at her. 'I hope…' His mouth was dry and he stumbled over the words. 'I hope that you and Sarah will be happy,' he said huskily.

'Thank you, Neil. I doubt if we shall see each other again before I go, so I'll say goodbye now.'

'Of course. Goodbye, Andrea.'

The door closed behind him and he was gone.

Andrea remained standing in the middle of the room. For a moment she had the strangest feeling that the walls of the room had vanished; that there was nothing; she was alone in the universe.

The feeling passed, and she just felt empty.

Monday, 11 January

MISS CROWTHER SHUT THE DOOR of the boardroom behind her and leaned against it. She felt completely drained.

She'd steeled herself for what she knew must come when she was summoned to attend an emergency meeting of the board. They would blame her for what Jane had done. They

would blame her for keeping her on all these years. Blame
her for tarnishing the reputation of the school.

And no one knew better than she that to a school, such
as Thornton Hill, reputation was everything. Someone
would have to be the scapegoat; parents would demand it,
and there was no doubt in her mind as to whom the board
would choose.

Her great-grandfather might have been the founder of
Thornton Hill, but the board still had the power to remove
her as headmistress.

She had been prepared for it. It had taken every ounce
of courage she possessed to walk into that room this morning. She would not resign; she had made up her mind to
that. Whatever they might say, none of this was her fault,
and she'd be damned if she was going to make it easy for
them. If she had to leave the school that was her very life,
they would have to dismiss her.

But now, standing there outside the room, she still could
not believe what had happened. Lady Tyndall, of all people,
had scotched the move to sack her almost before it had
begun. In her capacity as chair, she had opened the proceedings with a spirited defence of the school's past record
and Miss Crowther's contribution to that record. She had
concluded by saying it would be a gross miscarriage of
justice to try to lay the blame for what had happened on
any individual. No one could have foreseen such events,
she said, and if the school needed to be defended, then it
was up to them as members of the board to face the world
as one.

There had been some uncomfortable shuffling of feet.
Captain Wickstowe had harrumphed a bit, and the Right
Reverend Rowen-Jones had mumbled some platitude or
other, but none had found the courage to oppose the chair.

As to why Lady Tyndall had come so valiantly to her
defence, Miss Crowther did not understand. Nor, at this

moment, did she care. She just knew that her dream of finishing her days as headmistress of Thornton Hill could have ended here today. Now all that was changed, and she was very, very grateful.

RANSOM FOR A KILLING

FRED HUNTER

Eight years ago Ben Harvey was accused and convicted of raping Laura Shay, a high school classmate. Now, DNA tests prove he is innocent, and suddenly Harvey is free.

Then Laura Shay is murdered, and it's on Chicago police detective Jeremy Ransom's beat. The obvious suspect is Harvey. After all, who could blame him for wanting revenge? Not even Ransom's friend and unofficial partner, septuagenarian Emily Charters. But as Ransom is drawn into the case, he discovers the fine line of justice can be razor sharp....

Available December 1999 at your favorite retail outlet.

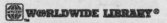 **WORLDWIDE LIBRARY®**

Visit us at www.worldwidemystery.com   WFH329